ALSO BY COLLEEN HOOVER

Slammed

Point of Retreat

This Girl

Hopeless

Losing Hope

Finding Cinderella

Maybe Someday

Ugly Love

Maybe Not

CONFESS

a novel

COLLEEN HOOVER

SIMON &
SCHUSTER

London · New York · Sydney · Toronto · New Delhi

ATRIA PAPERBACK
A Division of Simon & Schuster, Inc.
1230 Avenue of the Americas
New York, NY 10020

This book is a work of fiction. Any references to historical events, real people, or real places are used fictitiously. Other names, characters, places, and events are products of the author's imagination, and any resemblance to actual events or places or persons living or dead is entirely coincidental.

Artwork created by Danny O' Connor (aka DOC)

First Atria Paperback edition March 2015

ATRIA PAPERBACK and colophon are trademarks of Simon & Schuster, Inc.

Interior design by Kyoko Watanabe

Printed and bound by CPI Group (UK) Ltd, Croydon, CR0 4YY

18
The Library of Congress has catalogued this book as follows:

Hoover, Colleen.
Confess / by Colleen Hoover. — First Atria paperback edition.
pages ; cm
"ATRIA FICTION ORIGINAL TRADE."
I. Title.
PS3608.O623C66 2015
813'.6—dc23

2014043627

ISBN 978-1-4711-4859-0
ISBN 978-1-4767-9146-3 (ebook)

The confessions you read within this novel are true confessions, submitted anonymously by readers. This book is dedicated to all of you who found the courage to share them.

Part One

PROLOGUE

Auburn

I pass through the hospital doors knowing it'll be the last time.

On the elevator, I press the number three, watching it illuminate for the last time.

The doors open to the third floor and I smile at the nurse on duty, watching her expression as she pities me for the last time.

I pass the supply room and the chapel and the employee break room, all for the last time.

I continue down the hallway and keep my gaze forward and my heart brave as I tap lightly on his door, waiting to hear Adam invite me in for the very last time.

"Come in." His voice is somehow still filled with hope, and I have no idea how.

He's on his bed, lying on his back. When he sees me, he comforts me with his smile and lifts the blanket, inviting me to join him. The rail is already lowered, so I climb in beside him, wrap my arm over his chest, and lock our legs together. I bury my face into his neck, searching for his warmth, but I can't find it.

He's cold today.

He adjusts himself until we're in our usual position with his left arm under me and his right arm over me, pulling me to him. It takes him a little more time to get comfortable than it usually does, and I notice his breathing increase with each small movement he makes.

I try not to notice these things, but it's hard. I'm aware of his increased weakness, his slightly paler skin, the frailty in his voice. Every day during my allotted time with him, I can see that he's slipping further away from me and there's nothing I can do about it. Nothing anyone can do but watch it happen.

We've known for six months that it would end this way. Of course we all prayed for a miracle, but this isn't the kind of miracle that happens in real life.

My eyes close when Adam's chilled lips meet my forehead. I've told myself I'm not going to cry. I know that's impossible, but I can at least do everything I can to forestall the tears.

"I'm so sad," he whispers.

His words are so out of line with his usual positivity, but it comforts me. Of course I don't want him to be sad, but I need him to be sad with me right now. "Me too."

Our visits over the last few weeks have mostly been filled with a lot of laughter and conversation, no matter how forced.

I don't want this visit to be any different, but knowing it's our last makes it impossible to find anything to laugh about. Or talk about. I just want to cry with him and scream about how unfair this is for us, but that would tarnish this memory.

When the doctors in Portland said there was nothing more they could do for him, his parents decided to transfer him to a hospital in Dallas. Not because they were hoping for a miracle, but because their entire family lives in Texas, and they thought it would be better if he could be near his brother and everyone else who loved him. Adam had moved to Portland with his parents just two months before we began dating a year ago.

The only way Adam would agree to return to Texas was if they allowed me to come, too. It was a battle finally getting both sets of parents to agree, but Adam argued that he was the one dying, and he should be allowed to dictate who he's with and what happens when that time comes.

It's been five weeks now since I came to Dallas, and the two of us have run out of sympathy from both sets of parents. I was told I have to return to Portland immediately or my parents will be slapped with truancy charges. If it weren't for that, his parents might have let me stay, but the last thing my parents need right now is legal issues.

My flight is today, and we've exhausted all other ideas for how I can convince them that I don't need to be on that flight. I didn't tell Adam this and I won't, but last night after more pleas from me, his mother, Lydia, finally voiced her true opinion on the matter.

"You're fifteen, Auburn. You think what you feel for him is real, but you'll be over him in a month. Those of us who have loved him since the day he was born will have to suffer with his loss until the day we die. Those are the people he needs to be with right now."

It's a strange feeling when you know at fifteen that you just lived through the harshest words you'll ever hear. I didn't even know what to say to her. How can a fifteen-year-old girl defend her love when that love is dismissed by everyone? It's impossible to defend yourself against inexperience and age. And maybe they're right. Maybe we don't know love like an adult knows love, but we sure as hell feel it. And right now, it feels imminently heartbreaking.

"How long before your flight?" Adam asks as his fingers delicately trace slow circles down my arm for the last time.

"Two hours. Your mother and Trey are downstairs waiting for me. She says we need to leave in ten minutes in order to make it on time."

"Ten minutes," he repeats softly. "That's not enough time to share with you all the profound wisdom I've accrued while on my deathbed. I'll need at least fifteen. Twenty, tops."

I laugh what is probably the most pathetic, sad laugh to ever leave my mouth. We both hear the despair in it and he holds me tighter, but not much tighter. He has very little strength even compared to yesterday. His hand soothes my head and he presses his lips into my hair. "I want to thank you, Auburn," he says quietly. "For so many things. But first, I want to thank you for being just as pissed off as I am."

Again, I laugh. He always has jokes, even when he knows they're his last.

"You have to be more specific, Adam, because I'm pissed off about a whole hell of a lot right now."

He loosens his grip from around me and makes a tremendous effort to roll toward me so that we're facing each other.

One could argue that his eyes are hazel, but they aren't. They are layers of greens and browns, touching but never blending, creating the most intense, defined pair of eyes that have ever looked in my direction. Eyes that were once the brightest part of him but are now too defeated by an untimely fate that is slowly draining the color right out of them.

"I'm referring specifically to how we're both so pissed at Death for being such a greedy bastard. But I guess I'm also referring to our parents, for not understanding this. For not allowing me to have the one and only thing I want here with me."

He's right. I'm definitely pissed about both of those things. But we've been over it enough times in the last few days to know that we lost and they won. Right now I just want to focus on him and soak up every last ounce of his presence while I still have it.

"You said you have so many things to thank me for. What's the next one?"

He smiles and brings his hand up to my face. His thumb brushes over my lips and it feels as if my heart lunges toward him in a desperate attempt to remain here while my empty shell is forced to fly back to Portland. "I want to thank you for letting me be your first," he says. "And for being mine."

His smile briefly transforms him from a sixteen-year-old boy on his deathbed into a handsome, vibrant, full-of-life teenage boy who is thinking about the first time he had sex.

His words, and his own reaction to his words, force an embarrassed smile to cross my face as I think back to that night. It was before we knew he would be moving back to Texas. We knew his prognosis at that point and we were still trying to accept it. We spent an entire evening discussing all the things we could have experienced together if we had a possibility of forever. Traveling, marriage, kids (including what we would have named them), all the places we would have lived, and of course, sex.

We predicted that we would have had a phenomenal sex life, if given the chance. Our sex life would have been the envy of all our friends. We would have made love every morning before we left for work and every night before we went to bed and sometimes in between.

We laughed about it, but the conversation soon grew quiet as we both realized that this was the one aspect of our relationship that we still had control over. Everything else about the future, we had no voice in, but we could possibly have this one private thing that death could never take from us.

We didn't even discuss it. We didn't have to. As soon as he looked at me and I saw my own thoughts mirrored in his eyes, we began kissing and we didn't stop. We kissed while we undressed, we kissed while we touched, we kissed while we cried. We kissed until we were finished, and even then, we continued to kiss in celebration of the fact that we had won this one small battle against life and death and time. And we were still kissing when he held me afterward and told me he loved me.

Just like he's holding and kissing me now.

His hand is touching my neck and his lips are parting mine in what feels like the somber opening of a good-bye letter.

"Auburn," his lips are whispering against mine. "I love you so much."

I can taste my tears in our kiss and I hate that I'm ruining our good-bye with my weakness. He pulls away from my mouth and presses his forehead against mine. I'm struggling for more air than I even need, but my panic is setting in, burying itself in my soul and making it hard to think. The sadness feels like warmth creeping its way up my chest, creating an insurmountable pressure the closer it gets to my heart.

"Tell me something about yourself that no one else knows." His voice is laced with his own tears as he looks down at me. "Something I can keep for myself."

He asks this of me every day and every day I tell him something I've never said out loud before. I think it comforts him, knowing things about me that no one else will ever know. I close my eyes and think while his hands continue to run across all the areas of my skin he can reach.

"I've never told anyone what goes through my head when I fall asleep at night."

His hand pauses on my shoulder. "What goes through your head?"

I open my eyes and look back into his. "I think about all the people I wish could die instead of you."

He doesn't respond at first, but eventually his hand resumes its movements, tracing down my arm until he reaches my fingers. He slides his hand over mine. "I bet you don't get very far."

I force a soft smile and shake my head. "I do, though. I get really far. Sometimes I say every name I know, so I start saying names of people I've never met in person before. I even make up names sometimes."

Adam knows I don't mean what I'm saying, but it makes him feel good to hear it. His thumb swipes away tears from my cheek and it makes me angry that I couldn't even wait a whole ten minutes before crying.

"I'm sorry, Adam. I tried really hard not to cry."

His eyes grow soft with his response. "If you would have

walked out of this room today without crying, it would have devastated me."

I stop fighting it with those words. I fist his shirt in my hands and begin to sob against his chest while he holds me. Through my tears, I try to listen to his heart, wanting to curse his whole body for being so unheroic.

"I love you so much." His voice is breathless and full of fear. "I'll love you forever. Even when I can't."

My tears fall harder at his words. "And I'll love you forever. Even when I shouldn't."

We cling to one another as we experience a sadness so excruciating, it makes it hard to want to live beyond it. I tell him I love him because I need him to know. I tell him I love him again. I keep saying it, more times than I've ever said it out loud. Every time I say it, he tells me right back. We say it so much that I'm not sure who's repeating who now, but we keep saying it, over and over, until his brother, Trey, touches my arm and tells me it's time to go.

We're still saying it as we kiss for the last time.

We're still saying it as we hold on to each other.

We're still saying it as we kiss for the last time again.

I'm still saying it . . .

CHAPTER ONE

Auburn

I squirm in my chair as soon as he tells me his hourly rate. There's no way I can afford this with my income.

"Do you work on a sliding-scale basis?" I ask him.

The wrinkles around his mouth become more prominent as he attempts to keep from frowning. He folds his arms over the mahogany desk and clasps his hands together, pressing the pads of his thumbs against one other.

"Auburn, what you're asking me to do is going to cost money."

No shit.

He leans back in his chair, pulling his hands to his chest

and resting them on his stomach. "Lawyers are like weddings. You get what you pay for."

I fail to tell him what a horrible analogy that is. Instead, I glance down at the business card in my hand. He came highly recommended and I knew it was going to be expensive, but I had no idea it would be this expensive. I'll need a second job. Maybe even a third one. Actually, I'm going to have to rob a damn bank.

"And there's no guarantee the judge will rule in my favor?"

"The only promise I can make is that I'll do everything I can to ensure the judge does rule in your favor. According to the paperwork that was filed back in Portland, you've put yourself in a tough spot. This will take time."

"All I have is time," I mumble. "I'll be back as soon as I get my first paycheck."

He has me set up an appointment through his secretary and then sends me on my way, back out into the Texas heat.

I've been living here all of three weeks and so far it's everything I thought it would be: hot, humid, and lonely.

I grew up in Portland, Oregon, and assumed I would spend the rest of my life there. I visited Texas once when I was fifteen and although that trip wasn't a pleasant one, I wouldn't take back a single second of it. Unlike now, when I'd do anything to get back to Portland.

I pull my sunglasses down over my eyes and begin heading in the direction of my apartment. Living in downtown Dallas is nothing like living in downtown Portland. At least in Portland, I had access to almost everything the city had to offer, all within a decent walk. Dallas is spread out and expansive, and did I mention the heat? It's so hot. And I had to sell my car in order to afford the move, so I have the choice between public transportation and my feet, considering I'm now penny-pinching in order to be able to afford the lawyer I just met with.

I can't believe it's come to this. I haven't even built up a clientele at the salon I'm working at, so I'm definitely going to have to look for a second job. I just have no idea when I'll find time to fit it in, thanks to Lydia's erratic scheduling.

Speaking of Lydia.

I dial her number and hit send and wait for her to pick up on the other end. After it goes to voice mail, I debate whether to leave a message or just call back later tonight. I'm sure she just deletes her messages, anyway, so I end the call and drop the phone into my purse. I can feel the flush rising up my neck and cheeks and the familiar sting in my eyes. It's the thirteenth time I've walked home in my new state, in a city inhabited by nothing but strangers, but I'm determined to make it the first time I'm not crying when I reach my front door. My neighbors probably think I'm psychotic.

It's just such a long walk from work to home, and long walks make me contemplate my life, and my life makes me cry.

I pause and look into the glass window of one of the buildings to check for smeared mascara. I take in my reflection and don't like what I see.

A girl who hates the choices she's made in her life.

A girl who hates her career.

A girl who misses Portland.

A girl who desperately needs a second job, and now a girl who is reading the HELP WANTED sign she just noticed in the window.

Help Wanted.
Knock to apply.

I take a step back and assess the building I'm standing in front of; I've passed by it every day on my commute and I've never noticed it. Probably because I spend my mornings on the phone and my afternoon walks with too many tears in my eyes to notice my surroundings.

CONFESS

That's all the sign says. The name leads me to believe it might be a church, but that thought is quickly dismissed when I take a closer look at the glass windows lining the front of the building. They are covered with small scraps of paper in various shapes and sizes, concealing views into the building, removing any hope of taking a peek inside. The scraps of paper are all marked with words and phrases, written in different handwriting. I take a step closer and read a few of them.

> *Every day I'm grateful that my husband and his brother look exactly alike. It means there's less of a chance that my husband will find out that our son isn't his.*

I clutch my hand to my heart. What the hell is this? I read another.

> *I haven't spoken to my children in four months. They'll call on holidays and my birthday, but never in between. I don't blame them. I was a horrible father.*

I read another.

I lied on my résumé. I don't have a degree. In the five years I've been working for my employer, no one has ever asked to see it.

My mouth is agape and my eyes are wide as I stand and read all the confessions my eyes can reach. I still have no idea what this building is or what I even think about all these things being plastered up for the world to see, but reading them somehow gives me a sense of normalcy. If these are all true, then maybe my life isn't quite as bad as I think it is.

After no less than fifteen minutes, I've made it to the second window, having read most of the confessions to the right of the door, when it begins to swing open. I take a step back to avoid being hit, while I simultaneously fight the intense urge to step around the door and get a peek inside the building.

A hand reaches out and yanks down the HELP WANTED sign. I can hear a marker sliding across the vinyl sign as I remain poised behind the door. Wanting to get a better look at whoever or whatever this place is, I begin to step around the door just as the hand slaps the HELP WANTED sign back onto the window.

Help ~~Wanted~~.
~~Knock to apply~~.
DESPERATELY NEEDED!!
BEAT ON THE DAMN DOOR!!

I laugh when I read the alterations made to the sign. Maybe this is fate. I desperately need a second job and whoever this is desperately needs help.

The door then opens further, and I'm suddenly under the scrutiny of eyes that I guarantee are more shades of green than I could find on his paint-splattered shirt. His hair is black and thick and he uses both hands to push it off his forehead, revealing even more of his face. His eyes are wide and full of anxiety at first, but after taking me in, he lets out a sigh. It's almost as if he's acknowledging that I'm exactly where I'm supposed to be and he's relieved I'm finally here.

He stares at me with a concentrated expression for several seconds. I shift on my feet and glance away. Not because I'm uncomfortable, but because the way he stares at me is oddly comforting. It's probably the first time I've felt welcome since I've been back in Texas.

"Are you here to save me?" he asks, pulling my attention back to his eyes. He's smiling, holding the door open with his elbow. He assesses me from head to toe and I can't help but wonder what he's thinking.

I glance at the HELP WANTED sign and run through a million scenarios of what could happen if I answer his question with a yes and follow him inside this building.

The worst scenario I can come up with is one that would end with my murder. Sadly, that's not enough of a deterrent, considering the month I've had.

"Are you the one hiring?" I ask him.

"If you're the one applying."

His voice is overtly friendly. I'm not used to overt friendliness, and I don't know what to do with it.

"I have a few questions before I agree to help you," I say, proud of myself for not being so willingly killable.

He grabs the HELP WANTED sign and pulls it away from the window. He tosses it inside the building and presses his back against the door, pushing it open as far as it will reach, motioning for me to come inside. "We don't really have time for questions, but I promise I won't torture, rape, or kill you if that helps."

His voice is still pleasant, despite his phrase of choice. So is that smile that shows off two rows of almost perfect teeth and a slightly crooked front left incisor. But that little flaw in his smile is actually my favorite part of him. That and his complete disregard for my questions. I hate questions. This might not be such a bad gig.

I sigh and slip past him, making my way inside the building. "What am I getting myself into?" I mutter.

"Something you won't want to get out of," he says. The door closes behind us, blocking off all the natural lighting in the room. That wouldn't be a bad thing if there were interior lights on, but there aren't. Only a faint glow coming from what looks like a hallway on the other side of the room.

As soon as the beat of my heart begins to inform me of how stupid I am for walking into a building with a complete stranger, the lights begin to buzz and flicker to life.

"Sorry." His voice is close, so I spin around just as the first of the fluorescent lights reach their full power. "I don't usually work in this part of the studio, so I keep the lights off to save energy."

Now that the entire area is illuminated, I slowly scan the room. The walls are a stark white, adorned with various paintings. I can't get a good look at them, because they're all spread out, several feet away from me. "Is this an art gallery?"

He laughs, which I find unusual, so I spin around to face him.

He's watching me with narrowed, curious eyes. "I wouldn't

go so far as to call it an art gallery." He turns and locks the front door and then walks past me. "What size are you?"

He makes his way across the expansive room, toward the hallway. I still don't know why I'm here, but the fact that he's asking me what size I am has me a little more concerned than I was just two minutes ago. Is he wondering what size coffin I'll fit in? How to size the handcuffs?

Okay, I'm a lot concerned.

"What do you mean? Like as in my clothing size?"

He faces me and walks backward, still heading in the direction of the hallway. "Yes, your clothing size. You can't wear that tonight," he says, pointing at my jeans and T-shirt. He motions for me to follow him as he turns to ascend a flight of stairs leading to a room above the one we're in. I may be a sucker for a cute, crooked incisor, but following strangers into unknown territory is where I should probably draw the line.

"Wait," I say, stopping at the foot of the stairs. He pauses and turns around. "Can you at least give me a rundown of what's happening right now? Because I'm starting to second-guess my idiotic decision to place my trust in a complete stranger."

He glances over his shoulder toward wherever the stairs lead and then back at me. He lets out an exasperated sigh before descending several steps. He takes a seat, coming eye to eye with me. His elbows meet his knees and he leans forward, smiling calmly. "My name is Owen Gentry. I'm an artist and this is my studio. I have a showing in less than an hour, I need someone to handle all the transactions, and my girlfriend broke up with me last week."

Artist.

Showing.

Less than an hour?

And girlfriend? Not touching that one.

I shift on my feet, glance behind me at the studio once more and then back to him. "Do I get any kind of training?"

"Do you know how to use a basic calculator?"

I roll my eyes. "Yes."

"Consider yourself trained. I only need you for two hours tops and then I'll give you your two hundred bucks and you can be on your way."

Two hours.

Two hundred bucks.

Something isn't adding up.

"What's the catch?"

"There's no catch."

"Why would you need help if you pay a hundred dollars an hour? There has to be a catch. You should be swarmed with potential applicants."

Owen runs a palm across the scruff on his jaw, moving it back and forth like he's attempting to squeeze out the tension. "My girlfriend failed to mention she was also quitting her job the day she broke up with me. I called her when she didn't show to help me set up two hours ago. It's kind of a last-minute employment opportunity. Maybe you were just in the right place at the right time." He stands and turns around. I remain in my spot at the bottom of the stairs.

"You made your girlfriend an employee? That's never a good idea."

"I made my employee a girlfriend. An even worse idea." He pauses at the top of the stairs and turns around, looking down at me. "What's your name?"

"Auburn."

His gaze falls to my hair, which is understandable. Everyone assumes I was named Auburn due to my hair color, but it's strawberry blond at best. Calling it red is a stretch.

"What's the rest of your name, Auburn?"

"Mason Reed."

Owen slowly tilts his head in the direction of the ceiling as he blows out a breath of air. I follow his gaze and look at the ceiling with him, but nothing is up there other than white ceiling tiles. He takes his right hand and touches his forehead, then his chest, and then continues the movements from shoulder to shoulder, until he's just made the sign of the cross over himself.

What the hell is he doing? Praying?

He looks back down at me, smiling now. "Is Mason really your middle name?"

I nod. As far as I know, Mason isn't a strange middle name so I have no idea why he's performing religious rituals.

"We have the same middle name," he says.

I regard him silently, allowing myself to take in the probability of his response. "Are you serious?"

He nods casually and reaches into his back pocket, pulling out his wallet. He descends the stairs once more and hands me his license. I look it over, and sure enough, his middle name is Mason.

I press my lips together and hand him back his driver's license.

OMG.

I try to contain the laughter, but it's hard, so I cover my mouth, hoping I'm being inconspicuous about it.

He slides his wallet back into his pocket. His eyebrow raises and he shoots me a look of suspicion. "Are you that quick?"

My shoulders are shaking from the suppressed laughter now. I feel so bad. So, so bad for him.

He rolls his eyes and looks slightly embarrassed in the way he attempts to hide his own smile. He heads back up the stairs much less confidently than before. "This is why I never tell anyone my middle name," he mutters.

I feel guilty for finding this so funny, but his humility finally gives me the courage to climb the rest of the stairs. "Your initials are really OMG?" I bite the inside of my cheek, forcing back the smile I don't want him to see.

I reach the top of the stairs and he ignores me, heading straight for a dresser. He opens a drawer and begins rummaging through it, so I take the opportunity to look around the massive room. There's a large bed, probably a king, in the far corner. In the opposite corner is a full kitchen flanked by two doors, leading to other rooms.

I'm in his apartment.

He turns around and tosses me something black. I catch it and unfold it, revealing a skirt. "That should fit. You and the traitor look about the same size." He walks to the closet and removes a white shirt from a hanger. "See if this works. The shoes you have on are fine."

I take the shirt from him and glance toward the two doors. "Bathroom?"

He points to the door on the left.

"What if they don't fit?" I ask, worried he won't be able to use my help if I'm not dressed professionally. Two hundred dollars isn't easy to come by.

"If they don't fit, we'll burn them along with everything else she left behind."

I laugh and make my way to the bathroom. Once I'm inside, I pay no attention to the actual bathroom itself as I begin to change into the clothes he gave me. Luckily, they fit perfectly. I look at myself in the full-length mirror and cringe at the disaster that is my hair. I should be embarrassed to call myself a cosmetologist. I haven't touched it since I left the apartment this morning, so I do a quick fix and use one of Owen's combs to pull it up into a bun. I fold the clothes I just removed and set them on the countertop.

When I exit the bathroom, Owen is in the kitchen, pouring two glasses of wine. I contemplate whether or not I should tell him I'm a few weeks shy of being old enough to drink, but my nerves are screaming for a glass of wine right now.

"Fits," I say, walking toward him.

He lifts his eyes and stares at my shirt for much longer than it takes to acknowledge whether or not a shirt fits. He clears his throat and looks back down at the wine he's pouring. "Looks better on you," he says.

I slide onto the stool, fighting to hide my smile. It's been a while since I've been complimented and I've forgotten how good it feels. "You don't mean that. You're just bitter over your breakup."

He pushes a glass of wine across the bar. "I'm not bitter, I'm relieved. And I absolutely mean it." He raises his glass of wine, so I raise mine. "To ex-girlfriends and new employees."

I laugh as our glasses clink together. "Better than ex-employees and new girlfriends."

He pauses with his glass at his lips and watches me sip from mine. When I'm finished, he grins and finally takes a sip.

As soon as I set my wineglass back down on the countertop, something soft grazes my leg. My initial reaction is to scream, which is exactly what happens. Or maybe the noise that comes out of my mouth is more of a yelp. Either way, I pull both of my legs up and look down to see a black, long-haired cat rubbing the stool I'm seated on. I immediately lower my legs back to the floor and bend over to scoop up the cat. I don't know why, but knowing this guy has a cat eases my discomfort even more. It doesn't seem like someone could be dangerous if they own a pet. I know that isn't the best way to justify being in a stranger's apartment, but it does make me feel better.

"What's your cat's name?"

Owen reaches over and runs his fingers through the cat's mane. "Owen."

I immediately laugh at his joke, but his expression remains calm. I pause for a few seconds, waiting for him to laugh, but he doesn't.

"You named your cat after yourself? Seriously?"

He looks at me and I can see the slightest smile playing at the corner of his mouth. He shrugs, almost bashfully. "She reminded me of myself."

I laugh again. "She? You named a girl cat Owen?"

He looks down at Owen-Cat and continues to pet her as I hold her. "Shh," he says quietly. "She can understand you. Don't give her a complex."

As if he's right, and she can actually hear me making fun of her name, Owen-Cat jumps out of my arms and lands on the floor. She disappears around the bar, and I force myself to wipe the grin off my face. I love that he named a female cat after himself. Who does that?

I lean my arm on the counter and rest my chin in my hand. "So what do you need me to do tonight, OMG?"

Owen shakes his head and grabs the bottle of wine, storing it in the refrigerator. "You can start by never again referring to me by my initials. After you agree to that, I'll give you the rundown of what's about to happen."

I should feel bad, but he seems amused. "Deal."

"First of all," he says, leaning forward across the bar, "how old are you?"

"Not old enough for wine." I take another sip.

"Oops," he says dryly. "What do you do? Are you in college?" He rests his chin in his hand and waits for my response to his questions.

"How are these questions preparing me for work tonight?"

He smiles. His smile is exceptionally nice when accompanied by a few sips of wine. He nods once and stands straight. He takes the wineglass from my hand and sets it back down on the bar. "Follow me, Auburn Mason Reed."

I do what he asks, because for $100 an hour, I'll do almost anything.

Almost.

When we reach the main floor again, he walks into the center of the room and lifts his arms, making a full circle. I follow his gaze around the room, taking in the vastness of it. The track lighting is what catches my eye first. Each light is focused on a painting adorning the stark-white walls of the studio, pulling the focus to the art and nothing else. Well, there really *isn't* anything else. Just floor-to-ceiling white walls, a polished concrete floor, and art. It's both simple and overwhelming.

"This is my studio." He pauses and points to a painting. "That's the art." He points to a counter on the other side of the room. "That's where you'll be most of the time. I'll work the room and you ring up the purchases. That's pretty much it." He explains it all so casually, as if anyone is perfectly capable of creating something of this magnitude. He rests his hands on his hips and waits for me to absorb it all.

"How old are you?" I ask him.

His eyes narrow and he dips his head slightly before looking away. “Twenty-one.” He says it like his age embarrasses him. It’s almost as if he doesn’t like that he’s so young and already has what appears to be a successful career.

I would have guessed much older. His eyes don’t seem like the eyes of a twenty-one-year-old. They’re dark and deep, and I have the sudden urge to plunge into their depths so I can see everything he’s seen.

I glance away and place my attention on the art. I walk toward the painting closest to me, growing more and more aware of the talent behind the brush with each step. When I reach it, I suck in a breath.

It’s somehow sad and breathtaking and beautiful all at once. The painting is of a woman who seems to encompass both love and shame and every single emotion in between.

“What do you use besides acrylics?” I ask, taking a step closer. I run my finger across the canvas and hear his footsteps close in on me. He pauses next to me, but I can't take my eyes off the painting long enough to look at him.

"I use a lot of different mediums, from acrylic to spray paint. It just depends on the piece."

My eyes are drawn to a slip of paper next to the painting, adhered to the wall. I read the words sprawled across it.

Sometimes I wonder if being dead would be easier than being his mother.

I touch the paper and then look back at the painting. "A confession?" When I turn and face him, his playful smile is gone. His arms are folded tightly across his chest and his chin is tucked in. He looks at me as if he's nervous about my reaction.

"Yep," he says simply.

I glance toward the window—at all the pieces of paper lining the glass. My eyes move around the room to all the paintings and I notice strips of paper adhered to the walls next to every one.

"They're all confessions," I say in awe. "Are these from actual people? People you know?"

He shakes his head and motions toward the front door. "They're all anonymous. People leave their confessions in the slot over there, and I use some of them as inspiration for my art."

I walk to the next painting and look at the confession before I even look at the interpreted piece.

I've never let anyone see me without makeup. My greatest fear is what I'll look like at my funeral. I'm almost certain I'll be cremated, because my insecurities run so deep, they'll follow me into the afterlife. Thank you for that, Mother.

I immediately move my attention to the painting.

"It's incredible," I whisper, spinning around to take in more of what he's created. I walk to the window of confessions and find one written in red ink and highlighted.

I'm scared I'll never stop comparing my life without him to how my life was when I was with him.

I'm not sure if I'm more fascinated by the confessions, the art, or the fact that I feel like I can relate to everything in here. I'm a very closed-off person. I rarely share my true thoughts with anyone, regardless of how helpful it might be for me. Seeing all of these secrets and knowing that these people have more than likely never shared these with anyone, and never will, makes me feel a sense of connection to them. A sense of belonging.

In a way, the studio and the confessions remind me of Adam.

"Tell me something about yourself that no one else knows. Something I can keep for myself."

I hate how I always tie Adam in to everything I see and do, and I wonder if and when that will ever go away. It's been five years since I last saw him. Five years since he passed away. Five years, and I'm wondering if, like the confession in front of me, I'll forever be comparing my life with him to my life without him.

And I wonder if I'll ever not be disappointed.

CHAPTER TWO

Owen

She's here. Right here, standing in my studio, staring at my art. I never thought I'd see her again. I was so convinced that the likelihood of our paths ever crossing was minimal, I can't even remember the last time I thought about her.

But here she is, standing right in front of me. I want to ask her if she remembers me, but I know she doesn't. How could she when we never even exchanged words?

I remember her, though. I remember the sound of her laughter, her voice, her hair, even though her hair used to be a lot shorter. And even though I felt like I knew her back then, I never really got a good look at her face. Now that I'm seeing her up close, I have to force myself not to stare too hard. Not because of her unassuming beauty, but because it's exactly how I imagined she would look up close. I tried to paint her once, but I couldn't remember enough about her to finish it. I have a feeling I may attempt it again after tonight. And I already know I'll call the painting *More Than One*.

She moves her attention to another painting and I look away before she catches me staring at her. I don't want it to appear too obvious that I'm trying to figure out which colors to blend together to create her unique shade of skin tone, or whether I would paint her with her hair up or down.

There are so many things I should be doing right now other than staring at her. *What should I be doing?* Showering. Changing. Preparing for all the people who are about to show up for the next two hours.

"I need to take a quick shower," I say.

She turns around, fast, as if I startled her.

"Feel free to look around. I'll go over everything else when I'm finished. I won't take long."

She nods and smiles and for the first time I think, Hannah who?

Hannah, the last girl I hired to help me. Hannah, the girl who couldn't handle being second in my life. Hannah, the girl who broke up with me last week.

I hope Auburn isn't like Hannah.

There were so many things I didn't like about her, and that isn't how it should be. Hannah disappointed me when she spoke, which is why we spent a lot of our time together not speaking. And she always, always made it a point to tell me that her name, when spelled backward, was still Hannah.

"A palindrome," I said the first time she told me. She

looked at me, perplexed, and that's when I knew I could never love her. What a waste of a palindrome she was, that Hannah.

But I can already tell that Auburn isn't like Hannah. I can see the layers of depth in her eyes. I can see the way my art moves her by the way she focuses on it, ignoring everything else around her. I hope she isn't like Hannah at all. She already looks better in Hannah's clothes than Hannah did.

Did. Another palindrome.

I walk into the bathroom and look at her clothes, and I want to walk them back downstairs to her. I want to tell her never mind, that I want her to wear her *own* clothes tonight, not Hannah's clothes. I want her to be herself, to be comfortable, but my customers are wealthy and elite and they expect black skirts and white shirts. Not blue jeans and this pink (is it pink or red?) top that makes me think of Mrs. Dennis, my high school art teacher.

Mrs. Dennis loved art. Mrs. Dennis also loved artists. And one day, after seeing how incredibly talented with a brush she thought I was, Mrs. Dennis loved *me.* Her shirt was pink or red, or maybe both, that day, and that's what I remember as I look down at Auburn's shirt, because Mrs. Dennis who?

She was not a palindrome, but her name spelled backwards was still very fitting, because Dennis = Sinned, and that's precisely what we did.

We sinned for an entire hour. She more so than me.

And don't think that hasn't been a confession turned into a painting. It was one of the first I ever sold. I named it *She Sinned with Me. Hallelujah.*

But alas, I don't want to think about high school or Mrs. Dennis or Palindrome Hannah because they are the past and this is the present, and Auburn is . . . somehow both. She would be shocked if she knew how much of her past has affected my present, which is why I won't be sharing the truth with her. Some secrets should never turn into confessions. I know that better than anyone.

I'm not sure what to do with the fact that she just showed up at my doorstep, wide-eyed and quiet, because I don't know what to believe anymore. Half an hour ago I believed in coincidences and happenstance. Now? The idea that her being here is simply a coincidence is laughable.

When I make it back downstairs, she's standing statue-still, staring up at the painting I call *You Don't Exist, God. And If You Do, You Should Be Ashamed.*

I wasn't the one who named it, of course. I'm never the one who names the paintings. They are all titled by the anonymous confessions that inspire them. I don't know why, but this confession inspired me to paint my mother. Not as I remember her, but how I imagined she looked when she was my age. And

the confession didn't remind me of her because of her religious views. The words just reminded me of how I felt in the months following her death.

I'm not sure if Auburn believes in God, but something about this painting got to her. A tear rolls down her cheek and slides slowly toward her jaw.

She hears me, or maybe she sees me stand beside her, because she brushes her cheek with the back of her hand and takes a breath. She seems embarrassed to have connected with this piece. Or maybe she's just embarrassed that I saw her connect with it.

Instead of asking her what she thinks of the painting, or why she's crying, I just stare at the painting with her. I've had this one for over a year and just yesterday decided to put it in today's showing. I don't usually keep them for this long, but for reasons I don't understand, this one was harder to give up than the rest. They're all hard to give up, but some more so than others.

Maybe I'm afraid that once they leave my hands, the paintings will be misunderstood. Unappreciated.

"That was a fast shower," she says.

She's trying to change the subject, even though we weren't speaking out loud. We both know that even though we've been quiet, the subject for the last few minutes has been her tears and what prompted them and *why do you love this piece so much, Auburn?*

"I take fast showers," I say, and realize my response is unimpressive and *why am I even trying to be impressive?* I turn and face her and she does the same, but not before looking down at her feet first, because she's still embarrassed that I saw her connect with my art. I love that she looked at her feet first, because I love that she's embarrassed. In order to be embarrassed, a person has to care about the opinions of others first.

That means she cares about my opinion, even if only a fraction. And I like that, because I obviously care about her opinion of me, or I wouldn't be secretly hoping she doesn't do or say anything that reminds me of Palindrome Hannah.

She spins around, slowly, and I try to think of something more impressive to say to her. It's not enough time, though, because her eyes are back on mine and it looks like she's hoping I'm the confident one and will be the first to speak.

I'll speak first, although I don't think confidence has anything to do with it.

I look down at my wrist to check the time—*I'm not even wearing a watch*—and I quickly scratch at a nonexistent itch so that I don't look like I'm not confident. "We open in fifteen minutes, so I should explain how things work."

She exhales, seeming more relieved and relaxed than she did before that sentence left my mouth. "Sounds good," she says.

I walk to *You Don't Exist, God* and I point to the confession taped to the wall. "The confessions are also the titles of the pieces. The prices are written on the back. All you do is ring up the purchase, have them fill out an information card for delivery of the painting, and attach the confession to the delivery card so I'll know where to send it."

She nods and stares at the confession. She wants to see it, so I take it off the wall and hand it to her. I watch as she reads the confession again before flipping the card over.

"Do you think people ever buy their own confessions?"

I know they do. I've had people admit to me that they're the ones who wrote the confession. "Yes, but I prefer not to know."

She looks at me like I'm insane, but also with fascination, so I accept it.

"Why wouldn't you want to know?" she asks.

I shrug and her eyes drop to my shoulder and maybe linger on my neck. It makes me wonder what she's thinking when she looks at me like this.

"You know when you hear a band on the radio and you have this vision of them in your head?" I ask her. "But then you see a picture or a video of them and it's nothing like you assumed? Not necessarily better or worse than you imagined, just different?"

She nods in understanding.

"That's what it's like when I've finished a painting and someone tells me their confession inspired it. When I'm painting, I create a story in my head of what inspired the confession and who it came from. But when I find out that the image I had while painting doesn't fit the actual image standing in front of me, it somehow invalidates the art for me."

She smiles and looks at her feet again. "There's a song called 'Hold On' by the band Alabama Shakes," she says, explaining the reason behind her flushed cheeks. "I listened to that song for more than a month before I saw the video and realized the singer was a woman. Talk about a mind-fuck."

I laugh. She understands exactly what I'm saying, and I can't stop smiling because I know that band, and I find it hard to believe anyone would think the singer was a man. "She says her own name in the song, doesn't she?"

She shrugs and now I'm staring at her shoulder. "I thought he was referring to someone else," she says, still calling the singer a he even though she knows it's a she now.

Her eyes flutter away, and she walks around me toward the

counter. She's still holding the confession in her hand, and I let her hold it. "Have you ever thought of allowing people to purchase anonymously?"

I walk to the opposite side of the counter and I lean forward, closer to her. "Can't say that I have."

She runs her fingers over the counter, the calculator, the information cards, my business cards. She picks one up. She flips it over. "You should put confessions on the backs of these."

As soon as those words leave her mouth, her lips press into a tight line. She thinks I'm insulted by her suggestions, but I'm not.

"How would it benefit me if the purchases were anonymous?"

"Well," she says, treading carefully, "if I were one of the people who wrote one of these"—she holds up the confession in her hand—"I would be too embarrassed to buy it. I'd be afraid you would know it was me who wrote it."

"I think it's rare that people who write the confession actually come to a showing."

She hands me the confession, finally, and then crosses her arms over the counter. "Even if I didn't write the confession, I'd be too embarrassed to buy the painting for fear that you would assume I wrote it."

She makes a good point.

"I think the confessions add an element of realness to your paintings that can't be found in other art. If a person walks into a gallery and sees a painting they connect with, they might buy it. But if a person walks into your gallery and sees a painting or a confession they connect with, they might not want to connect with it. But they do. And they're embarrassed that they connect with a painting about a mother admitting she might not love her own child. And if they hand the confession card to whoever is going to ring up their purchase, they're essentially saying to that person, 'I connected with this horrible admission of guilt.'"

I might be in awe of her, and I try not to look at her with so much obvious fascination. I straighten up but can't shake the sudden urge to hibernate inside her head. Ferment in her thoughts. "You make a good argument."

She smiles at me. "Who's arguing?"

Not us. Definitely not us.

"So let's do it, then," I say to her. "We'll place a number below every painting and people can bring you the number rather than the confession card. It'll give them a sense of anonymity."

I notice every tiny detail of her reaction as I walk around the counter toward her. She grows an inch taller and sucks in a small breath. I reach around her and pick up a piece of paper, and then reach across her for the scissors. I don't make eye contact with her when I do these things so close to her, but she's staring at me, almost as if she's willing me to.

I look around the room and begin counting the paintings when she interrupts and says, "There are twenty-two." She almost seems embarrassed that she knew how many paintings there were, because she glances away and clears her throat. "I counted them earlier . . . while you were in the shower." She takes the scissors from my hands and begins cutting the paper. "Do you have a black marker?"

I retrieve one and set it down on the counter. "Why do you think I need confessions on my business cards?"

She continues to meticulously cut the squares while she answers me. "The confessions are fascinating. It sets your studio apart from all the rest. If you have confessions on your business cards, it'll pique interest."

She's right again. I can't believe I haven't thought of that yet. She must be a business major. "What do you do for a living, Auburn?"

"I cut hair at a salon a few blocks away." Her answer lacks pride and it makes me sad for her.

"You should be a business major."

She doesn't respond, and I'm afraid I may have just insulted her profession. "Not that cutting hair is something you shouldn't be proud of," I say. "I just think you have a brain for business." I pick up the black marker and begin writing numbers on the squares, one to twenty-two, because that's how many paintings she said are hanging and I believe her enough not to recount them.

"How often are you open?" She completely ignores my insult/compliment regarding her profession.

"First Thursday of every month."

She looks at me, perplexed. "Only once a month?"

I nod. "I told you it's not really an art gallery. I don't show other artists, and I'm rarely open. It's just something I started doing a few years back and it took off, especially after I got a front-page feature last year in the *Dallas Morning News*. I do well enough the one night I'm open to make a living."

"Good for you," she says, genuinely impressed. I've never really tried to be impressive before, but she makes me a little bit proud of myself.

"Do you always have a set number of paintings available?"

I love that she's so interested.

"No. One time, about three months ago, I opened with only one painting."

She turns and faces me. "Why only one?"

I shrug, playing it off. "I wasn't very inspired to paint that month."

This isn't entirely the truth. It was when I first began seeing Palindrome Hannah, and most of my time was spent inside of her that month, attempting to focus on her body and ignore the fact that I didn't connect as much with her mind. Auburn doesn't need to know any of that though.

"What was the confession?"

I look at her questioningly, because I'm not sure what she's talking about.

"The one painting you did that month," she clarifies. "What was the confession that inspired it?"

I think back to that month and back to the only confession I seemed to want to paint. Even though it wasn't my confession, it somehow feels like it was now that she's asking me to tell her what my only inspiration was for that entire month.

"The painting was called *When I'm with You, I Think of All the Great Things I Could Be If I Were Without You.*"

She keeps her focus on me and her eyebrows are furrowed as if she's trying to get to know my story through this confession.

Her expression relaxes and keeps falling until she looks disturbed. "That's really sad," she says.

She glances away, either to hide that this confession bothered her or to hide that she's still trying to decipher me through the confession. She glances at some of the paintings closest to us so that she's not looking directly at me anymore. We're playing a game of hide-and-seek and the paintings are home base, apparently.

"You must have been extremely inspired this month,

because twenty-two is a big number. That's almost a painting a day."

I want to say, "Just wait until next month," but I don't.

"Some of these are old paintings. They weren't all made this month." I reach around her again, for the tape this time, but it's different. It's different because I accidentally touch her arm with my hand, and I haven't actually touched her until now. But we definitely just made contact, and she's absolutely real, and I hold on extra tight to the tape because I want more of whatever that was she just unintentionally delivered.

I want to say, "Did you feel that, too?" but I don't have to because I can see the chills run up her arm. I want to put down the tape and touch one of those tiny bumps I just created on her skin.

She clears her throat and takes a quick step back into the expansiveness of the room and away from the closeness of us.

I breathe, relieved by the space she just put between us. She seems uncomfortable, and honestly, I was becoming uncomfortable, because I'm still trying to wrap my mind around the fact that she's actually here.

If I had to guess, I would say that she's an introvert. Someone who isn't used to being around other people, much less people who are complete strangers to her. She seems a lot like me. A loner, a thinker, an artist with her life.

And it appears as though she's afraid I'll alter her canvas if she allows me too close.

She doesn't need to worry. The feeling is mutual.

We spend the next fifteen minutes hanging the numbers below each painting. I watch as she writes down the name of each confession on a piece of paper and correlates it with its number. She acts like she's done this a million times. I think she might be one of those people who are good at everything they do. She has a talent for life.

"Do people always show up to these things?" she asks as we walk back to the counter. I love the fact that she has no idea about my studio or my art.

"Come here." I walk toward the front door, smiling at her innocence and curiosity. It gives me a nostalgic feeling reminiscent of the first night I opened over three years ago. She brings back a little of that excitement, and I wish it could always be like this.

When we reach the front door, I pull away one of the confessions so she can take a peek outside. I watch her eyes grow wide as she takes in the line of people that I know are standing at the door. It didn't always used to be like this. Since the front-page feature last year, word of mouth has increased the amount of traffic I get, and I've been very lucky.

"Exclusivity," she whispers, taking a step back.

I attach the confession back to the window. "What do you mean?"

"That's why you do so well. Because you restrict the amount of days you're open and you can only make so many paintings in a month. It makes your art worth more to people."

"Are you saying I don't do well because of my talent?" I smile when I say this so she knows I'm only teasing.

She shoves my shoulder playfully. "You know what I mean."

I want her to shove my shoulder again, because I loved the way she smiled when she did it, but instead she turns and faces the open floor of the studio. She draws in a slow breath.

It makes me wonder if seeing all the people outside has made her nervous.

"You ready?"

She nods and forces a smile. "Ready."

I open the doors and the people begin pouring in. There's a big crowd tonight and for the first several minutes, I worry that this will intimidate her. But regardless of how quiet and a little bit shy she seemed when she first showed up here, she's the exact opposite now. She's flourishing, as if she's somehow in her element, when this probably isn't a situation she's ever been in before.

I wouldn't know that from watching her, though.

For the first half hour, she mingles with the guests and discusses the art and some of the confessions. I recognize a few faces, but most of them are people I don't know. She acts like she knows all of them. She eventually walks back to the counter when she sees someone pull the number five down. Number five correlates to the painting titled *I went to China for two weeks without telling anyone. When I returned, no one noticed I'd been gone.*

She smiles at me from across the room as she's ringing up her first transaction. I continue to work the crowd, mingling, all the while watching her out of the corner of my eye. Tonight, everyone's focus is on my art, but my focus is on her. She's the most interesting piece in this entire room.

"Will your father be here tonight, Owen?"

I look away from her long enough to answer Judge Corley's question with a shake of my head. "He couldn't make it tonight," I lie.

If I were a priority in his life, he would have made it.

"That's a shame," Judge Corley says. "I'm having my office

redecorated, and he suggested I stop by to check out your work."

Judge Corley is a man with a height of five feet six but an ego twice as tall. My father is a lawyer and spends a lot of time in the courthouse downtown, where Judge Corley's office is. I know this because my father isn't a fan of Judge Corley's, and despite Judge Corley's show of interest, I'm pretty sure he's not a fan of my father's.

"Surface friends" is what I call it. When your friendship is merely a façade and you're enemies on the inside. My father has a lot of surface friends. I think it's a side effect of being a lawyer.

I don't have any. I don't want any.

"You have exceptional talent, although I'm not sure it's quite my taste," Judge Corley says, moving around me to view another painting.

An hour quickly passes. She's been busy most of the time, and even when she isn't, she finds something to do. She doesn't just sit behind the counter and look bored like Palindrome Hannah did. Hannah perfected the art of boredom, filing her nails so much during the two showings she worked for me, I'm surprised she even had nails left by the end of it.

Auburn doesn't look bored. She looks like she's having fun. Whenever there isn't someone at the counter, she's up and mingling and smiling and laughing at the jokes that I know she thinks are lame.

She sees Judge Corley approach the table with a number. She smiles at him and says something, but he just grunts. When she looks down at the number, I see a frown form on her lips, but she quickly shoves it away with a fake smile. Her eyes briefly meet the painting titled *You Don't Exist, God . . .*, and I immediately understand the look on her face. Judge Corley is buying the painting and she knows as well as I do that he doesn't deserve it. I quickly make my way to the counter.

"There's been a misunderstanding."

Judge Corley looks at me, annoyed, and Auburn glances up at me in surprise. I take the number out of her hand. "This painting isn't for sale."

Judge Corley huffs and points to the number in my hand. "Well, the number was still on the wall. I thought that meant it was for sale."

I put the number in my pocket. "It sold before we opened," I say. "I guess I forgot to take down the number." I wave toward the painting behind him. One of the few left. "Would something like this work for you?"

Judge Corley rolls his eyes and puts his wallet back in his pocket. "No, it won't," he says. "I liked the orange in the other painting. It matches the leather in my office sofa."

He likes it for the orange. Thank God I saved it from him.

He motions for a woman standing several feet away and he begins walking toward her. "Ruth," he says, "let's just stop by the Pottery Barn tomorrow. There's nothing here I like."

I watch as they leave, then turn and face Auburn again. She's grinning. "Couldn't let him take your baby, could you?"

I let out a breath of relief. "I would have never forgiven myself."

She glances behind me at someone approaching so I step aside and let her work her magic. Another half hour passes and most of the paintings have been purchased when the last person leaves for the night. I lock the door behind them.

I turn around and she's still standing behind the counter, organizing the sales. Her smile is huge and she isn't trying to hide it at all. Whatever stress she walked into this studio with, it's not plaguing her right now. Right now, she's happy and it's intoxicating.

"You sold nineteen!" she says, almost in a squeal. "OMG, Owen. Do you realize how much money you just made? And do you realize I just used your initials in my sentence?"

I laugh because yes, I realize how much money I just made, and yes, I realize she just used my initials in a sentence. But it's okay, because she was adorable doing it. She also must have a natural ability to conduct business, because I can honestly say I've never sold nineteen paintings in one night.

"So?" I ask, hopeful that this won't be the last time she helps me. "You busy next month?"

She's already smiling, but my job offer makes her smile even bigger. She shakes her head and looks up at me. "I'm never busy when it comes to a hundred dollars an hour."

She's counting the money, separating the bills into piles. She takes two of the one-hundred-dollar bills and holds them up, smiling. "These are mine." She folds them and tucks them into the front pocket of her (or Palindrome Hannah's) shirt.

My high from the night begins to fade the moment I realize she's finished, and I don't know how to prolong the time between us. I'm not ready for her to leave yet, but she's tucking the cash away in a drawer and stacking the orders into a pile on the counter.

"It's after nine," I say. "You're probably starving."

I use this as an opening to see if she wants something to eat, but her eyes immediately grow wide and her smile disappears. "It's already after nine?" Her voice is full of panic and she quickly turns and sprints for the stairs. She takes them two at a time; I had no idea she was capable of displaying so much urgency.

I expect her to come rushing back down the stairs with the same haste, but she doesn't, so I make my way toward the stairs. When I reach the top step, I can hear her voice.

"I'm so sorry," she says. "I know, I know."

She's quiet for several seconds, and then she sighs. "Okay. That's okay, I'll talk to you tomorrow."

When the call comes to an end, I walk up the stairs, curious what kind of phone call could cause someone to feel so much panic. I see her, sitting quietly at the bar, staring at the phone in her hands. I watch her wipe away the second tear tonight, and I immediately dislike whoever was on the other end of that call. I don't like the person who made her feel this way, when just a few minutes ago she couldn't stop smiling.

She lays her phone facedown on the bar when she notices me standing at the top of the stairs. She isn't sure if I saw that tear just now—I did—so she forces a smile. "Sorry about that," she says.

She's really good at hiding her true emotions. So good, it's scary.

"It's okay," I say.

She stands up and glances toward the bathroom. She's about to suggest that it's time to change her clothes and go home. I'm scared if she does that, I'll never see her again.

We have the same middle name. That could be fate, you know.

"I have a tradition," I tell her. I'm lying, but she seems like the type of girl who wouldn't want to break a guy's tradition. "My best friend is the bartender across the street. I always go have a drink with him after my showings are over. I want you to come with me."

She glances at the bathroom once more. Based on her hesitation, I can only conclude that either she doesn't frequent bars or she's just not sure if she wants to go to one with *me*.

"They also serve food," I say, attempting to downplay the fact that I just asked her to a bar for a drink. "Appetizers mostly, but they're pretty good and I'm starving."

She must be hungry because her eyes light up when I mention appetizers. "Do they have cheese sticks?" she asks.

I'm not sure if they have cheese sticks, but I'll say anything at this point just to spend a few more minutes with her. "The best in town."

Again, her expression is hesitant. She glances down at the phone in her hands and then looks back up at me. "I . . ." She bites her bottom lip, embarrassed. "I should probably call my roommate first. Just to let her know where I am. I'm usually home by now."

"Of course."

She looks down at her phone and dials a number. She waits for the other person to pick up.

"Hey," she says into the phone. "It's me." She smiles at me reassuringly. "I'll be late tonight, I'm having drinks with someone." She pauses for a second and then looks up at me with a twisted expression. "Um . . . yeah, I guess. He's right here."

She holds the phone out toward me. "She wants to talk to you."

I step toward her and take the phone.

"Hello?"

"What's your name?" a girl on the other end of the line says.

"Owen Gentry."

"Where are you taking my roommate?"

She's grilling me in a monotone, authoritative voice. "To Harrison's Bar."

"What time will she be home?"

"I don't know. A couple of hours from now, maybe?" I look to Auburn for confirmation, but she just shrugs her shoulders.

"Take care of her," she says. "I'm giving her a secret phrase to use if she needs to call me for help. And if she doesn't call me at midnight to let me know she's home safe, I'm calling the police and reporting her murder."

"Um . . . okay," I say with a laugh.

"Let me talk to Auburn again," she says.

I hand the phone back to Auburn, a little more nervous than before. I can tell by the confused expression on her face that she's hearing about the secret-phrase rule for the first time. I'm guessing either she and this roommate haven't been living together for very long, or Auburn never goes out.

"What?!" Auburn says into the phone. "What kind of secret phrase is 'pencil dick'?"

She slaps her hand over her mouth and says, "Sorry," after accidentally blurting it out. She's quiet for a bit and then her face contorts into confusion. "Seriously? Why can't you choose normal words, like raisin or rainbow?" She shakes her head with a quiet laugh. "Okay. I'll call you at midnight."

She ends the call and smiles. "Emory. She's a little strange."

I nod, agreeing with the strange part. She points to the bathroom. "Can I change first?"

I tell her to go ahead, relieved that she'll be back in the clothes I found her in. When she disappears into the bathroom, I pull out my phone to text Harrison.

Me: I'm coming for a drink. Do you serve cheese sticks?

Harrison: Nope.

Me: Do me a favor. When I order cheese sticks, don't say you don't serve them. Just say you ran out.

Harrison: Okay. Random request, but whatever.

CHAPTER THREE

Auburn

Life is strange.

I have no idea how I went from working at the salon this morning, to an appointment at a law office this afternoon, to working at an art studio tonight, to walking into a bar for the first time in my life.

I was too embarrassed to tell Owen I've never been to a bar before, but I'm pretty sure he could tell by my hesitation at the door. I didn't know what to expect when we walked in because I'm not yet twenty-one. I reminded Owen of this and he shook his head and told me not to mention it if Harrison asks for ID. "Just tell him you left it at the studio and I'll vouch for you."

It's definitely not what I expected a bar would look like. I imagined disco balls and a huge, central dance floor, and John Travolta. In reality, this bar is much less dramatic than I imagined. It's quiet, and I could probably count the number of occupants on both hands. There are more tables covering the floor than there is room to dance. And there's no disco ball anywhere in sight. I'm a little disappointed by that.

Owen weaves through a few tables until he gets to the back of the dimly lit room. He pulls out a stool and motions for me to sit while he takes the one next to it.

There's a guy at the other end of the bar who looks up at us just as I'm taking my seat, and I assume this is Harrison. He looks to be in his late twenties, with a head full of curly, red hair. The combination of his fair skin and the fact that there are four-leaf clovers on almost every sign in this place makes me wonder if he's Irish or if he just wishes he were.

I know it shouldn't surprise me that this guy owns a bar and appears this young, because if everyone around here is anything like Owen, this city must be full of young entrepreneurs. *Great.* Makes me feel even more out of place.

Harrison nods his head in Owen's direction and then briefly glances at me. He doesn't stare long, and then his eyes are back on Owen's with a perplexed look. I don't know what has this guy confused, but Owen ignores the look he shoots him and turns to face me.

"You were great tonight," he says. His chin is resting in his hand and he's smiling. His compliment makes me smile back, or maybe it's just him. He's got such an innocent, charming vibe. The way his eyes crinkle in the corners makes his smile seem more genuine than other people's.

"So were you." We both just continue to smile at each other

and I realize that although bars aren't typically my scene, I'm actually enjoying myself. I haven't in so long, and I don't know why Owen seems to extract a whole different side of me, but I like it. I also know that I have so many other things I should be focusing on right now, but it's one night. One drink. What harm can it do?

He lays his arm on the bar and swivels his chair until he's facing me full-on. I do the same, but the chairs are really close together and our knees end up overlapping. He adjusts himself until one of my knees is between both of his, and one of his is between both of mine. We aren't too close and it's not as though we're rubbing our legs together, but they're definitely touching and it's kind of an intimate way to be seated with someone I barely know. He looks down at our legs.

"Are we flirting?"

Now we're looking at each other again and we're both still grinning and it hits me that I don't think either of us has stopped grinning since we left his studio.

I shake my head. "I don't know how to flirt."

He looks back down at our legs and is about to comment when Harrison approaches us. He leans forward and casually rests his arms on the bar, placing his attention on Owen.

"How'd it go?"

Harrison is definitely Irish. I almost can't even understand him, his accent is so thick.

Owen smiles in my direction. "Pretty damn good."

Harrison nods and then focuses on me. "You must be Hannah." He reaches his hand out to me. "I'm Harrison."

I don't look at Owen, but I can hear him clearing his throat. I take Harrison's hand and shake it. "Nice to meet you, Harrison, but I'm actually Auburn."

Harrison's eyes grow wide and he slowly turns back to Owen. "Shit, man," he says, laughing apologetically. "I can't keep up with you."

Owen waves it off. "It's fine," he says. "Auburn knows about Hannah."

I don't really. I'm assuming Hannah is the girl who just dumped him. The only thing I do know is that Owen told me coming to this bar after a showing was tradition. So I'm curious how Harrison has never met Hannah if she's worked shows for Owen before. Owen looks at me and can see the confusion on my face.

"I never brought her here."

"Owen has never brought anyone here," Harrison offers. He looks back at Owen. "What happened to Hannah?"

Owen shakes his head like he doesn't really want to talk about it. "The usual."

Harrison doesn't ask what "the usual" is, so I'm assuming he understands exactly what happened to Hannah. I just wish I knew what "the usual" meant.

"What can I get you to drink, Auburn?" Harrison asks.

I look at Owen a little wide-eyed, because I have no idea what to order. I've never ordered a drink before, considering I'm not yet old enough to do so. He understands my expression and immediately turns back to Harrison. "Bring us two Jack and Cokes," he says. "And an order of cheese sticks."

Harrison taps the bar with his fist and says, "Coming right up." He begins to turn around but quickly faces Owen again. "Oh, we're all out of cheese sticks. Travesty. Cheese fries okay?"

I try not to frown, but I was really looking forward to cheese sticks. Owen looks at me and I nod. "Sounds good," I say.

Harrison smiles and begins to turn around but then faces me yet again. "You're over twenty-one, right?"

I quickly nod, and for a second I see doubt appear in his expression, but he turns and walks away without asking for my identification.

"You're a horrible liar," Owen laughs.

I expel a breath. "I don't normally lie."

"I can see why," he says.

He adjusts his position on the stool, and our legs brush together again. He smiles. "What's your story, Auburn?"

Here we go. The moment when I usually call it a night before the night even gets started.

"Whoa," he says. "What's the look for?"

I realize I must be frowning when he says this. "My story is that I have a very private life and I don't like to talk about it."

He smiles, which isn't the reaction I was expecting. "Sounds a lot like my story."

Harrison is back with the drinks, saving us from what was about to become a failed conversation. We both take a drink at the same time, but his goes down a whole lot smoother than mine does. Despite being underage, I've had a few drinks in the past with friends back in Portland, but this is a tad strong for my taste. I cover my mouth to cough and Owen, of course, smiles again.

"Well, since neither of us feels like talking at all, do you at least dance?" He glances over my shoulder at the small, empty dance floor on the opposite side of the room.

I immediately shake my head.

"How did I know that would be your answer?" He stands up. "Come on."

I shake my head again and almost instantly, my mood

changes. There's no way I'm dancing with him, especially to whatever slow song just started playing. He grabs my hand and tries to pull me up, but I'm gripping my chair with my other hand, ready to fight him off if I have to.

"You really don't want to dance?" he asks.

"I really don't want to dance."

He stares at me for a few quiet seconds and then takes a seat back in his chair. He leans forward and motions for me to come closer. He still has hold of my hand, and I feel his thumb brush slightly over mine. He continues to lean toward me until his mouth is close to my ear. "Ten seconds," he whispers. "Just give me ten seconds on the dance floor. If you still don't want to dance with me after my time is up, you can walk away."

There are chills on my arms and legs and neck, and his voice is so soothing and convincing, I can feel myself nodding before I even know what I'm agreeing to.

But ten seconds is simple. Ten seconds I can do. Ten seconds isn't enough time to embarrass myself. And after his time is up, I'll come back and sit down and he'll leave me alone about dancing, hopefully.

He's standing again, pulling me toward the dance floor. I'm relieved the place is relatively empty. Even though we'll be the only ones dancing, the place is deserted enough that I won't feel like I'm the center of attention.

We reach the dance floor and he slips a hand to my lower back.

"One," I whisper.

He smiles when he realizes I'm actually counting. He uses his other hand to position my hands around his neck. I've seen couples dance enough to know how to stand, at least.

"Two."

He shakes his head with a laugh and wraps his free hand around my lower back, pulling me against him.

"Three."

He begins to sway, and this is where dancing becomes confusing to me. I have no idea what to do next. I look down at our feet, hoping to get an idea of what I'm supposed to do with mine. He rests his forehead against mine and also looks down at our feet. "Just follow my lead," he says. His hands slide to my waist and he gently guides my hips in the direction he wants me to move.

"Four," I whisper as I move with him.

I can feel him relaxing just a little bit when he sees I've got it down. His hands slip to my back once again and he pulls me even closer. Naturally, my arms loosen slightly and I lean into him.

His smell is intoxicating and before I realize what I'm doing, my eyes are closed and I'm inhaling the scent of him. He still smells like he just stepped out of the shower, even though it's been hours.

I think I like dancing.

It feels very natural, as if dancing is part of a human's biological purpose.

It's a lot like sex, actually. I have about as much experience with sex as I do with dancing, but I definitely remember every moment I spent with Adam. It can be very intimate, the way two bodies come together and somehow know exactly what to do and exactly how to fit while doing it.

I can feel my pulse getting faster and warmth spreading over me, and it's been so long since I've felt this way. I wonder if it's the dancing that's doing this to me or if it's Owen. I've never slow-danced before, so I have no other dance to compare it to. The only thing I have to measure this feeling against is the way Adam used to make me feel, and this is pretty close to that. It's been a long time since I've wanted someone to kiss me.

Or maybe it's just been a long time since I've allowed myself to feel this way.

Owen lifts his hand to the back of my head and lowers his mouth to my ear. "It's been ten seconds," he whispers. "Do you want to stop?"

I shake my head softly.

I can't see his face, but I know he's smiling. He pulls me against his chest and rests his chin on top of my head. I close my eyes and breathe him in again.

We dance like this until the song ends, and I'm not sure if I'm supposed to let go first or if he's supposed to let go first, but neither of us does. Another song begins and luckily, it's slow like the last one, so we just keep moving as though the first song never ended.

I don't know when Owen began moving his hand away from the back of my head, but it's slowly moving down my back, making my arms and legs feel so weak, I question their existence. I find myself wishing he would pick me up and carry me, preferably straight to his bed.

His initials are very appropriate for the way he's making me feel right now. I want to whisper, "OMG," over and over.

I pull away from his chest and look up at him. He's not smiling right now. He's piercing me with eyes that seem a thousand shades darker than when we walked into this bar.

I unlock my hands, and I slide one against his neck. I'm surprised I feel comfortable enough to do this, and even more surprised by his reaction. He exhales softly and I can feel the chills erupt over the skin on his neck as his eyes fall shut and his forehead meets mine.

"I'm pretty sure I just fell in love with this song," he says. "And I hate this song."

I laugh a little and he pulls me closer, resting my head against his chest. We don't speak, and we don't stop dancing until the song ends. The third song begins to play and it isn't something I'm willing to dance to, considering it's not a slow song. When we both accept that the dance is over, we inhale simultaneous breaths and begin to separate.

His expression is full of concentrated intent, and as much as I like his smile, I also really like it when he looks at me like this. My arms leave his neck and his hands leave my waist and we're both standing on the dance floor, staring at each other awkwardly, and I'm not sure what to do now.

"The thing about dancing," he says, folding his arms across his chest, "is that no matter how good it feels when you're doing it, it's always extremely awkward when it's over."

It makes me feel good to know that it's not just me who doesn't know what to do now. His hand touches my shoulder, and he urges me back toward the bar. "We have drinks to finish."

"And fries to eat," I add.

He didn't ask me to dance again. In fact, as soon as we got back to the bar, he seemed like he was in a hurry to get out of there. I ate most of the fries while he chatted with Harrison a little more. He could tell I wasn't really digging my drink, so he finished it for me. Now we're walking back outside and it feels a little bit awkward again, like when the dance came to an end. Only now, it's the entire night that's coming to an end, and I hate that I really don't want to say good-bye to him yet. But I'm certainly not about to suggest we go back to his studio.

"Which way is your place?" he asks.

My eyes swing to his and I'm shocked by his forwardness. "You aren't coming over," I immediately say.

"Auburn," he says, laughing, "it's late. I'm offering to walk you home, not asking to spend the night."

I inhale, embarrassed at my assumption. "Oh." I point to the right. "I'm about fifteen blocks that way."

He smiles and waves a hand in that direction, and we both begin walking. "But if I *were* asking to spend the night . . ."

I laugh and push him playfully. "I would tell you to fuck off."

CHAPTER FOUR

Owen

If I were eleven years old again, I would shake my Magic 8 Ball and ask it silly questions, like "Does Auburn Mason Reed like me? Does she think I'm cute?"

And I might be making assumptions based on the way she's looking at me right now, but I expect the answer would be "It is decidedly so."

We continue walking away from the bar, toward her apartment, and considering it's quite a few blocks away, I can probably think of enough questions between here and there to get to know her a whole lot better. The one thing I've been wanting to know most since I saw her standing in front of my studio tonight is why she's back in Texas.

"You never told me why you moved to Texas."

She looks alarmed by my comment, but I don't know why. "I never told you I wasn't from Texas."

I smile to cover up my mistake. I shouldn't know she isn't from Texas, because as far as she knows, I know nothing about her other than what she's told me tonight. I do my best to hide what's really going through my head, because if I were to come clean with her now, it would make me look like I've been hiding something from her for the majority of the night. I have, but it's too late for me to admit that now. "You didn't have to tell me. Your accent told me."

She watches me closely, and I can tell she's not going to answer my question, so I think of a different question to replace that one, but the next question is even more rushed. "Do you have a boyfriend?"

She quickly looks away and it makes my heart sting because for some reason, she looks guilty. I assume this means she does have a boyfriend, and dances like the one I just shared with her shouldn't happen with girls who have boyfriends.

"No."

My heart instantly feels better. I smile again, for about the millionth time since I first saw her at my door tonight. I don't know if she knows this about me yet, but I hardly ever smile.

I wait for her to ask me a question, but she's quiet. "Are you gonna ask me if I have a girlfriend?"

She laughs. "No. She broke up with you last week."

Oh, yeah. I forgot we've already visited this subject. "Lucky me."

"That's not very nice," she says with a frown. "I'm sure it was a hard decision for her."

I disagree with a shake of my head. "It was an easy decision for her. It's an easy decision for all of them."

She pauses for a second or two, eyeing me warily before she begins walking again. "All of them?"

I realize this doesn't make me sound good, but I'm not about to lie to her. Plus, if I tell her the truth, she might continue to trust me and ask me even more questions.

"Yes. I get broken up with a lot."

She squints her eyes and scrunches her nose up at my response. "Why do you think that is, Owen?"

I try to pad the harshness of the sentence about to come out of my mouth by speaking softer, but it's not a fact I necessarily want to admit to her. "I'm not a very good boyfriend."

She looks away, probably not wanting me to see the disappointment in her eyes. I saw it anyway, though. "What makes you a bad boyfriend?"

I'm sure there are lots of reasons, but I focus on the most obvious answers. "I put a lot of other things before my relationships. For most girls, not being a priority is a pretty good reason to end things."

I glance at her to see if she's still frowning or if she's judging me. Instead, she has a thoughtful look on her face and she's nodding.

"So Hannah broke up with you because you wouldn't make time for her?"

"That's what it boiled down to, yes."

"How long were the two of you together?"

"Not long. A few months. Three, maybe."

"Did you love her?"

I want to look at her, to see the look on her face after she asks me this question, but I don't want her to see the look on my face. I don't want her to think my frown means I'm heart-broken, because I'm not. If anything, I'm sad that I couldn't love her.

"I think love is a hard word to define," I say to her. "You can love a lot of things about a person but still not love the whole person."

"Did you cry?"

Her question makes me laugh. "No, I didn't cry. I was pissed. I get involved with these girls who claim they can handle it when I need to lock myself up for a week at a time. Then when it actually happens, we spend the time we are together fighting about how I love my art more than I love them."

She turns and walks backward so she can peg me with her stare. "Do you? Love your art more?"

I look straight at her this time. "Absolutely."

Her lips curl up into a hesitant grin, and I don't know why this answer pleases her. It disturbs most people. I should be able to love people more than I love to create, but so far that hasn't happened yet.

"What's the best anonymous confession you've ever received?"

We haven't been walking long. We aren't even to the end of the street, but the question she just asked could open up a conversation that could last for days.

"That's a tough one."

"Do you keep all of them?"

I nod. "I've never thrown one away. Even the awful ones."

This gets her attention. "Define awful."

I glance over my shoulder to the end of the street and look at my studio. I don't know why the thought to show her even crosses my mind, because I've never shared the confessions with anyone.

But she isn't just anyone.

When I look at her again, her eyes are hopeful. "I can show you some," I say.

Her smile widens with my words, and she immediately stops heading in the direction of her apartment in favor of my studio.

Once upstairs, I open the door and let her cross the threshold that has, up to this point, only been crossed by me. This is the room I paint in. This is the room I keep the confessions in. This is the room that is the most private part of me. In a way, I guess you could say this room holds my confession.

There are several paintings in here I've never shown anyone. Paintings that will never see the light of day—like the one she's looking at right now.

She touches the canvas and runs her fingers over the face of the man in the picture. She traces his eyes, his nose, his lips. "This isn't a confession," she says, reading the piece of paper attached to it. She glances at me. "Who is this?"

I walk to where she is and stare at the picture with her. "My father."

She gasps quietly, running her fingers over the words written on the slip of paper. "What does *Nothing but Blues* mean?"

Her fingers are now trailing over the sharp white lines in the painting and I wonder if anyone has ever told her that artists don't like it when you touch their paintings.

That's not true in this case, because I want to watch her touch every single one of them. I love how she can't seem to look at one without feeling it with both her eyes and her hands. She looks up at me expectantly, waiting for me to explain what the title of this one means.

"It means nothing but lies." I walk away before she can see the expression on my face. I lift the three boxes I keep in the corner and take them to the center of the room. I take a seat on the concrete floor and motion for her to do the same.

She sits cross-legged in front of me with the boxes stacked between us. I take the two smaller boxes off the top and set them aside, then open the lid on the larger box. She peeks inside and shoves her hand into the pile of confessions, pulling out a random one. She reads it out loud.

"'I've lost over one hundred pounds in the past year.

Everyone thinks it's because I've discovered a new healthy way of living, but really it's because I suffer from depression and anxiety and I don't want anyone to know.'"

She places the confession back in the box and grabs another. "Will you ever use any of these for paintings? Is that why you keep them in here?"

I shake my head. "This is where I keep the ones I've seen in one form or another before. People's secrets are a lot alike, surprisingly."

She reads another. "'I hate animals. Sometimes when my husband brings home a new puppy for our children, I'll wait a few days and then drop it off miles from our house. Then I pretend it ran away.'"

She frowns at that confession.

"Jesus," she says, picking up several more. "How do you retain faith in humanity after reading these every day?"

"Easy," I say. "It actually makes me appreciate people more, knowing we all have this amazing ability to put on a front. Especially to those closest to us."

She stops reading the confession in her hands and her eyes meet mine. "You're amazed that people can lie so well?"

I shake my head. "No. Just relieved to know that everyone does it. Makes me feel like maybe my life isn't as fucked up as I thought it was."

She regards me with a quiet smile and continues sifting through the box. I watch her. Some of the confessions make her laugh. Some make her frown. Some make her wish she'd never read them.

"What's the worst one you've ever received?"

I knew this was coming. I almost wish I had lied to her and said I throw a lot of them away, but instead I point to the smaller box. She leans forward and touches it, but she doesn't pull it toward her.

"What's in here?"

"The confessions I never want to read again."

She looks down at the box and slowly pulls the lid off of it. She grabs one of the confessions from the top. "'My father has been . . .'" Her voice grows weak and she looks up at me with daunting sadness. I can see the gentle roll of her throat as she swallows and then looks back down to the confession. "'My father has been having sex with me since I was eight years old. I'm thirty-three now and married with children of my own, but I'm still too scared to say no to him.'"

She doesn't just place this confession back into the box. She crumples it up into a tight fist and she throws the confession at the box, like she's angry at it. She puts the lid back on it and shoves the box several feet away. I can see that she hates that box as much as I do.

"Here," I say, handing her the box she hasn't opened. "Read a couple of these. You'll feel better."

She hesitantly removes one of the confessions. Before she reads it, she straightens up and stretches her back, and then inhales a deep breath.

"'Every time I go out to eat, I secretly pay for someone's meal. I can't afford it, but I do it because it makes me feel good to imagine what that moment must be like for them, to know a complete stranger just did something nice for them with no expectations in return.'"

She smiles, but she needs another good one. I sift through the box until I find the one printed on blue construction paper. "Read this one. It's my favorite."

"'Every night after my son falls asleep, I hide a brand-new

toy in his room. Every morning when he wakes up and finds it, I pretend not to know how it got there. Because Christmas should come every day and I never want my son to stop believing in magic.'"

She laughs and looks up at me appreciatively. "That kid's gonna be sad when he wakes up in his college dorm for the first time and doesn't have a new toy." She places it back in the box and continues sifting through them. "Are any of these your own?"

"No. I've never written one."

She looks at me in shock. "Never?"

I shake my head and she tilts hers in confusion. "That's not right, Owen." She immediately stands and leaves the room. I'm confused as to what's going on, but before I take the time to stand up and follow her, she returns. "Here," she says, handing me a sheet of paper and a pen. Sitting back down on the floor in front of me, she nods her head at the paper and encourages me to write.

I look down at the paper when I hear her say, "Write something about yourself that no one else knows. Something you've never told anyone."

I smile when she says this, because there is so much I could tell her. So much that she probably wouldn't even believe, and so much I'm not even sure I want her to know.

"Here." I tear the paper in half and hand a piece of it to her. "You have to write one, too."

I write mine first, but as soon as I'm done, she takes the pen from me. She writes hers without hesitation. She folds it and begins to throw it in the box, but I stop her. "We have to trade."

She immediately shakes her head. "You aren't reading mine," she says firmly.

She's so adamant, it makes me want to read it even more. "It's not a confession if no one reads it. It's just an unshared secret."

She shoves her hand inside the box and releases her confession into the pile of other confessions. "You don't have to read it in front of me in order for it to be considered a confession." She grabs the paper out of my hands and shoves it into the box along with hers and all the others. "You don't read any of the others as soon as they write them."

She makes a good point, but I'm extremely disappointed that I don't know what she just wrote down. I want to pour the box out onto the floor and sift through the confessions until I find hers, but she stands up and reaches down for my hand.

"Walk me home, Owen. It's getting late."

We walk most of the way to her apartment in complete silence. Not an uncomfortable silence in any way. I think we're both quiet because neither of us is ready to say good-bye just yet.

She doesn't pause when we reach her apartment building in order to say good-bye to me. She keeps walking, expecting that I'll follow her.

I do.

I follow behind her, all the way to apartment 1408. I stare at the pewter number plaque on her door, and I want to ask her if she's ever seen the horror movie *1408*, with John Cusack. But I'm afraid if she's never heard of it, she might not like that there's a horror movie with the same name as her apartment number.

She inserts her key into the lock and pushes open the door. After it's open she turns around to face me, but not before motioning toward the apartment number. "Eerie, huh? You ever seen the movie?"

I nod. "I wasn't going to bring it up."

She glances at the number and sighs. "I found my roommate online, so she already lived here. Believe it or not, Emory had a choice between three apartments and actually chose this one because of the creepy correlation to the movie."

"That's a little disturbing."

She nods and inhales a breath. "She's . . . different."

She looks down at her feet.

I inhale and look up at the ceiling.

Our eyes meet in the middle, and I hate this moment. I hate it because I'm not finished talking to her, but it's time for her to go. It's way too soon for a kiss, but the discomfort of a first date coming to an end is there. I hate this moment because I can feel how uncomfortable she is as she waits for me to tell her good night.

Rather than do the expected, I point inside her apartment. "Mind if I use your restroom before I head back?"

That's platonic enough but still gives me an excuse to talk to her a little more. She glances inside, and I see a flash of doubt cross her face because she doesn't know me, and she doesn't know that I would never hurt her, and she wants to do the right thing and protect herself. I like that. It makes me worry a little less, knowing she has a semblance of self-preservation.

I smile innocently. "I already promised I wouldn't torture, rape, or kill you."

I don't know why this makes her feel better, but she laughs. "Well, since you promised," she says, holding the door open wider, allowing me inside her apartment. "But just in case, you should know I'm very loud. I can scream like Jamie Lee Curtis."

I shouldn't be thinking about what she sounds like when she's loud. But she brought it up.

She points me in the direction of her restroom, and I walk inside, closing the door behind me. I grip the edges of her sink while looking in the mirror. I try to tell myself again that this is nothing more than a coincidence. Her showing up at my doorstep tonight. Her connecting with my art. Her having the same middle name as I do.

That could be fate, you know.

CHAPTER FIVE

Auburn

What the hell am I doing? I don't do this kind of thing. I don't invite guys into my home.

Texas is turning me into a whore.

I put on a pot of coffee, knowing full well I don't need caffeine. But after the day I've had, I know I won't be able to sleep anyway, so what the hell?

Owen walks out of the restroom, but he doesn't make his way back to the door. Instead, a painting catches his eye on the far wall of the living room. He walks slowly to it and studies it.

He better not say anything negative about it. He's an artist, though. He'll probably critique it. What he doesn't realize is that painting is the last thing Adam made me before he passed away, and it means more to me than anything else I own. If Owen criticizes it, I'll kick him out. Whatever this flirtation is that's going on between us will be over faster than it started.

"Is this yours?" he asks, pointing at the painting.

Here we go.

"It's my roommate's," I lie.

I feel like he'll be more honest in his critique if he doesn't think it belongs to me.

He glances back at me and watches me for a few seconds before facing the painting again. He runs his fingers over the center of it, where the two hands are being pulled apart. "Incredible," he says quietly, as if he's not even speaking to me.

"He was," I say under my breath, knowing he can hear me, but not really caring. "Do you want a cup of coffee?"

He says yes without turning to face me. He stares at the painting for a while longer and then continues around the living room, taking everything in. Luckily, since most of my stuff is still back in Oregon, the only trace of me in this entire apartment is that painting, so he won't be able to learn anything else about me.

I pour him a cup of coffee and slide it across the bar. He makes his way into the kitchen and takes a seat, pulling it to him. I pass him the cream and sugar when I finish with them, but he waves them away and takes a sip.

I can't believe he's sitting here in my apartment. What shocks me even more is that I feel somewhat comfortable with it. He's probably the only guy since Adam that I've had the urge to flirt with. Not that I haven't dated at all since then. I've been on a few dates. Well, two. And only one of those ended with a kiss.

"You said you met your roommate online?" he asks. "How did that happen?"

He just seems to want to cut right to the core with his heavy questions, so I'm relieved he's finally given me a light one. "I applied for a job online when I decided to move here from Portland. She spoke with me over the phone and by the end of the conversation, she'd invited me to move in with her and share the lease."

He smiles. "Must have been a great first impression."

"It wasn't that," I say. "She just needed someone to split her rent or she would have been evicted."

He laughs. "Talk about perfect timing."

"You can say that again."

"Talk about perfect timing," he says again with a grin.

I laugh at him. He's not what I initially expected when I first walked into his studio. I assumed artists were quiet, brooding, and emotional creatures. Owen actually seems very put together. He's definitely mature for his age, considering he runs a successful business, but he's also very down-to-earth and . . . fun. His life seems to have a good balance, and that's probably the thing I find most attractive about him.

And yet, a conflicted feeling consumes me, because I can see where this is headed. And for a typical girl in her twenties, this would be exciting and fun. Something you would be texting your best friend about. *Hey, I met this really attractive, successful guy, and he actually seems normal.*

But my situation is anything but typical, which explains the mound of hesitation that keeps growing alongside my nervousness and anticipation. I find myself curious about him, and every now and then, I catch myself staring at his lips or his neck or those hands, which seem capable of doing a hell of a lot of magnificent things, aside from just painting.

But the hesitation I'm feeling is due in large part to me and my inexperience, because I'm not sure I'd know what to do with my hands if it came down to it. I try to remind myself of scenes in movies or books where the guy and girl are attracted to each other and how they go from that initial moment of attraction to the point of . . . acting on it. It's been so long since I was with Adam, I forget what comes next.

Of course I'm not sleeping with him tonight, but it's been so damn long since I've even felt comfortable enough to consider someone worthy of kissing. I just don't want my inexperience to reveal itself, which I'm sure it already has.

This lack of confidence is really getting in the way of my thoughts, and apparently our conversation, because I'm not speaking and he's just staring.

And I like it. I like it when he stares at me, because it's been a long time since I've felt beautiful in someone else's eyes. And right now, he's watching me so closely and with such a satisfied, heated look in his eyes, I would be fine if we spent the rest of the night just doing this and not speaking at all.

"I want to paint you," he says, breaking the silence. His voice is full of all the confidence I lack.

Apparently my heart is worried I forgot it existed, because it's giving me a loud and fast reminder of its presence in my chest. I do my best to swallow without his noticing. "You want to paint me?" I ask in an embarrassingly weak voice.

He nods slowly. "Yes."

I smile and try to play off the fact that his words just became the most erotic thing a guy has ever said to me. "I don't . . ." I release a breath to try to calm myself down. "Would it be . . . you know . . . with clothes on? Because I'm not posing nude."

I expect him to smile or laugh at this comment, but he doesn't. He stands up, slowly, and brings his cup of coffee back to his mouth. I like how he drinks his coffee. Like his coffee is so important, it deserves all of his attention. When he's finished, he sets it on the bar and gives me his focus, fixing me with a pointed stare. "You don't even have to be there when I paint you. I just want to paint you."

I don't know why he's standing now, but it makes me nervous. The fact that he's standing means either he's about to leave, or he's about to make a move. Neither of which I'm ready for quite yet.

"How will you paint me if I'm not there?" I hate that I can't fake the confidence that surrounds him like an aura.

He confirms my fear that he's about to make a move, because he slowly works his way around the bar, toward me. I'm eyeing him the entire time until my back is against the counter and he's standing directly in front of me. He lifts his right hand and—yes, I know you're in there, heart—his fingers brush lightly beneath my chin, slowly tilting my face upward. I gasp. His eyes fall to my mouth before scanning slowly over my features, lingering on each one, giving every part of me from the neck up his complete and total focus. I watch his eyes as they move from my jaw, to my cheekbones, to my forehead, back to my eyes again.

"I'll paint you from memory," he says as he releases my face. He takes two steps back until he meets the counter behind him. I don't realize how heavily I'm breathing until I see his gaze fall to my chest for a brief second. But I honestly don't have time to worry about whether or not my reaction is obvious to him, because all I can focus on right now is how to get oxygen back into my lungs and a voice back into my throat. I inhale a shaky breath and realize it isn't coffee I need right now. It's water. Ice water. I walk toward him and open a cabinet and proceed to pour myself a glass of water. He props his hands on the counter behind him and crosses one foot over the other, grinning at me the entire time I down half the glass.

The sound the glass makes when I set it on the counter is a little loud and dramatic, and it makes him laugh. I wipe my mouth and curse myself for being so obvious.

His laugh is cut short when his cell phone rings. He quickly stands and pulls it out of his pocket. He glances at the screen, silences his phone, and slides it back into his pocket. His eyes move around the living room once more before they land on me again. "I should probably go."

Wow. This went well.

I nod and take his cup when he slides it toward me. I turn around and begin washing it. "Well, thanks for the job," I say. "And for walking me home."

I don't turn around to watch him leave. I feel like my obvious inexperience just killed the entire vibe we had going. And I'm not upset with myself for that; I'm upset with him. I'm upset that he would be turned off by the fact that I'm not being forward or throwing myself at him. I'm upset that he gets one phone call, more than likely from Hannah, and he immediately uses it as his opportunity to hightail it out of here.

This is exactly why I never do things like this.

"It wasn't a girl."

His voice startles me and I immediately spin around to find him standing right behind me. I start to respond, but I don't know what to say, so I just clamp my mouth shut. I feel stupid for getting so angry just now, even though he has no idea what was going through my head.

He takes a step closer and I press myself against the counter behind me, leaving the two feet of space between us that I need in order to remain coherent.

"I don't want you to think I'm leaving because another girl just called me," he says, explaining his remark in more detail.

I love that he just said this, and it makes all the negative thoughts I was having about him disappear. Maybe I was wrong. I do tend to have irrational reactions from time to time.

I turn around and face the sink again because I don't want him to see how much it pleases me that he wasn't making up an excuse to leave. "It's not my business who calls you, Owen."

I'm still facing the sink when his hands grip the counter on either side of me. His face moves close to the side of my head and I can feel his breath on my neck. I don't know how it happens, but my entire body moves involuntarily until his chest is flush against my back. We aren't nearly as close as we were during our dance, but it feels a whole hell of a lot more intimate considering we aren't actually dancing.

He rests his chin on my shoulder and I close my eyes and inhale. The way he makes me feel is so overwhelming; I find it difficult to continue standing. I'm gripping the counter, hoping he doesn't notice how white my knuckles are.

"I want to see you again," he whispers.

I don't think about all the reasons why that's such a bad idea. I don't think about what my focus should be on. Instead, I think about how good it feels when he's this close to me and how I want so much more of it. All the bad parts of me answer him and force my voice to say, "Okay," because all the good parts of me are too weak to offer up a defense.

"Tomorrow night," he says. "Will you be home?"

I think about tomorrow, and for a few seconds I have no idea what month it is, much less what day of the week it is. After grasping where and who I am, and remembering that this is still Thursday and tomorrow is Friday, I conclude that I am, in fact, free tomorrow night.

"Yes," I whisper.

"Good," he says. I'm almost positive he's smiling right now. I can hear it in his voice.

"But . . ." I turn and face him. "I thought you learned your lesson about mixing business with pleasure. Isn't that how you found yourself in a bind today?"

He grins with a very subtle laugh. "Consider yourself fired."

I smile, because I'm not sure I've ever been so happy to lose a job. I would choose his coming over tomorrow night over working for $100 an hour any day. And that surprises me. A lot.

He turns and heads toward the front door. "I'll see you tomorrow night, Auburn Mason Reed."

We're both smiling when we lock eyes for the two seconds it takes for him to close the door behind him. I fall forward and lay my head on my arms, sucking in all the air I've been missing tonight, straight into my lungs.

"Oh, em, gee," I exhale. This was definitely an unexpected departure from my usual routine.

A sudden knock on my door startles me, and I stand upright just as the door begins to crack open. He reappears in the doorway. "Will you lock your door behind me? You don't live in the best neighborhood."

I can't help but grin at his request. I walk to the door and he pushes it open a little further. "And one more thing," he adds. "You shouldn't be so quick to follow strangers into random buildings. That's not very smart for someone who doesn't know anything about Dallas."

I narrow my eyes at him. "Well, you shouldn't be so desperate for employees," I say in my own defense. I lift my hand to the lock on the door, but instead of pulling it shut, he opens it even further.

"And I don't know how it is in Portland, but you also shouldn't allow strangers inside your apartment."

"You walked me home. I couldn't deny you the use of my restroom."

He laughs. "Thank you. I appreciate that. Just don't let anyone else in to use your restroom, okay?"

I grin at him flirtatiously, proud that I even have it in me. "We haven't even been on a date yet and you're already trying to dictate who can and can't use my restroom?"

He shoots me the same grin in return. "I can't help it if I'm a little possessive. It was a really nice restroom."

I roll my eyes and begin to close the door. "Good night, Owen."

"I'm serious," he says. "You even have those cute little seashell soaps. I love those."

We're both laughing now as he watches me through the crack in the door. Right when the door shuts and I lock the latch, he knocks again. I shake my head and open the door, but it catches with the chain lock this time.

"What now?"

"It's midnight!" he says frantically, slapping at the door. "Call her. Call your roommate!"

"Oh, shit," I mutter. I retrieve my phone and begin to dial Emory's number.

"I was about to dial 911," Emory says as she answers.

"Sorry, we almost forgot."

"Do you need to use the code word?" she asks.

"No, I'm fine. I already locked him out, so I don't think he's going to murder me tonight."

Emory sighs. "That sucks," she says. "Not that he didn't murder you," she adds quickly. "I just really wanted to hear you say the code word."

I laugh. "I'm sorry my safety disappoints you."

She sighs again. "Please? Just say it for me one time."

"Fine," I say with a groan. "Meat dress. Are you happy?"

There's a quiet pause before she says, "I don't know. Now I'm not sure if you said the code word just to make me happy or if you're really in danger."

I laugh. "I'm fine. I'll see you when you get home." I hang up the phone and glance at Owen through the opening in the door. His eyebrow is cocked and his head is tilted.

"Your code word was *meat dress?* That's kind of morbid, isn't it?"

I smile, because it kind of is. "So is choosing an apartment based on its connection to a horror film. I told you Emory is different."

He nods in agreement.

"I had fun tonight," I tell him.

He smiles. "I had funner."

We're both smiling, almost cheesily, until I straighten up and decide to close the door for good this time.

"Good night, Owen."

"Good night, Auburn," he says. "Thank you for not correcting my grammar."

"Thank you for not killing me," I say in response.

His smile disappears. "Yet."

I don't know if I should laugh at that comment.

"I'm kidding," he says as soon as he sees the hesitation on my face. "My jokes always fail when I'm trying to impress a girl."

"Don't worry," I say to reassure him. "I was kind of impressed as soon as I walked into your studio tonight."

He smiles appreciatively and slips his hand through the opening in the door before I can shut it again. "Wait," he says, wiggling his fingers. "Give me your hand."

"Why? So you can lecture me about how I shouldn't touch strangers' hands through locked doors?"

He dismisses my question with a shake of his head. "We're far from being strangers, Auburn. Give me your hand."

I tentatively bring my fingers up and barely touch them to his. I'm not sure what he's doing. His eyes drop to our fingers, and he leans his head against the door frame. I do the same and we both watch our hands as he slides his fingers between mine.

We're on two separate sides of a locked door, so I have no idea how simply touching his hand can make me have to lean against the wall for support, but that's exactly what I'm doing. Chills run up my arms and I close my eyes.

His fingers brush delicately over my palm and trace their way around my hand. My breaths are shaky and my hand is growing even shakier. I have to stop myself from unlocking the door so I can pull him inside and beg him to do to the rest of me what he's doing to my hand.

"You feel that?" he whispers.

I nod, because I know he's looking right at me. I can feel his stare. He doesn't speak again and his hand eventually stills against mine, so I slowly open my eyes. He's still watching me through the crack in the door, but as soon as my eyes are all the way open, he quickly lifts his head away from the door frame and pulls his hand back, leaving mine empty.

"Fuck," he says, standing up straight. He runs his hand through his hair and then grips the back of his neck. "I'm sorry. I'm ridiculous." He releases his neck and grips the doorknob. "I'm leaving for real this time. Before I scare you away," he says with a smile.

I grin. "Good night, OMG."

He slowly shakes his head back and forth while his eyes narrow playfully. "You're lucky I like you, Auburn Mason Reed."

With that, he closes the door.

"Oh my God," I whisper. I think I might have a crush on that boy.

"Auburn."

I groan, not ready to wake up, but someone's hand is on my shoulder, shaking me.

Rude.

"Auburn, wake up." It's Emory's voice. "The police are here."

I immediately roll onto my side and see her standing over me. She's got mascara under her eyes and her blond hair is sticking out in all directions. Her unexpected, unkempt appearance scares me more than the fact that she just said the police are here. I sit straight up in bed. I try to find my alarm clock to check the time, but my eyes won't open enough for me to see it. "What time is it?"

"After nine," she says. "And . . . did you hear me? I said there's a cop here. He's asking for you."

I scoot myself off the bed and look for my jeans. I find them crumpled on the floor on the other side of my bed. As soon as I get them buttoned, I reach into the closet for a shirt.

"Are you in some kind of trouble?" Emory asks, standing by my door now.

Shit. I forgot she doesn't know anything about me.

"It's not the police," I tell her. "It's just Trey, my brother-in-law."

I can see she's still confused, and that makes sense since he's not really my brother-in-law. It's just easier to refer to him that way sometimes. I also have no idea why he's here. I open my bedroom door and see Trey standing in the kitchen, making himself a cup of coffee.

"Is everything okay?" I ask him. He spins around and as soon as I see his smile, I know everything is fine. He's just here for a visit.

"All good," he says. "Shift just ended and I was in the neighborhood. Thought I'd bring you breakfast." He holds up a sack and tosses it toward me on the counter. Emory walks around me and grabs the bag, opening it.

"Is it true?" she asks, looking up at Trey. "Do cops really get all the free doughnuts they want?" She grabs one of the pastries and shoves it in her mouth while making her way toward the living room. Trey is looking at her with contempt, but she doesn't notice. I wonder if she's aware that she hasn't looked in a mirror today. I doubt she cares. I love that about her.

"Thank you for the breakfast," I tell him. I take a seat at the bar, confused as to why he would think it's okay to just stop by without notice. Especially this early in the morning. But I don't say anything, because I'm sure it's just me being cranky due to my late night and lack of sleep. "Is Lydia coming home today?"

He shakes his head. "Tomorrow morning." He sets his cup on the bar. "Where were you last night?"

I cock my head, wondering why he would even ask that. "What do you mean?"

He glances back at me. "She says you called over an hour late."

Now I get why he's here. I sigh. "Did you really want to bring me breakfast or are you using it as an excuse to check up on me?"

The offended look he shoots me makes me regret my comment. I blow out an exasperated breath and rest my arms on the bar. "I was working," I say. "I filled in at an art gallery for extra money."

Trey is standing in the exact spot Owen was standing in last night. Trey and Owen are probably the same height, but for some reason Trey just appears more intimidating. I don't know if it's because he's always in a police uniform, or if it's the hardened facial features. His dark eyes always seem to be frowning, whereas Owen can't seem to help smiling. Just thinking about Owen and the fact that I'll see him again tonight instantly puts me in a better mood.

"An art gallery? Which one?"

"The one on Pearl, near my work. It's called Confess."

Trey's jaw tenses and he sets his cup of coffee on the counter. "I know the one," he says. "Callahan Gentry's son owns that building."

"Am I supposed to know who Callahan Gentry is?"

He shakes his head and pours his coffee in the sink. "Cal's an attorney," he says. "And his son is trouble."

I wince at his insult, because I don't understand it. Owen is the last person I would associate with the word trouble. Trey grabs his keys off the bar and begins making his way out of the kitchen. "I don't like the idea of you working for him."

Not that Trey's opinion matters to me in any way, but I'm a little put off that he even made that comment. "You don't have to worry about it," I say. "I was fired last night. Not what he was looking for in an employee, I guess." I fail to tell him the true reason I was fired last night. I'm sure that would upset him even more.

"Good," he says. "You coming to dinner Sunday night?"

I follow him to the door. "Haven't missed it yet, have I?"

Trey turns to face me after he opens the door. "Well, you've also never missed a phone call, and look what happened last night."

Touché, Trey.

I hate confrontation, and my attitude is going to start one if I don't backtrack. The last thing I need is tension with Trey or Lydia. "Sorry," I mutter. "It was a late night last night with working two jobs yesterday. Thank you for the breakfast. I'll be nicer next time you show up unannounced."

He smiles and reaches up to tuck a lock of hair behind my ear. It's an intimate gesture, and I don't like that he feels comfortable enough to do it. "It's fine, Auburn." He drops his hand and steps out into the hall. "See you Sunday night."

I close the door and lean against it. I've been getting a very different vibe from him lately. When I lived in Portland, I never saw him. However, moving to Texas put me in his presence a lot more, and I'm not sure we're on the same page when it comes to how we define our friendship.

"I don't like him," Emory says. I glance toward the living room and she's seated on the couch, eating her doughnut while flipping through a magazine.

"You don't even know him," I say in Trey's defense.

"I liked the guy you had over last night much better." She doesn't bother looking up from her magazine as she judges me.

"You were here last night?"

She nods and takes a long sip of her soda, again not bothering to give me eye contact. "Yep."

What? Why does she think this is okay?

"Were you here when I called you about the code word?"

She nods again. "I was in my room. I'm really good at eavesdropping," she says flatly.

I nod once and make my way back toward my bedroom. "That's good to know, Emory."

CHAPTER SIX

Owen

If I were smarter, I would be at my place right now, getting dressed.

If I were smarter, I'd be mentally preparing to show up at Auburn's apartment, since that's what I promised her I would do tonight.

If I were smarter, I wouldn't be sitting here. Waiting for my father to walk through the door and see my hands cuffed behind my back.

I don't really know how I should feel right now, but numbness probably isn't the appropriate response. I just know he's about to walk through that door any second and the last thing I want to do is look him in the eyes.

The door opens.

I look away.

I hear his footsteps as he slowly enters the room. I shift in my seat, but I can barely move thanks to the metal digging into my wrists. I bite my bottom lip to stop myself from saying something I'll regret. I bite it so hard I taste blood. I continue to avoid looking at him and choose to focus on the poster hanging on the wall. It's a photo timeline, depicting the progression of meth use over a ten-year span. I stare at it, aware of the fact that all ten pictures are of the same man, and all of them are mug shots. That means the guy was arrested no fewer than ten times.

He's got nine arrests on me.

My father sighs from where he's seated, directly across from me. He sighs so heavily his breath reaches me from across the table. I scoot back a few inches.

I don't even want to know what's going through his head right now. I just know what's going through my head, and that's nothing but a sea of disappointment. Not as much for my arrest as for the fact that I've let Auburn down. She seems to live a life where a lot of people let her down and I hate that I'm about to become one of them.

I hate it.

"Owen," my father says, requesting my attention.

I don't give it to him. I wait for him to finish, but he doesn't say anything beyond my name.

I don't like that all he said was my name, because I know there are a hell of a lot of other things he wants to say to me right now. There are certainly a lot of things I want to say to him, but Callahan Gentry and his son are not the best communicators.

Not since the night Owen Gentry became Callahan Gentry's only son.

That's probably the *only* day out of my entire life I wouldn't trade this one for. That day is the reason why I continue to do the shit I do. That day is the reason I'm sitting here, about to have to talk to my father about my options.

Sometimes I wonder if Carey can still see us. I wonder what he would think of what's become of us.

I look away from the meth poster and stare at my father. We've perfected the art of silence over the past few years. "Do you think Carey can see us right now?"

My father's face remains expressionless. The only thing I see in his eyes is disappointment, and I don't know if it's disappointment because he failed at being a father or if it's disappointment that I'm in this situation or if it's disappointment that I just brought up Carey.

I never bring up my brother. My father never brings up my brother. I don't know why I'm doing it now.

I lean forward and I keep my eyes locked with his.

"What do you think he thinks of me, Dad?" I say quietly. So quietly. If my voice were a color, it would be white.

My father's jaw clenches, so I keep going.

"Do you think he's disappointed in my inability to just say no?"

My father inhales and looks away, breaking eye contact with me. I'm making him uncomfortable. I can't lean forward any more than I already am, so I scoot my chair toward him until my chest meets the table between us. I'm as close as I can get now.

"What do you think Carey thinks of *you*, Dad?"

That sentence would be painted black.

My father's fist meets the table and his chair falls backward when he stands abruptly. He paces the room, twice, and kicks the chair, causing it to crash against the wall. He continues to pace from one end of the small room to the other, which is only about seven feet or so. He's so pissed, I feel bad that we're in such a tiny room. The man needs space to release all of his aggression. They should take these types of situations into consideration when they arrest people and stick them in tiny square rooms to meet with their lawyers. Because you never know when a lawyer is also a father and that father needs space to fit all his *anger*.

He takes several deep breaths, in and out, in and out. Just like he used to teach Carey and me to do when we were younger. Being brothers, we used to fight a lot. No more so than other brothers, but back then, when Callahan Gentry was a father, he would do everything he could to teach us how to deal with our anger internally, rather than physically.

"Only you can control your reactions," he would say to us. "No one else. You control your anger and you control your happiness. Get it under control, boys."

I wonder if I should repeat those words to him right now.

Get it under control, Dad.

Probably not. He doesn't want me to interrupt him as he silently attempts to convince himself that I didn't mean what I said. He tries to tell himself that I only said it because I'm under a lot of stress.

Callahan Gentry is good at lying to himself.

If I had to paint him right now, I would paint him every shade of blue I could find. He calmly places his palms flat on the table between us. He stares down at his hands and fails to make eye contact with me. He inhales one long, slow breath, and then releases it even slower. "I'm posting your bail as soon as I can."

I want him to think I'm indifferent. I'm not indifferent, though. I don't want to be here, but there's nothing I can do about it.

"Not like I have anywhere else to be," I say to him.

I mean, I don't, do I? I'd already be late if I were to even show up, plus there's no way I could show up now and tell Auburn where I've been. Or why. Besides, I was more or less warned to stay away from her last night, so there's also that.

So yeah. Who needs bail? Not me.

"Not like I have anywhere else to be," I repeat.

My father's eyes meet mine and it's the first time I notice the tears. With those tears comes hope. Hope that he's reached his breaking point. Hope that this was the last straw. Hope that he'll finally say, "How can I help you, Owen? How can I make this better for you?"

None of those things happen, though, and my hope disappears right along with the tears in his eyes. He turns and walks to the door. "We'll talk tonight. At the house."

And he's gone.

"What in the hell happened to you?" Harrison asks. "You look like shit."

I take a seat at the bar. I haven't slept in over twenty-four hours. As soon as my bail cleared a few hours ago, I went straight to my studio. I didn't even bother going to my father's house to discuss this situation, because I need a little more time before I can face him.

It's almost midnight now, so I know Auburn is probably asleep, or *too pissed off* to sleep, because I never showed up tonight like I promised I would. It's probably for the best though. I need to get my life straightened out enough for her to want to be a part of it.

"I was arrested last night."

Harrison immediately stops pouring the glass of beer he was about to hand me. He squares up and faces me full-on. "I'm sorry . . . did you just say *arrested*?"

I nod and reach across the bar, taking the half-full beer from him.

"I hope you're about to elaborate," he says, watching me take a long drink. I set the glass down on the bar and wipe my mouth.

"Arrested for possession."

Harrison's expression becomes a mixture of anger and nervousness. "Wait a second," he says. He leans in and lowers his voice to a whisper. "You didn't tell them I—"

I'm offended he would even ask that, so I cut him off before he even finishes the question. "Of course not," I say. "I refused to say anything about where the pills came from. Unfortunately, that won't help my situation when I show up for court. Apparently they cut you slack when you rat people out." I laugh and shake my head. "That's fucked up, huh? We teach kids that tattling is wrong but as adults, we're rewarded for it."

Harrison doesn't respond. I can see all the words he wants to say, he's just doing his best to keep them in.

"Harrison," I say, leaning forward. "It's fine. It'll be fine. It's my first offense, so I doubt I'll get much . . ."

He shakes his head. "It's *not* fine, Owen! I've been telling you to stop this shit for over a year now. I knew it would catch up with you and I hate being the one to say I told you so, but I fucking told you so about a million goddamn times."

I exhale. I'm too tired to listen to this right now. I stand up and set a ten-dollar bill on the bar and I turn around and leave.

He's right, though. He told me so. And he's not the only one, because I've been telling myself this would catch up to me for a hell of a lot longer than Harrison has.

CHAPTER SEVEN

Auburn

"Do you want a refill?"

I smile and say, "Sure," to the waitress, even though I know I don't need a refill. I should just leave, but there's still a small part of me that hopes Lydia will show up. Surely she didn't forget.

I debate whether or not to text her again. She's over an hour late and I'm sitting here, pathetically waiting, hoping I don't get stood up.

Not that she's the first person to stand me up. That award goes to Owen Mason Gentry.

I should have known. I should have been prepared for it.

That entire night with him seemed too good to be true, and the fact that I haven't heard from him after three solid weeks only proves that my decision to forgo guys was a smart one.

It still stings, though. It hurts like hell because when he walked out my door that Thursday night, I felt so hopeful. Not just about meeting him, but because it made me think Texas wouldn't be all that bad. I thought maybe for once, things were going to go my way and karma was going to cut me some slack.

As much as it hurt to realize he was full of shit, being stood up by Lydia hurts a little bit more than being stood up by Owen, because at least Owen didn't stand me up on my birthday.

How could she forget?

I won't cry. I won't do it. I've shed enough tears over that woman and she's not causing any more.

The waitress is back at the table, refilling my drink. My nonalcoholic drink.

I'm drinking a pathetic soda, sitting alone in a restaurant, being stood up for the second time this month, and it's my twenty-first birthday.

"I'll take the bill," I say, defeated. The waitress gives me a look of pity as she lays the bill on the table. I pay it and leave.

I hate that I still have to walk past his studio on my way home from work. Or in this case, on my way home from being stood up. Sometimes the light is on in his apartment upstairs and I get the urge to set the place on fire.

Not really. That's a little bit harsh. I wouldn't burn his beautiful art.

Just him.

When I reach his building, I stop and stare at it. Maybe it's worth walking an extra block or two from now on, just so

I'll never have to pass it again. Before I reroute myself, maybe I should leave a confession. I've been wanting to leave one for three weeks and tonight everything has lined up perfectly for me to finally be pissed enough to do so.

I walk to the front door of his building and stare at the slot while I reach inside my purse and pull out a pen. I don't have any paper, so I dig around until I find the receipt from the fantastic birthday dinner I just shared with myself. I flip it over and press the receipt to the window and begin my confession.

I met this really great guy three weeks ago. He taught me how to dance, reminded me of what it feels like to flirt, walked me home, made me smile, and then YOU'RE AN ASSHOLE, OWEN!

I press the button on the end of the pen to retract it. I put it back in my purse. Oddly enough, getting that out on paper actually made me feel a little better. I begin to fold the receipt but flatten it back out and retrieve my pen in order to add another sentence.

PS: *Your initials are so stupid.*

Much better. I slip the confession through the slot before I give myself enough time to think it through. I take a few steps away from the building and bid it farewell.

I turn toward my apartment and my phone sounds off. I pull it out and open my text.

Lydia: *Sorry! I got sidetracked and it's been such a crazy day. I hope you didn't wait long. Heading back to Pasadena in the morning, but you'll be at dinner Sunday, right?*

I read the text and all I can think is, Bitch, bitch, bitch, bitch.

I'm so immature. But come on, she couldn't even tell me happy birthday?

God, my heart hurts.

I begin to put the phone back into my pocket when it sounds off again. Maybe she remembered it was my birthday. At least she'll feel a little guilty about it. Maybe I shouldn't have called her a bitch.

Lydia: *Next time, remind me before I'm supposed to be there. You know I have my hands full.*

Bitch, bitch, bitch, big *huge* bitch.

I clench my teeth and scream out of frustration. I can't win with her. I'll never win with her.

I can't believe I'm about to do this, but I need a drink. An alcoholic drink. And lucky for me, I know just where to get one.

"You lied."

Harrison is looking at my ID.

I assume he just noticed that today is my birthday and I wasn't at all twenty-one when I walked in here with Owen the first time.

"Owen made me."

Harrison shakes his head and hands me back my ID. "Owen does a lot of things Owen shouldn't do." He wipes down the bar between us and tosses the rag aside, but I'm hoping he'll elaborate on that comment. "So what'll it be, Ms. Reed? Jack and Coke again?"

I immediately shake my head. "No thanks. Something a little less assaulting."

"Margarita?"

I nod.

He turns around to make my first legally ordered alcoholic beverage. I hope he puts one of those tiny umbrellas in it.

"Where's Owen?" he asks.

I roll my eyes. "Do I look like Owen's keeper? He's probably inside Hannah."

Harrison spins around, wide-eyed. I shrug off my insult and he laughs before returning his attention to my drink. When he's finished making it, he sets it on the bar in front of me. I begin to frown, but he reaches to his right, plucks an umbrella out of a jar, and places it in the drink. "See how you like this one."

I bring the margarita to my lips and lick the salt off first, then take a sip. My eyes light up, because this is so much better than the shit Owen ordered for me. I nod and motion for him to go ahead and make me another one.

"Why don't you finish that one first," he suggests.

"Another one," I say, wiping my mouth. "It's my birthday and I'm a responsible adult who wants two drinks."

His shoulders rise with his intake of breath and he shakes his head, but he does what I ask. Which is a good thing, because as soon as he finishes making my second one, I'm ordering a third one. Because I can. Because it's my birthday and I'm all alone, and Portland is way on top of the country and I'm way down here, all the way at the bottom, and *Owen Mason Gentry is a huge asshole*!

And Lydia is a bitch.

CHAPTER EIGHT

Owen

"There's someone here who belongs to you."

It takes me a few seconds to adjust to the middle-of-the-night phone call. I sit up in bed and rub my eyes. "Harrison?"

"You're asleep?" He sounds shocked. "It's not even one in the morning."

I swing my legs to the side of the bed and press my palm to my forehead. "Been a rough week. Haven't slept much." I stand up and look for my jeans. "Why are you calling?"

There's a pause and I hear a clatter come from his end of the line. "No! You can't touch that! Sit down!"

I pull the phone away from my ear to salvage my eardrum.

"Owen, you better get your ass over here. I close in fifteen minutes and she doesn't take last call well."

"What are you talking about? Who are you talking about?"

And then it hits me.

Auburn.

"Shit. I'll be right there."

Harrison hangs up without saying good-bye and I'm pulling a T-shirt over my head as I make my way downstairs.

Why are you there, Auburn? And why are you there alone?

I make it to the front door and kick a few of the confessions that have piled in front of it out of the way. I average about ten most weekdays, but the downtown traffic triples the number on Saturdays. I usually throw them all in a pile until I'm ready to begin a new painting before I read them, but one of the confessions on the floor catches my eye. I notice it because it has my name on it, so I pick it up.

> *I met this really great guy three weeks ago. He taught me how to dance, reminded me of what it feels like to flirt, walked me home, made me smile, and then* YOU'RE AN ASSHOLE, OWEN!
>
> *PS: Your initials are so stupid.*

The confessions are supposed to be anonymous, Auburn. This isn't anonymous. As much as I want to laugh, her confession also reminds me of how much I let her down and how I'm probably the last person she wants to see come rescue her from a bar.

I walk across the street anyway and open the door, immediately searching for her. Harrison notices me approaching and nods his head toward the restroom. "She's hiding from you."

I grip the back of my neck and look in the direction of the restrooms. "What's she doing here?"

Harrison lifts his shoulders in a shrug. "Celebrating her birthday, I guess."

You've got to be kidding me. Could I feel any more like shit?

"It's her birthday?" I begin making my way toward the bathroom. "Why didn't you call me sooner?"

"She made me swear I wouldn't."

I knock on the restroom door but get no response. I slowly push it open and immediately see her feet protruding from the last stall.

Shit, Auburn.

I rush to where she is but stop just as fast when I see she isn't passed out. In fact, she's wide awake. She looks a little too comfortable for someone sprawled out in a bar bathroom. She's resting her head against the wall of the stall, looking up at me.

I'm not surprised by the anger in her eyes. I probably wouldn't want to speak to me right now, either. In fact, I'm not even going to make her speak to me. I'll just take a seat right here on the floor with her.

She watches me as I walk into the stall and take a seat directly in front of her. I pull my knees up and wrap my arms around them and then lean my head back against the stall.

She doesn't look away from me, she doesn't speak, she doesn't smile. She just inhales a slow breath and gives her head the slightest disappointed shake.

"You look like shit, Owen."

I smile, because she doesn't sound as drunk as I thought she might be. But she's probably right. I haven't looked in a mirror in over three days. That happens when I get caught up in my work. I haven't shaved, so I more than likely have a good case of stubble going on.

She doesn't look like shit, though, and I should probably say that out loud. She looks sad and a little bit drunk, but for a girl sprawled out on a bathroom floor, she looks pretty damn hot.

I know I should apologize to her for what I did. I know that's the only thing that should be coming out of my mouth right now, but I'm scared if I apologize then she'll start asking questions, and I don't want to have to tell her the truth. I would rather she be disappointed that I stood her up than know the truth about why I stood her up.

"Are you okay?"

She rolls her eyes and focuses on the ceiling and I can see her attempt to blink back her tears. She brings her hands up to her face and rubs them up and down in an attempt to sober herself up, or maybe because she's frustrated that I'm here. Probably a little of both.

"I got stood up tonight."

She continues to stare up at the ceiling. I'm not sure how to feel about this confession of hers, because my first reaction is jealousy and I know that isn't fair. I just don't like the thought of her being so upset over someone who isn't me, when really it's none of my business.

"You get stood up by a guy so you spend the rest of the night drinking in a bar? That doesn't sound like you."

Her chin immediately drops to her chest and she looks up at me through her lashes. "I didn't get stood up by a guy, Owen. That's very presumptuous of you. And for your information, I happen to like drinking. I just didn't like your drink."

I shouldn't be focusing on that one word in her sentence, but . . .

"You got stood up by a girl?"

I have nothing against lesbians, but please don't be one. That's not how I envision this ending between us.

"Not by a girl, either," she says. "I got stood up by a bitch. A big, mean, selfish bitch."

Her words make me smile even though I don't mean for them to. There's nothing about her situation worth smiling over, but the way her nose crinkled up while she insulted whoever stood her up was really cute.

I straighten my legs out, placing them on the outsides of her legs. She looks as defeated as I feel.

What a pair we make.

I want so badly to tell her the truth, but I also know that the truth won't make things any better between us than they are now. The truth makes less sense than the lie, and I don't even know which one I should go with anymore.

The only thing I do know is that, whether she's mad or happy or sad or excited, she has this calming energy that radiates from her. Every day of my life it feels as if I'm fighting my way up an escalator that only goes down. And no matter how fast or how hard I run to try to reach the top, I stay in the same place, sprinting, getting nowhere. But when I'm with her it doesn't feel like I'm on that escalator. It feels as if I'm on a moving walkway, and I'm effortlessly just carried along. Like I can finally relax and take a breath and not feel the constant pressure to sprint in order to prevent hitting rock bottom.

Her presence calms me, relaxes me, makes me feel as though maybe things aren't as hard as they appear to be when she isn't around. So no matter how pathetic we may seem right now, sitting on the floor of the women's restroom, there isn't anywhere else I would rather be at this moment.

"OMG," she says, leaning forward to pull at my hair. Her entire face contorts into a frown and I can't understand how my hair is displeasing her so much right now. "We need to fix this shit," she mutters.

She puts one hand on the wall and one on my shoulder and she pushes herself up. When she's standing, she reaches for my hand. "Come on, Owen. I'm gonna fix your shit."

I don't know that she's sober enough to fix anything, really. But that's okay, because I'm still on my moving walkway, so I'll effortlessly follow her anywhere she wants to go.

"Let's wash our hands, Owen. The floor is gross." She walks to the sink and squirts soap on my palm. She glances at me in the mirror and looks down at my hand. "Here's you some soap," she says, wiping the soap across my hand.

I can't tell with her. I don't know how much she's had to drink, but this interaction isn't what I was expecting tonight. Especially after reading her confession.

We wash our hands in silence. She pulls two paper towels out and hands one to me. "Dry your hands, Owen."

I take the paper towels from her and do as she says. She's confident and in charge right now and I think it's best to leave it that way. Until I figure out her level of sobriety, I don't want to do anything to trigger any type of reaction from her other than what I'm getting right now.

I walk to the door and open it. She steps away from the sink and I watch her stumble slightly, but she catches herself on the wall. She immediately looks down at her shoes and glares at them.

"Fucking heels," she mumbles. Only she isn't wearing heels. She's wearing black flats, but she blames them, anyway.

We make our way back out into the bar and Harrison has

already closed up and shut off some of the lights. He raises a brow as we pass by him.

"Harrison?" she says to him, pointing a finger in his direction.

"Auburn," he says flatly.

She wags her finger and I can tell Harrison wants to laugh, but he keeps it in check. "You put those wonderful drinks on my tab, okay?"

He shakes his head. "We close out all tabs at the end of the night."

She places her hands on her hips and pouts. "But I don't have any money. I lost my purse."

Harrison leans over and grabs a purse from behind the bar. "You didn't lose it." He shoves it across the bar and she stares at the purse like she's upset she didn't lose it.

"Well, shit. Now I have to pay you." She steps forward and opens her purse. "I'm only paying you for one drink because I don't even think you put alcohol in that second one."

Harrison looks at me and rolls his eyes, then pushes her money away. "It's on the house. Happy birthday," he says. "And for the record, you had three drinks. All with alcohol."

She throws her purse over her shoulder. "Thank you. You're the only person in the entire state of Texas to tell me happy birthday today."

Is it possible to hate myself more than I did three weeks ago? Yes, it absolutely is.

She turns to me and tucks her chin in when she sees the look on my face. "Why do you look so sad, Owen? We're going to fix your shit, remember?" She takes a step toward me and grabs my hand. "Bye, Harrison. I hate you for calling Owen."

Harrison smiles and gives me a nervous look as if he's

silently saying, "Good luck." I shrug and allow her to pull me behind her as we walk toward the exit.

"I got presents from Portland today," she says as we near the exit. "People love me in Portland. My mom and dad. My brother and sisters."

I push the door open and wait for her to walk outside first. It's the first day of September—happy birthday—and the night has an unseasonable chill to it for Texas.

"But how many people who claim to love me from Texas got me a present? Take a wild guess."

I really don't want to guess. The answer is obvious, and I want to rectify the fact that no one from Texas got her a present today. I would say we should go get one right now, but not while she's drunk and angry.

I watch her rub her hands up the bare skin of her arms and look up at the sky. "I hate your Texas weather, Owen. It's dumb. It's hot during the day and cold at night and unreliable the rest of the time."

I want to point out that the inclusion of both day and night leaves little room for a "rest of the time." But I don't think now is a good time to get into specifics. She continues to pull me in a direction that isn't across the street to my studio, nor is it in the direction of her apartment.

"Where are we going?"

She drops my hand and slows down until we're walking next to each other. I want to put my arm around her so that she doesn't trip over her "heels," but I also know that she's probably slowly sobering up, so I highly anticipate her coming to her senses soon. I doubt she wants me near her, much less with my arm around her.

"We're almost there," she says, rummaging through her

purse. She stumbles a few times and each time, my hands fly up, preparing to break her fall, but somehow she always recovers.

She pulls her hand out of her purse and holds it up, jiggling a set of keys so close to my face they touch my nose. "Keys," she says. "Found 'em."

She smiles like she's proud of herself, so I smile with her. She swings her arm against my chest so that I stop walking. She points to the salon we're now standing in front of, and my hand immediately flies up to my hair in a protective response.

She inserts the key in the lock and sadly, the door opens with ease. She pushes it and motions for me to walk in first. "Lights are on the left by the door," she says. I turn to my left and she says, "No, O-wen. The *other* left."

I keep my smile in check and reach to the right and flip the lights on. I watch her walk with purpose toward one of the stations. She drops her purse on the counter and then grips the back of the salon chair and spins it around to face me. "Sit."

This is so bad. What guy would allow an inebriated girl to come near him with a pair of scissors?

A guy who stood up said inebriated girl and feels really guilty about it.

I inhale a nervous breath as I take a seat. She spins me around until I'm facing the mirror. Her hand lingers over a selection of combs and scissors as if she's a surgeon attempting to decide what tool she wants to slice me open with.

"You've really let yourself go," she says as she grabs a comb. She stands in front of me and concentrates on my hair as she begins to comb through it. "Are you at least showering?"

I shrug. "Occasionally."

She shakes her head, disappointed, as she reaches behind

her for the scissors. When she faces me again, her expression is focused. As soon as the scissors begin to come at me, I panic and try to stand up.

"Owen, stop," she says, pushing my shoulders back against the chair. I try to gently brush her aside with my arm so I can stand, but she shoves me back in the chair again. The scissors are still in her left hand, and I know it's not intentional, but they're a little too close to my throat for comfort. Her hands are on my chest and I can tell I just made her angry with my failed attempt at escaping.

"You need a haircut, Owen," she says. "It's okay. I won't charge you, I need the practice." She brings one of her legs up and presses her knee onto my thigh, then brings the other leg up and does the same. "Be still." Now that she physically has me locked to my chair, she lifts herself up and begins messing with my hair.

She doesn't have to worry about my trying to escape now that she's in my lap. That won't happen.

Her chest is directly in front of me, and even though her button-up shirt isn't at all revealing, the fact that I'm this close to such an intimate part of her has me glued to my seat. I gently lift my hands to her waist to keep her steady.

When I touch her, she pauses what she's doing and looks down at me. Neither of us speaks, but I know she feels it. I'm too close to her chest not to notice her reaction. Her breath halts right along with mine.

She looks away nervously as soon as we make eye contact and she begins snipping at my hair. I can honestly say I've never had my hair cut quite like this before. They aren't as accommodating at the barbershop.

I can feel the scissors sawing through my hair and she

huffs. "Your hair is really thick, Owen." She says it like it's my fault and it's irritating her.

"Aren't you supposed to wet it first?"

Her hands pause in my hair as soon as I ask her that question. She relaxes and lowers herself until her thighs meet her calves. We're eye to eye now. My hands are still on her waist and she's still on my lap and I'm still thoroughly enjoying the position of this spontaneous haircut, but I can see from the sudden trembling of her bottom lip that I'm the only one enjoying it.

Her arms fall limply to her sides and she drops the scissors and the comb on the floor. I can see the tears forming and I don't know what to do to stop them, since I'm not sure what started them.

"I forgot to wet it," she says with a defeated pout. She begins to shake her head back and forth. "I'm the worst hairdresser in the whole world, Owen."

And now she's crying. She brings her hands up to her face, attempting to cover her tears, or her embarrassment, or both. I lean forward and pull her hands away. "Auburn."

She won't open her eyes to look at me. She keeps her head tucked down and she shakes it, refusing to answer me.

"Auburn," I say again, this time raising my hands to her cheeks. I hold her face in my hands, and I'm mesmerized by how soft she feels. Like a combination of silk and satin and sin, pressing against my palms.

God, I hate that I've already fucked this up so bad. I hate that I don't know how to fix it.

I pull her toward me and surprisingly, she lets me. Her arms are still at her sides, but her face is buried against my neck now, and why did I fuck this up, Auburn?

I brush my hand over the back of her head and move my lips to her ear. I need her to forgive me, but I don't know if she can do that without an explanation. The only problem is, I'm the one who reads the confessions. I'm not used to writing them and I'm certainly not used to speaking them. But I still need her to know that I wish things were different right now. I wish things would have been different three weeks ago.

I hold on to her tightly so that she'll feel the sincerity in my words. "I'm sorry I didn't show up."

She immediately stiffens in my arms, as if my apology sobered her up. I don't know if that's a good thing or a bad thing. I watch closely as she slowly lifts herself away from me. I wait for a response, or more of a reaction from her, but she's so guarded.

I don't blame her. She doesn't owe me anything.

She turns her head to the left in an effort to remove my hand from around the back of her head. I pull it away and she grips the arms of the chair and pushes herself out of it.

"Did you get my confession, Owen?"

Her voice is firm, void of the tears that were consuming her a few moments ago. When she stands, she wipes her eyes with her fingers.

"Yes."

She nods, pressing her lips together. She glances at her purse and grabs both it and her keys.

"That's good." She begins walking toward the door. I slowly stand, afraid to look in the mirror at the unfinished haircut she's just given me. Luckily, she switches the lights off before I have the chance to see it.

"I'm going home," she says, holding the door open. "I don't feel so well."

CHAPTER NINE

Auburn

I have four younger siblings ranging in age from six to twelve years old. My parents had me when they were still in high school and waited several years before having more kids. Neither of my parents went to college and my father works for a manufacturing company, where he's been since he was eighteen. Because of this, we grew up on a budget. A very strict budget. A budget that didn't allow for air conditioners to be turned on at night. "That's what windows are for," my father used to say if anyone complained.

I may have adopted his penny-pinching habit, but it hasn't really been an issue since moving in with Emory. She was on the verge of being evicted after her old roommate stuck her with half of the lease, so things like air-conditioning aren't considered necessities. They're considered luxuries.

This was fine when I lived back in Portland, but having lived in the bipolar weather of Texas for an entire month, I've had to adjust my sleeping habits. Instead of using a comforter, I sleep with layers of sheets. That way, if it gets too hot in the middle of the night, I can just push one or two of the sheets off the bed.

With all that considered, why am I so cold right now? And why am I wrapped up in what feels like a down comforter? Every time I try to open my eyes and wake up to find answers to my own questions, I go right back to sleep, because I've never been this comfortable. I feel like I'm a little cherub angel sleeping peacefully on a cloud.

Wait. I shouldn't feel like an angel. Am I dead?

I sit straight up in the bed and open my eyes, I'm too confused and scared to move, so I keep my head completely still and slowly move my eyes around the room. I see the kitchen, the bathroom door, the stairwell leading down to the studio.

I'm in Owen's apartment.

Why?

I'm in Owen's big, comfortable bed.

Why?

I immediately turn and look down at the bed, but Owen isn't in it, thank God. The next thing I do is check my clothes. I'm still fully dressed, thank God.

Think, think, think.

Why are you here, Auburn? Why does your head feel like someone used it as a trampoline all night?

It comes back to me, slowly. First, I remember being stood

up. *Bitch.* I remember Harrison. I remember running to the bathroom after he betrayed me by calling Owen. *I hate Harrison.* I also remember being at the salon and . . . Oh, God. Really, Auburn?

I was in his lap. In his lap, cutting his damn hair.

I bring my hand to my forehead. That's it. I'm never drinking again. Alcohol makes people do stupid things, and I can't afford to be caught doing stupid things. The smart thing to do right now would be to get the hell out of here, which sucks because I really wish I could take this bed with me.

I quietly slip out of it and head toward the restroom. I close the door behind me and immediately begin looking through drawers in order to hopefully find an unused toothbrush, but I come up empty-handed. Instead, I use my finger, some toothpaste, and an ungodly amount of amazing wintergreen mouthwash. Owen has great taste in bathroom products, that's for sure.

Where is he, anyway?

Once I'm finished in the restroom, I search for my shoes and find my Toms at the foot of his bed. I could have sworn I was in heels at some point last night. Yep, definitely never drinking again.

I make my way to the stairs, hoping Owen isn't in the studio. He doesn't appear to be here, so maybe he left to avoid having to face me once I woke up. He obviously has his reasons for not showing up, so I doubt he's changed his mind about how he feels. Which means this is probably the perfect opportunity to get the hell out of here and never come back.

"You can't keep avoiding me, Owen. We need to talk about this before Monday."

I pause at the foot of the stairs and press my back against

the wall. Shit. Owen is still here, and he's got company. Why, why, why? I just want to leave.

"I know what my options are, Dad."

Dad? Great. The last thing I want right now is to do the walk of shame in front of his freaking father. This isn't good. I hear footsteps approaching, so I immediately begin to scale the stairs again, but the footsteps fade just as fast.

I pause, but then the footsteps grow louder. I take two more steps, but the footsteps fade again.

Whoever is walking, they're just pacing back and forth. After several back-and-forths, they come to a stop.

"I need to prepare to shut down the studio," Owen says. "It might be a few months before I can open it again, so I really just want to focus on that today."

Shut down the studio? I catch myself creeping back to the bottom of the stairs to hear more of the conversation. I'm being so uncharacteristically nosy, it makes me feel a bit like Emory right now.

"This studio is the last thing you should be worried about right now," his father says angrily.

More pacing.

"This studio is the *only* thing I'm worried about right now," Owen says loudly. He sounds even angrier than his father. The pacing stops.

His father sighs so heavily I could swear it echoes across the studio. There's a long pause before he speaks again. "You have options, Owen. I'm only trying to help you."

I shouldn't be listening to this. I'm not the type of person to invade someone's privacy and I feel guilty for doing it. But for the life of me, I can't make myself walk back up the stairs.

"You're trying to help me?" Owen says, laughing in disbelief. He's obviously not pleased with what his father is saying. Or failing to say. "I want you to leave, Dad."

My heart skips an entire beat. I can feel it in my throat. My stomach is telling me to find an alternate escape route.

"Owen—"

"Leave!"

I squeeze my eyes shut. I don't know who to feel sorry for right now, Owen or his father. I can't tell what they're arguing about and of course it's none of my business, but if I'm about to have to face Owen, I want to be prepared for whatever mood he's going to be in.

Footsteps. I hear footsteps again, but some are coming and some are going and . . .

I slowly open one eye and then the other. I try to smile at him, because he looks so defeated standing at the bottom of the stairs, looking up at me. He's wearing a blue baseball cap that he lifts up and flips around after running his hand over the top of his head. He squeezes the back of his neck and exhales. I've never seen him with a hat on before, but it looks good on him. It's hard to picture an artist wearing a baseball cap, for some reason. But he's an artist, and he definitely makes it work.

He doesn't look nearly as angry as he sounded a minute ago, but he definitely looks stressed. He doesn't seem like the same wide-eyed guy I met at the door three weeks ago.

"Sorry," I say, attempting to prepare an excuse for why I'm standing here eavesdropping. "I was about to leave and then I heard you—"

He scales the first few steps, coming closer to me, and I stop speaking.

"Why are you leaving?"

His eyes are searching mine and he looks disappointed.

I'm confused by his reaction, because I assumed he'd want me to leave. And honestly, I don't know why he seems confused that I would choose to leave after he failed to contact me for three weeks. He can't expect me to want to spend the day here with him.

I shrug, not really knowing what to say in response. "I just . . . I woke up and . . . I want to leave."

Owen reaches his hand around to my lower back and urges me up the stairs. "You aren't going anywhere," he says.

He tries to walk me up the stairs with him, but I push his hand off of me. He can more than likely see by the shock on my face that I'm not about to take orders from him. I open my mouth to speak, but he beats me to it.

"Not until you fix my hair," he adds.

Oh.

He pulls his cap off and runs his hand through his choppy hair. "I hope you're better at cutting hair when you're sober."

I cover my mouth with my hand to stifle my laughter. There are two huge chunks cut out of his hair, one of them front and center. "I'm so sorry."

I would say we're even now. Destroying hair as beautiful as his should definitely make up for the asshole move he made three weeks ago. Now if I could just get my hands on Lydia's hair, I'd feel a whole lot better.

He slides his cap back on his head and begins walking up the stairs. "Mind if we go now?"

Today is my day off, so I'm free to correct the damage I've done to his hair, but it kind of stinks that I have to go to the salon when I otherwise wouldn't have to. Emory marked the weekend off on the schedule for me since it was my birthday yesterday. She probably did this because most twenty-one-year-olds do fun things on their birthday and want the weekend to celebrate. I've been living with her for a month now, so if she hasn't noticed already, she'll soon discover that I have no life and don't need special "recovery days" reserved on the calendar.

I realize I've been paused on the steps and Owen is upstairs, so I make my way back up to his apartment. When I reach the top of the stairs, my feet stop moving again. He's in the process of changing his shirt. His back is to me, and he's pulling his paint-splattered T-shirt off over his head. I watch as the muscles in his shoulders move around and contract, and I wonder if he's ever painted a self-portrait.

I would buy it.

He catches me staring at him when he turns to reach for his other shirt. I do that thing where I quickly glance away and make it completely obvious that I was staring, since I'm now looking at nothing but a blank wall and I know he's still looking at me and oh, my word, I just want to leave.

"Is that okay?" he asks, pulling my attention back to him.

"Is what okay?" I say quickly, relieved by the sound of our voices, which is now eliminating the awkwardness I was about to drown in.

"Can we go right now? To fix my hair?"

He pulls the clean shirt on and I'm disappointed that I now have to stare at a boring gray T-shirt instead of the masterpiece beneath it.

What are these ridiculous, shallow thoughts that are plaguing my brain? I don't care about muscles or six-packs or skin that looks so flawless, it makes me want to chase his father down and give him a high five for creating such an impeccable son.

I clear my throat. "Yeah, we can go now. I don't have plans."

Way to appear more pathetic, Auburn. Admit you have nothing to do on a Saturday after ogling his half-naked body. Real attractive.

He picks the baseball cap up and puts it back on before stepping into his shoes. "Ready?"

I nod and turn to head back down the stairs. I'm beginning to hate these stairs.

When he opens the front door, the sun is so bright, I start to question my own mortality and entertain the thought that maybe I became a vampire overnight. I cover my eyes with my arms and stop walking. "Damn it, that's bright."

If this is a hangover, I have no idea how anyone could become an alcoholic.

Owen closes the door and takes a few steps toward me. "Here," he says. He places his cap on my head and pulls it down close to my eyes. "That should help."

He smiles, and I get a glimpse of that crooked left incisor and it makes me smile, despite the fact that my head hates me for moving any facial muscles. I lift my hand and adjust the hat, pulling it down a little more. "Thank you."

Owen opens the door, and I look at my feet to avoid the assault from the sun. I step outside and wait for him to lock it, and then we begin walking. Luckily, we're walking in the opposite direction of the sun, so I'm able to look up and pay attention to where we're going.

"How are you feeling?" Owen asks.

It takes me about six steps to answer him. "Confused," I say. "Why in the world do people drink if it makes them feel like this the next day?"

I continue counting steps, and it takes him about eight before he answers me. "It's an escape," he says.

I glance at him but quickly look straight ahead again, because turning my head doesn't feel so hot, either. "I get that, but is escaping for a few hours really worth the hangover the next day?"

He's quiet for eight steps. Nine. Ten. Eleven.

"I guess that would depend on the reality you're trying to escape."

That's deep, Owen.

I would think my reality is pretty bad, but definitely not bad enough to endure this every morning. But maybe that would explain what turns people into alcoholics. You drink to escape the emotional pain you're in, and then the next day you do it all over again to get rid of the physical pain. So you drink more and you drink more often and pretty soon you're drunk all the time and it becomes just as bad, if not worse, than the reality you were attempting to escape from in the first place. Only now, you need an escape from the escape, so you find something even stronger than the alcohol. And maybe that's what turns alcoholics into addicts.

A vicious cycle.

"You want to talk about it?" he asks.

I don't make the mistake of looking at him again, but I'm curious where he's going with his question. "Talk about what?"

"What you were trying to escape last night," he says, glancing at me.

I shake my head. "No, Owen. I don't." I look at him this time, even though it hurts my head to do so. "You want to talk about why you're shutting down the studio?"

My question catches him by surprise. I can see it in his eyes before he looks away. "No, Auburn. I don't."

We both stop walking when we reach my salon. I put my hand on the door and take his cap off my head. I place it back on top of his head, even though I have to lift up onto the tips of my toes to do it. "Great talk. Let's shut up now and fix your hair."

He holds the door open for me to walk in first. "Sounds a lot like what I had in mind."

We enter the salon, and I motion for him to follow me. I know now that his hair will be a lot more cooperative if it's wet, so I take him straight back to the room with the sinks. I can feel Emory watching me as we make our way past her and it makes me curious as to why she didn't freak out that I didn't show up last night, or at the least, call with a code word.

Before she has the chance to yell at me, I offer up an apology as I pass her station. "Sorry I didn't call last night," I say quietly.

She glances at Owen trailing behind me. "No worries. Someone made sure I knew you were alive."

I immediately turn and look at Owen, and it's obvious with his shrug that he's the one responsible for Emory being notified. I'm not sure if I like this, because it's just another considerate thing of him to do, which makes it even harder to stay mad at him.

When we reach the back room, all the sinks are empty, so I walk to the farthest one. I adjust the height of it and then motion for Owen to sit. I adjust the temperature of the water and watch as he leans his head back into the groove of the sink. I keep my focus trained on anything but his face while I begin to wet his hair. He keeps his eyes on me the entire time I'm working my hands through it, creating a thick lather with the shampoo. I've been doing this for over a month now and the majority of the clients at this salon are women. I've never noticed how intimate washing someone's hair can be.

Then again, no one else stares so unabashedly while I'm trying to work. Knowing he's watching my every move makes me incredibly nervous. My pulse speeds up and my hands grow fidgety. After a while, he opens his mouth to speak.

"Are you mad at me?" he asks quietly.

My hands pause what they're doing. It's such a juvenile question to ask. I feel like we're kids and we've been giving each other the silent treatment. But for such a simple question, it's a really hard one to answer.

I was mad at him three weeks ago. I was mad at him last night. But right now I don't feel angry. Actually being near him and seeing how he looks at me makes me think he must have had a very valid excuse for not showing up, and it had nothing to do with how he felt about me. I just wish he would explain himself.

I shrug as I begin to work the shampoo through his hair again. "I was," I tell him. "But you did warn me, didn't you? You said everything else comes before the girls. So mad might be a bit harsh. Disappointed, yes. Annoyed, yes. But I'm not really mad."

That was way too much of an explanation. One he didn't really deserve.

"I did say that my work is my number one priority, but I never said I was an asshole. I let a girl know beforehand if I need space to work."

I glance at him, briefly, and then give my attention to the bottle of conditioner. I squirt some in my hands and spread it through his hair.

"So you have the courtesy to warn your girlfriends that

you're about to disappear, but you don't have the courtesy to warn the girls who *aren't* screwing you?" I'm working the conditioner through his hair, not being nearly as gentle as I should be.

I think I changed my mind . . . I'm mad now.

He shakes his head and sits straight up, turning around to face me. "That's not what I meant, Auburn." Water is dripping down the side of his face. Down his neck. "I meant that I didn't disappear on you because of my art. It wasn't that type of situation. I don't want you to think I didn't want to come back, because I did."

My jaw is tense and I'm grinding my teeth together. "You're dripping everywhere," I say as I pull him back to the sink. I pick up the sprayer and begin rinsing his hair. Again, his eyes are on me the whole time, but I don't want to make eye contact with him. I don't want to care what his excuse is, because I honestly don't want to be involved with anyone right now. But damn it, I care. I want to know why he didn't show up and why he hasn't made an effort to contact me at all since then.

I finish rinsing his hair and I wash the suds down the drain. "You can sit up."

He sits up and I grab a towel and squeeze the excess water out of his hair. I toss the towel in the hamper on the other side of the room and begin to walk around him, but he grabs my wrist and stops me. He stands up, still holding on to my wrist.

I don't try to pull away from him. I know I should, but I'm too curious to see what his next move is to care what I should be doing. I also don't pull away because I love how the slightest touch from him leaves me breathless.

"I lied to you," he says quietly.

I don't like those words, and I certainly don't like the truthfulness on his face right now.

"I didn't . . ." His eyes narrow in contemplation as he exhales slowly. "I didn't come back because I didn't see the point. I'm moving on Monday."

He says the rest of the sentence like he can't get it out fast enough. I don't like this confession. At all.

"You're moving?" My voice is full of disappointment. I feel like I was just dumped, and I don't even have a boyfriend.

"You're moving?" Emory asks.

I spin around, and she's walking a client to one of the sinks, staring at Owen, waiting for an answer. I face Owen again and can see that this moment of truth is over for now. I walk away from him and head out of the room, toward my station. He follows quietly.

Neither of us speaks as I comb through his hair and try to figure out how I'm going to fix the mess I made of it last night. I'll have to cut most of it off. He'll look so different and I'm not sure I'm happy about his having much shorter hair.

"It'll be short," I say. "I messed it up pretty bad."

He laughs, and his laugh is exactly what I need in this moment. It alleviates the heaviness of what was happening back in the other room. "Why would you let me do this to you?"

He smiles up at me. "It was your birthday. I would have done anything you asked."

Flirtatious Owen is back, and I both love it and hate it. I take a step away from him to study his hair. When I'm positive I know how to fix it, I turn around and grab the scissors and comb, which are right where they're supposed to be. I remember dropping them on the floor last night, and it occurs to me that Emory more than likely walked into a mess this morning.

I didn't sweep up what I did cut of Owen's hair before we left the salon, but it's gone, so I'll have to thank her later.

I begin cutting his hair, and I do my best to focus on that and not so much on him. Somewhere between the beginning of the haircut and this moment, Emory returned to her station. She's now seated in her own salon chair, watching us. She kicks off the cabinet with her foot and begins spinning.

"Are you moving forever or just for a little while?" Emory asks. Owen looks in my direction and raises an eyebrow.

"Oh," I say, forgetting they haven't been formally introduced yet. I point to Emory. "Owen, this is Emory. My strange roommate."

He nods slightly and looks in her direction without turning too much. I think he's nervous I'll mess his hair up even more, so he's being as still as he can possibly be. "A few months, probably," he says in response to her. "It's not permanent. A work thing."

Emory frowns. "That's too bad," she says. "I already like you a whole lot better than the other guy."

My eyes grow wide and my head swings in her direction. "Emory!"

I can't believe she just said that.

Owen slowly turns his attention back to me and cocks an eyebrow. "Other guy?"

I shake my head and wave her off. "She's misinformed. There is no other guy." I glare at her. "There can't be another guy when there's not even a guy."

"Oh, please." She catches the cabinet with her foot and stops spinning. She points to Owen. "He's a guy. A guy you apparently spent the night with last night. A guy I think is a lot nicer than the other guy, and a guy I think you're sad is moving."

What is wrong with this girl? I can feel Owen staring at me, but I'm too embarrassed to look at him. I glare at Emory again instead. "I was actually beginning to respect you because you never gossip."

"It's not gossip when I'm saying it to both your faces. It's called conversation. We're discussing how you guys are attracted to each other and you want to fall in love like . . . like . . . two . . ." She pauses for a moment and then shakes her head. "I suck at metaphors. You want to fall in love, but now he has to move and you're sad. But you don't have to be sad because thanks to me, you now know he's only moving for a few months. Not forever. Just don't give in to the other guy first."

Owen is laughing, but I'm not. I grab the blow dryer to drown out her words and I finish styling his now-short hair, which actually looks really good. His eyes stand out even more. A lot more. They look brighter. So much so that I'm finding it really hard not to stare at them.

I turn off the blow dryer and Emory immediately begins speaking again. "So when are you moving, Owen?"

He stares at me when he answers her. "Monday."

Emory slaps the arm of the chair. "That's perfect timing," she says. "Auburn is off today and tomorrow. You guys can spend the whole weekend together."

I don't tell her to shut up, because I know it wouldn't stop her. I step behind Owen and untie the smock wrapped around him and then shove it into a drawer, all the while giving her a death stare.

"I actually like that idea," Owen says.

His voice makes me fear for the safety of the world, because I'm single-handedly depleting the oxygen supply with all the deep breaths I take every time I hear it. I look at him in the mirror and he's leaning forward in the salon chair, staring at my reflection.

He wants to spend the weekend with me? Hell no. If that happens, then it means other things will happen and I don't know if I'm ready for other things yet. Besides, I'll be busy with . . . Crap. I'm not busy at all. This is the weekend Lydia goes to Pasadena. There goes that excuse.

"Look at her trying to come up with excuses," Emory says, amused.

They're both staring at me now, waiting on me to respond. I grab Owen's hat and put it on my head and walk straight for the front door. I don't owe Owen a weekend and I definitely don't owe Emory a sideshow. I swing open the door and begin walking in the direction of my apartment, which also happens to be the direction of Owen's studio, so I'm not surprised when he appears next to me.

Our steps fall into sync, and I begin to count them. I wonder if we'll make it all the way to his studio without speaking.

Thirteen, fourteen, fifteen . . .

"What are you thinking?" he asks quietly.

I stop counting our steps, because I'm not walking anymore. Owen isn't walking either, because Owen is standing directly in front of me, looking at me with those big, noticeable Owen-eyes this haircut just created.

"I'm not spending the weekend with you. I can't believe you would even suggest that."

He shakes his head. "I didn't suggest it. Your inappropriate roommate did. I just said I liked the idea of it."

I huff and fold my arms tightly over my chest. I look down

at the sidewalk between us and try to figure out why I'm so mad right now. Walking away from him won't make me any less mad, because that's actually the problem. Thinking about spending the weekend with him excites me, and the fact that I can't come up with a reason as to why it's a bad idea is pissing me off. I guess I still feel like he owes me more of an explanation. Or more of an apology. If Harrison hadn't called him last night, I'd have probably never heard from or seen him again. That's a little bit crushing to my self-confidence, so I find it hard to just accept that he suddenly wants to spend time with me.

I unfold my arms and rest my hands on my hips, then look up at him. "Why didn't you at least let me know you were moving before standing me up?"

I know he tried to explain himself earlier, but it wasn't good enough, because I'm still upset about it. Sure, he may have not wanted to start anything if he was moving, but if that's really the case, he never should have told me he'd come back the next night.

His expression doesn't waver, but he does take a step closer. "I didn't show up the next night because I like you."

I close my eyes and drop my head in disappointment. "That's such a dumb answer," I mutter.

He takes another step closer, and he's right here, right in front of me. When he speaks again, his voice is so low I can feel it in my stomach. "I knew I was moving and I like you. Those two things don't make a very good combination. I should have let you know I wasn't coming back, but I didn't have your number."

Nice try. "You knew where I lived."

He gives no response to that comeback other than a sigh.

He shifts on his feet, and I finally allow my eyes to make the brave journey to his face. He actually looks very apologetic, but I know better than to trust the expression on a man's face. The only things worth trusting are actions, and so far he hasn't proven very trustworthy.

"I messed up," he says. "I'm sorry."

At least he's not giving me an excuse. I guess it takes a little bit of honesty to be able to admit when you're wrong, even if you aren't very forthcoming with the *why*. He has that going for him.

I'm not sure when he moved this close to me, but he's so close—really close—that to passersby it would look like either we're in the middle of a breakup or we're about to make out.

I step around him and begin walking again until we reach his studio. I'm not sure why I stop when we reach his door. I should keep going. I should be walking all the way to my apartment, but I'm not. He unlocks his door and glances over his shoulder to make sure I'm still here.

I shouldn't be. I should be separating myself from what I know could be two of the best days I've had in a long time, but will be followed by one of the worst Mondays I've had in a long time.

If I spend the weekend with him, it'll feel just like how drinking went for me last night. It'll be fun and exciting while it's happening and I'll forget about everything else while I'm with him, but then Monday will come. He'll move and I'll have an Owen hangover that'll be so much worse than the Owen hangover I'll have if I would just walk away from him right now.

He opens the door to his studio and a blast of cool air surrounds me, luring me in. I look inside and then at Owen. He can see the apprehension in my eyes and he reaches down for my hand. He walks me into the studio and for some reason, I don't resist. The door closes behind us and we're engulfed by the darkness.

I listen for the echo of my heart, because I'm certain it's beating loud enough to hear one. I can feel him standing close to me, but neither of us is moving. I can hear his breaths, I feel his closeness, I smell the clean scent of conditioner mixed with whatever makes him smell like rain.

"Is it the thought of spending the weekend with someone you barely know that's making you doubt this? Or is it just the thought of spending the weekend with me in particular?"

"I'm not scared because it's you, Owen. I'm *considering* it because it's you."

He takes a step back and my eyes have adjusted enough to the darkness that I can see his face clearly now. He's hopeful. Excited. Smiling. How can I say no to that face?

"What if I agree to just spend the day with you for right now? And we'll go from there?"

He laughs at my suggestion, as if he thinks it's silly that I wouldn't want to stay the entire weekend after spending the day with him.

"That's cute, Auburn," he says. "But okay."

His grin is huge when he pulls me to him. He wraps his arms around me and lifts me off the floor, squeezing the breath out of me. He sets me back down and pushes open the door. "Come on. Let's go to Target."

I pause. "Target?"

He smiles and adjusts his cap on my head as he pushes me out into the sunlight again. "I don't have anything to feed you. We're going grocery shopping."

CHAPTER TEN

Owen

I'm losing track of the lies I'm telling her, and lying to someone like her isn't normally something I would do. But I didn't know how to tell her the truth. I was scared to let her go and scared to admit that I'm not actually moving on Monday, because the truth is, I'll be in court on Monday. And after my hearing, I'll be in either jail or rehab, depending on who gets his way. Me or Callahan Gentry.

When my father stopped by the studio this morning, I was careful not to say too much because I knew Auburn might be listening. But keeping my cool was harder than I thought it would be. I just wanted him to see what this is doing to me. I wanted to grab his hand and pull him up the stairs and point down at her, sleeping on my bed. I wanted to say, "Look at her, Dad. Look at what your selfishness is costing me."

Instead, I did what I always do. I allowed the memories of my mother and my brother to talk me out of standing up to him. They're my excuse. They're his excuse. They've been our excuse for the last several years, and I'm afraid if I don't find a way to stop using that night as my excuse, then Callahan and Owen Gentry will never be father and son again.

Nothing has made me want to stop this way of life like she has, though. As much as I've tried and as much as I've thought about it and as much as it defeats me every time my guilt wins, I've never felt stronger than I feel when I'm with her. I've never felt like I had purpose like I feel when I'm with her. I think about the first words I said to her when she showed up at my door. "Are you here to save me?"

Because are you, Auburn? It sure feels that way, and it's been a long time since I've felt any semblance of hope.

"Where are you going?" she asks me.

Her voice could be used as a form of therapy. I'm convinced of that. She could walk into a room full of severely depressed people and all she would have to do to heal them is open a book and read out loud.

"Target."

She shoves my shoulder and laughs, and I'm glad to see this side of her is back. She's hardly laughed all day.

"I don't mean right now, dummy. I mean Monday. Where are you going? Why are you moving?"

I glance across the street.

I look up at the sky.

I focus on my feet.

I look everywhere but into her eyes, because I don't want to lie to her again. I've already lied to her once today, and I can't do it again.

I reach out and take her hand in mine. She lets me, and the simple fact that I know she wouldn't let me hold her hand if she knew the truth makes me regret ever having lied to her in the first place. But the longer I wait to admit the truth, the harder it becomes.

"Auburn, I don't really want to answer that question, okay?"

I continue to stare at my feet, not wanting her to see in my face that I think she's crazy for agreeing to spend the weekend with me, because she deserves so much better than what I can give her. I don't, however, think she deserves better than me. I think she would be perfect for me and I would be perfect for her, but all the bad choices I've made in my life are what she doesn't deserve to be a part of. So until I can figure out how to right all my wrongs, two days with her is all I'm really worthy of. And I know she said we would focus on today first before she decides to spend the entire weekend, but I think we both know that's bullshit.

She squeezes my hand. "If you aren't going to tell me why you're moving away, then I'm not going to tell you why I ended up moving here."

I was hoping to learn everything there is to know about her this weekend. I had questions lined up and ready to be fired, and now I have to withdraw, because there's no way in hell I'm telling her about my life. Not right now, anyway.

"That's fair," I say, finally able to look at her again.

She smiles and squeezes my hand again, and I can't fucking take how beautiful you look right now, Auburn. Free of worry, free of anger, free of guilt. The wind blows a piece of her hair across her mouth and she pulls it away with her fingertips.

I'm going to paint this moment later.

But right now, I'm taking her to Target. For groceries.

Because she's staying with me.

All weekend.

She's modest in a lot of areas, but definitely not when it comes to her food. I know she understands that she'll only be at my house for two days, but she's grabbed enough food to last two weeks.

I let her, though, because I want this to be the best weekend she's ever had, and frozen pizza and cereal will definitely help me make that happen.

"I think we're good." She's looking down at the cart, digging through it, making sure she got everything she wanted. "We'll have to take a cab back to your place, though. We can't carry all this."

I turn the cart around right before we hit the checkout line. "We forgot something," I say.

"How? We bought the entire store."

I head in the opposite direction. "Your birthday present."

I expect her to run up behind me and protest, like most girls would probably do. Instead, she starts clapping. I think she might have just squealed, too. She grabs my arm with both hands and says, "How much can I spend?"

Her excitement reminds me of one of the times my father took Carey and me to Toys "R" Us. Carey was two years older, but our birthdays were only a week apart. Our father used to do things like that, back when Callahan Gentry knew how to be a father. I remember one particular trip; he wanted to turn the present buying into a game. He told us to pick an aisle number and a shelf number, and said we could pick anything we wanted from that particular shelf. Carey went first, and we wound up on the Lego aisle, which was typical of Carey's good luck. When it was my turn, I didn't fare so well. My numbers put us on the Barbie aisle and to say I was upset is an understatement. Carey was the type of brother who, when he wasn't beating me up, was fiercely protective of me. He looked at my father and said, "What if he reversed the numbers? Maybe instead of aisle four and shelf three, we're supposed to be on shelf four and aisle three."

My father grinned proudly. "That's pretty lawyerly of you, Carey." We moved over to aisle three, which was the sports aisle. I don't even remember what I ended up choosing. I just remember the day and how, despite that moment of terror in the Barbie aisle, it ended up being one of my favorite memories of the three of us.

I take her hand in mine, and I stop pushing the buggy. "Pick an aisle number."

She arches an eyebrow and glances behind her, trying to peek at the aisle signs, so I block her view. "No cheating. Pick an aisle number and a shelf number. I'll buy you anything you want off the shelf we end up at."

She smiles. She likes this game.

"Lucky thirteen," she says to me. "But how do I know how many shelves there are?"

"Just guess. You might get lucky."

She squeezes her bottom lip between her thumb and forefinger, concentrating her gaze on me. "If I say shelf one, would that be considered the top shelf or the bottom?"

"Bottom."

She smiles and her eyes light up. "Row thirteen, shelf number two it is." She's so excited I would think she's never been given a gift before. She also bites her bottom lip to keep from appearing as excited as she is.

God, she's adorable.

I turn around, and we're standing on the opposite side of the store from aisle thirteen. "Looks like either sporting goods or electronics."

She jumps a little and says, "Or jewelry."

Oh, shit. Jewelry is close to electronics. This may be the most expensive birthday present I've ever bought. She lets go of my hand and grabs the end of the cart, pulling it faster. "Hurry up, Owen."

If I knew birthday presents made her this excited, I would have bought her one the day I met her. And every day since then.

We're still walking toward aisle thirteen when we pass jewelry, then electronics, eliminating both of those possibilities. We pause on aisle twelve, and even though we're standing in front of sporting goods, she still looks excited.

"I'm so nervous," she says, tiptoeing toward aisle thirteen. She rounds the corner first and peeks down the aisle. She looks back at me and breaks out into a huge grin. "Tents!"

And then she disappears.

I follow after her and round the corner with the cart, but she's already pulling one off the shelf. "I want this one," she says with excitement. But then she pushes it back on the shelf. "No, no, I want this one," she mumbles to herself. "Blue is his favorite color." She grabs the blue one, and I would help her, but I'm not sure I can move just yet. I'm still trying to absorb her words.

"Blue is his favorite color."

I want to ask her who he is, and why she's thinking about camping with someone whose favorite color is blue, blue, nothing but blue. But I don't say anything, because I don't have a right to say anything. She's giving me two days, not forever.

Two days.

That won't be enough for me, Auburn. I can already tell. And whoever's favorite color is blue won't stand a chance in this tent, because I'm about to make sure that the only thing she ever thinks about when she sees a tent again is Oh My God.

I get all the groceries loaded into the taxi and turn around to grab the tent. She takes it from my hands before I can put it in the trunk. "I'll carry this. I want to go to my apartment for a little while before I go to yours, so I'll just take it with me."

I glance at the groceries and then back at her. "Why?" I shut the trunk and watch her cheeks flush when she shrugs.

"Can you just drop me off there first? I'll meet you at your apartment in a couple of hours."

I don't want to drop her off. She might change her mind. "Yeah," I say. "Sure." I walk around to the back and open the door for her. I think she can tell that I don't want her to go home, but I'm trying to hide my disappointment. When I get into the cab I grab her hand and close the door. She tells the cab driver her address.

I'm looking out the window when I feel her squeeze my hand. "Owen?"

I face her and her smile is so sweet, it makes my jaw ache.

"I just really want to shower and grab some clothes before

I come over. But I promise I'm still coming over, okay?" Her expression is reassuring.

I nod, still not sure that I believe her. This may be her way of getting back at me for standing her up. She can still see the hesitation in my eyes, so she laughs.

"Owen Mason Gentry," she says, pushing the tent out of her lap and onto the seat next to her. She slides onto my lap and I grab her waist, not at all sure where she's going with this, but not really concerned enough to stop it. She looks me in the eyes while holding on to both sides of my face. "You better stop pouting. And doubting."

I grin. "That rhymed."

She laughs loudly, and have I mentioned I love her? No, I haven't. Because that would be crazy. And impossible.

"I'm the queen of rhyming," she says with a grin. "It's all about the timing." Her hands drop to my chest and she looks up at the roof of the car for a second, contemplating her next line before dropping her gaze to mine again. "So trust me, Owen. My desire for you is growin'."

She's trying to be seductive, and it's working, but she also can't stop laughing at herself, which is even better.

The cab comes to a stop in front of her apartment. She starts to reach for the tent, but I grab her face and pull her back to me, moving my lips to her ear. "So go take your shower. Come back over in an hour. Then you, Auburn Mason Reed, I will completely devour."

When I pull back and look at her, her smile is gone. She swallows dramatically and her reaction to my words makes me grin. I push open the back door and she breaks out of her trance.

"You're such a one-upper, Owen." She leans across the seat

and reaches for her tent. After she exits the cab, I smile at her and she smiles at me, but neither of us tells the other good-bye. I'm only saying good-bye to her once, and that won't be until Monday morning.

I'm about to ring her doorbell. I know it's only been an hour and she hasn't even had time to make it back to my studio, but I couldn't stop thinking about her walking all that way by herself. I hate that she makes that walk twice a day when she goes to work.

I don't want to rush her, though, and I don't want it to feel like I'm showing up because I doubt her. Maybe I should sit on the stairs and wait for her to open the door. That way, it'll look like I got here just as she was leaving. And also, if she never opens her door, then I'll know in a couple hours that she changed her mind. If that happens, I can just leave and she won't even know I was here in the first place.

But what if she already left, and I just missed her because she took a cab? She could be at my place, and now I've made the idiotic decision to show up at her place. *Shit.*

"Do you want to come inside?"

I quickly turn, and Emory is standing in the doorway, staring at me. She's holding her purse in one hand and her keys in the other.

"Is Auburn still here?"

Emory nods and holds the door open wider. "She's in her room. She just got out of the shower."

I hesitate, not feeling comfortable entering her apartment without her knowing. Emory can see the hesitation on my face, so she leans back into the apartment. "Auburn! That guy you should totally sleep with is here! Not the cop, the other one!"

The cop.

Emory faces me again and nods her head like she's saying you're welcome. I would say I like her, but every time she speaks, she's bringing up the "other" guy. I wonder if he's the one who likes the color blue.

I hear Auburn groan from inside the apartment. "I swear to God, Emory. You need to take a class on social skills." She appears in the doorway and Emory ducks out, heading for the exit. Her hair is damp, and she's changed clothes. She's still in jeans and a simple top, but they're different from the ones she had on earlier. I like that she's so casual. She's eyeing me up and down. "It hasn't even been an hour, Mr. Impatient."

She doesn't seem annoyed, which is good. She motions for me to come inside, so I follow her into the apartment. "I was going to wait outside," I say.

She walks into her bedroom and walks back out with a backpack. She tosses it on the bar and turns and looks at me expectantly.

"I was bored," I say. "I thought I'd walk with you to my studio."

Her lips curl up into a grin. "You're way too into me, Owen. Monday won't be good for you."

She says this like she's kidding, but she has no idea how right she is.

"Oh!" She turns toward the living room and retrieves the tent from the couch. "Help me set up the tent before we go." She walks toward her bedroom with the tent in her hands. "It's tiny, it won't take long."

I shake my head, completely confused as to why she wants

to set up a tent in her bedroom. But she doesn't seem bothered by it, so I don't question her. Because what girl doesn't deserve a tent in her bedroom?

"I want it over here." She points to a spot close to her bed as she kicks a yoga mat out of the way. I look around her room, trying to see what I can figure out about her without having to ask questions. There aren't any pictures on her walls or her dresser, and her closet door is shut. It's like she decided one day that she was leaving Portland and she didn't bring a single thing with her when she came. I wonder why that is? Is this not a permanent move for her?

I help her unpack the tent. I didn't notice at the store, but it really is a small tent. It fits two people and has an optional divider down the middle of it. We have it set up in less than five minutes, but simply setting it up isn't good enough for her, apparently. She walks to her closet and grabs two blankets that are on the top shelf. She lays them down in the tent and crawls inside.

"Grab two pillows off my bed," she says. "We have to lie in it for a few minutes before we leave."

I grab the pillows and kneel down in front of the tent. I push them inside and she takes them from me. I pull the flap back and crawl in with her, but I go to my side instead of doing what I really want to do, which is crawl on top of her.

I'm too big for the tent and my feet hang out of it, but so do hers.

"I think you bought a tent for fictional characters."

She shakes her head and lifts up onto her elbow. "I didn't buy it; you bought it. And it's a kid tent, Owen. Of course we don't fit."

Her eyes move to the zipper hanging from the top of the

tent. "Look." She grabs it and begins zipping. A net lowers from the top and she continues to zip up the sides of it until a mesh screen separates us. She lays her head on her arm and smiles at me. "Feels like we're in a confessional."

I roll onto my side and rest my head in my hand and stare back at her. "Which one of us is confessing?"

She narrows her eyes and lifts her finger, pointing at me. "I think it's safe to say you owe the world a few more confessions of your own."

I lift my hand and touch her finger through the mesh. She opens up her palm and presses it against mine. "We could be here all night, Auburn. I have a lot of confessions."

I could tell her how I know her. Make her realize why I have this overwhelming urge to protect her. But some secrets I'll take to my grave, and this is definitely one of them.

Instead, I give her a different confession. One that doesn't mean as much to me. I give her something safe. "I have three numbers in my phone. My father's. Harrison's. My cousin Riley's, but I haven't talked to him in over six months. That's it."

She's quiet. She doesn't know what to say, because who only has three numbers in his phone? Someone who has issues, obviously.

"Why don't you have more phone numbers?"

I like her eyes. They're very telling, and right now she hurts for me, because she realizes that she isn't the only lonely person in Dallas.

"After I graduated high school, I kind of went my own way. I focused on my art and nothing else. I lost all my old contacts when I switched phones about a year ago, and when that happened, I realized I didn't really talk to anyone. My grandparents passed away years ago. I only have one cousin, and like I said, we don't really talk much. Other than Harrison and my father, there isn't a phone number I need."

Her fingers are tracing my palm now. She's staring at her hands and no longer at me. "Let me see your phone."

I pull it out of my pocket and hand it to her beneath the mesh, because I told her the truth. She can check for herself. Three numbers and that's it.

Her fingers move over the screen for several seconds before she hands me back my phone. "There. Now you have four."

I look down at my screen and read her contact. I laugh when I see the name she entered for herself.

Auburn Mason-is-the-best-middle-name Reed.

I slide my phone back in my pocket and touch her hand against the mesh again. "Your turn," I say to her.

She shakes her head. "You still have a lot of catching up to do. Keep going."

I sigh and roll onto my back. I don't want to tell her anything else yet, but I'm scared if we don't get out of this tent soon, I'll tell her everything I know and everything she doesn't want to hear. But maybe it's best that way. Maybe if I tell her the truth, she can accept it and trust me and know that as soon as I get back, things will be different. Maybe if I tell her the truth, we'll have a chance of making it beyond Monday.

"That night I didn't show up here?" I pause, because my heart is beating so fast I'm finding it hard to think around it. I know I need to admit this to her, but I haven't known how to bring it up. No matter how I spin it, I know she'll react negatively, and I get that. But I'm tired of not being honest with her.

I roll onto my side and face her. I open my mouth to confess, but I'm spared by the knock on her front door.

Her confused expression reveals that she isn't used to visitors. "I need to get that. Wait here." She immediately climbs out of the tent, and I roll onto my back and exhale. In a matter of seconds, she's back in her room and kneeling down in front of the tent.

"Owen."

Her voice is frantic, and I lift up on my elbows as she pokes her head inside. Her eyes are full of worry. "I have to get the door, but please don't come out of my room, okay? I'll explain everything as soon as she leaves. I promise."

I nod, hating the fear in her voice. I also hate that she suddenly wants to hide me from whoever is at her door.

She backs away and closes the bedroom door. I fall back onto the pillow and listen, aware that I'm about to get one of her confessions, even though she doesn't quite seem ready to share it with me.

I hear the front door open and the first thing I hear is a child's voice. "Mommy, look! Look what Nana Lydia bought me."

And then I hear her respond. "Wow. That's exactly the one you wanted."

Did he just call you Mommy?

I hear feet shuffling across the floor. I hear a woman's voice say, "I know this is last-minute, but we were supposed to leave for Pasadena hours ago. However, my mother-in-law was admitted to the hospital and Trey is on duty—"

"Oh no, Lydia," Auburn interrupts.

"Oh, she's fine. Diabetic issues again, which wouldn't happen if she'd just take care of herself like I tell her. But she doesn't, and then expects the entire family to give up their plans in order to take care of her."

I hear a doorknob turning. "AJ, no," I hear Auburn say. "Stay out of Mommy's room."

"Anyway," the woman says, "I have to take some things to her but they don't allow children in the ICU, so I need you to watch him for a couple of hours."

"Of course," she says. "Here?"

"Yes, I don't have time to drive you to our house."

"Okay," she says. She sounds excited. She sounds like she's not used to the woman trusting her to do this. She's so excited, I don't think she notices AJ is opening her bedroom door again.

"I'll pick him up later tonight," the woman says.

"He can spend the night," Auburn replies, hopeful. "I'll bring him back in the morning."

Her bedroom door is open now and a little boy falls to his knees directly in front of the tent. I lift up on my elbows and smile at him, because he's smiling at me.

"Why are you in a tent?" he asks.

I bring my finger up to my mouth. "Shhh."

He grins and crawls inside the tent. He looks to be about four or five years old, and his eyes aren't green like Auburn's. They're all different colors. Browns and grays and greens. Like a canvas.

He doesn't have her unique shade of hair color, as his is dark brown. I'm assuming he gets that from his father, but I still see a lot of Auburn in him. Mostly in his expression, and how he seems so curious.

"Is the tent a secret?" he asks.

I nod. "Yes. And no one knows this tent is here, so we need to keep it between us, okay?"

He smiles and nods, like he's excited to have a secret. "I can keep secrets."

"That's good," I say to him. "Because it's not muscles that make men strong. Secrets do. The more secrets you keep, the stronger you are on the inside."

He grins. "I want to be strong."

I'm about to tell him to go back to the living room before any attention is brought to me, but I can hear the opening of the bedroom door.

"AJ, come give Nana Lydia a hug," the woman says. Her footsteps grow louder and AJ's eyes grow wide.

"Lydia, wait," I hear Auburn say to her with panic in her voice. But she says it a second too late, because I don't have time to pull my feet inside the tent before Lydia walks into the room.

I can see her steps come to an immediate halt. I don't have to see her face to know that she's not very happy about the fact that AJ is in this tent right now.

"AJ," her voice is firm. "Come out of the tent, sweetie."

AJ grins at me and puts his finger to his mouth. "I'm not in a tent, Nana Lydia. There's no tent in here."

"Lydia, I can explain," Auburn says, bending down. She motions for AJ to come out of the tent, and her eyes only meet mine for a second. "He's just a friend. He was helping me put up this tent for AJ."

"AJ, let's go, honey." Lydia grabs his hand, pulling him out of the tent. "You may be okay with allowing your son to be around complete strangers, but I'm not."

I can see the disappointment wash over Auburn. It washes over AJ, too, when he realizes Lydia isn't letting him stay. I follow after him, crawling out of the tent, standing up. "It's fine, I'll go," I say. "We just finished setting it up for him."

Lydia looks me up and down, unimpressed with whatever

she thinks she sees. I want to eye her the same way, but I don't want to do anything to make this worse for Auburn. When I get a good look at her, I realize I've seen her before. It's been a while, but she hasn't changed a bit, other than having a little more gray in her straight, black hair. She still looks just as stoic and intimidating as she did all those years ago.

She faces AJ.

"AJ, get your toy. We need to go."

Auburn follows Lydia out of the room. "Lydia, please." She waves her hand in my direction. "He's leaving. It'll just be me and AJ here, I promise."

Lydia's hand pauses on the front door, and she turns to face Auburn. She releases a quick sigh. "You can see him Sunday night, Auburn. Really, it's fine. I should have known not to stop by unannounced."

She looks over Auburn's shoulder to AJ. "Tell your mother good-bye, AJ."

I can see Auburn grimace and then just as fast, her frown turns into a smile as she turns around and kneels down in front of AJ. She pulls him to her and hugs him. "I'm sorry, but you're gonna go with Nana Lydia tonight, okay?" She pulls away from him and brushes her hand through his hair. "I'll see you Sunday night."

"But I want to stay here," he says with genuine disappointment.

Auburn tries to hide it with her smile, but I can see how his words have gutted her. She ruffles his hair and says, "Another night, okay? Mommy has to get up really early and work tomorrow and you won't have any fun if all we do is go to sleep."

"It'll be fun," he says. He points toward the bedroom. "You have a tent and we could sleep in—" AJ's eyes cut to mine and he realizes he just mentioned the secret tent. He looks back at Auburn and shakes his head. "Never mind, you don't have a tent. I was wrong, you don't."

As shitty as I feel about what's happening right now, the kid makes me smile.

"AJ, let's go."

Auburn gives him another tight hug and whispers, "I love you. I'll love you forever." She kisses his forehead and he kisses her cheek before taking Lydia's hand. Auburn doesn't even turn around to tell Lydia good-bye, and I don't blame her one bit. As soon as the door closes, she stands and brushes past me, heading straight to her bedroom. I watch as she pulls back the flap and crawls into the tent.

I stand at her door and listen to her cry.

It all makes sense now. Why she was so upset that Lydia stood her up on her birthday, because that meant she didn't get to spend it with AJ.

Why she said his favorite color is blue.

Why she moved to Texas, when she seems so unhappy here.

And why there is no way in hell I'll be able to walk away from her now. Not after witnessing that. Not after seeing how incredible she is when she loves that little boy.

CHAPTER ELEVEN

Auburn

I hear the partition being unzipped, and then I feel a hand on my arm, followed by an arm sliding beneath my pillow. Owen pulls me against him and I immediately want to pull away, but at the same time I'm surprised at the level of comfort I feel wrapped in his arms. I close my eyes and wait for his questions to come. I'll just lie here and enjoy the comfort until he strips it away with his curiosity.

His hand moves up and down my arm, stroking me gently. After several minutes of silence, he finds my fingers and slides his through mine.

"When I was sixteen," he says quietly, "my mother and older brother died in a car wreck. I was driving."

I squeeze my eyes shut. I can't even imagine. Suddenly my issues don't seem like issues at all.

"My father was in a coma for several weeks after that. I stayed by his side the entire time. Not because I necessarily wanted to be there when he woke up, but because I didn't know where else to go. Our home was empty. My friends had lives they continued to live, so I rarely saw them after the funeral. I had relatives who would stop by in the beginning, but even that faded. By the end of that first month, it was just my father and me. And I was terrified that if he died, too, I wouldn't have anything left to live for."

I slowly roll onto my back and look up at him. "What happened?"

Owen reaches his fingers to my forehead and brushes back my hair. "He lived, obviously," he says quietly. "He woke up right before the one-month anniversary of the wreck. And as happy as I was that he was okay, I don't think reality sank in until I had to tell him what happened. He couldn't recall anything from the day leading up to the wreck, nor could he recall anything after that point. And when I had to tell him that my mother and Carey were dead, I saw it. I saw the life seep right out of his eyes. And I haven't seen it return since the night it happened."

I wipe tears from my eyes. "I'm so sorry," I tell him.

He shakes his head, like he doesn't need my condolences. "Don't be," he says to me. "It's not something I dwell on. The wreck wasn't my fault. Of course I miss them, and it hurts every day, but I also know that life has to go on. And my mother and Carey weren't the type of people who would want me to use their deaths as an excuse." His fingers move gently, back and forth, across my jaw. He's not looking me in the eyes. He's looking beyond me, over my head, contemplating.

"Sometimes I miss them so much, it hurts me right here," he says, making a tight fist with his hand against his chest. "It feels like someone is squeezing my heart with the strength of the entire goddamn world."

I nod, because I know exactly what he means. I feel that way every time I think of AJ and the fact that he's not living with me.

"Every time I get that feeling in my chest, I start to think about the things I miss most about them. Like my mother, and the way she used to smile at me. Because no matter what, no matter where we were, her smile would always comfort me. We could have been in the middle of a war and all she had to do was kneel down and look me in the eyes with that smile, and it would take away every single fear or worry I had. And somehow, even on her bad days, when I know she didn't feel like smiling, she would anyway. Because to her, nothing else mattered but my happiness. And I miss that. Sometimes I miss it so much, the only way I can make myself feel better is to paint her."

He laughs under his breath. "I have about twenty paintings of my mother stowed away. It's kind of creepy."

I laugh with him, but seeing how much he loves his mother puts the ache back in my chest, and my laugh turns into a frown. It makes me wonder if AJ will ever feel that for me, since I'm not able to be the type of mother I want to be to him right now.

Owen cups my cheek in his hand and looks me very seriously in the eyes. "I saw the way you looked at him, Auburn.

I saw the way you smiled at him. You smiled at him the same way my mother used to smile at me. And I don't care what that woman may think of you as a mother; I barely know you, and I could feel how much you love that little boy."

I close my eyes and let his words seep over every doubtful thought I've ever had when it comes to my abilities as a mom.

I've been a mother for over four years now.

Four.

And in those four years, Owen is the first person to ever say anything that makes me feel like I'm capable of being a good mother. And even though he hardly knows me, and he doesn't know a thing about my situation, I can feel the belief he holds in the words he's saying to me. The simple fact that he believes what he's saying makes me want to believe it, too.

"Really?" I say quietly. I open my eyes and look up at him. "Because sometimes I feel like—"

He cuts me off with an adamant shake of his head. "Don't," he says firmly. "I don't know your situation, and I assume if you wanted me to know, you would have told me. So I'm not going to ask. But I can tell you that what I just witnessed was a woman who takes advantage of your insecurities. Don't allow her to make you feel that way, Auburn. You're a good mother. A good mother."

Another tear escapes, and I quickly turn my head away. I know in my heart that I could be a good mother if Lydia would give me the chance. I know that the way things have turned out isn't my fault. I was sixteen and unprepared when I had him. But I never knew how good it could feel for someone else to believe in me.

Finding out about AJ could have sent Owen out the door in a flash. Finding out I don't have custody of my son could have filled him with misjudgments about me. Neither of those things happened, though. Instead, he used this opportunity to encourage me. To make me feel better. And no one has made me feel this way since the day Adam passed away.

Thank you just doesn't seem like enough, so instead of speaking, I face him again. He's still hovering over me, looking down on me. I reach my hand up and around the back of his head, and I lift my mouth to his.

I kiss him softly, and he does nothing to try to stop it, nor does he try to prolong it. He just accepts the kiss as he inhales slowly. I don't part my lips, and neither of us attempts to take the kiss further. I think we both know that this kiss was more of a "Thank you" than an "I want you."

When I pull away, his eyes are closed and he looks as peaceful as he just made me feel.

I lie back against the pillow and watch as he slowly opens his eyes. A smile forms on his lips and he lies down next to me, both of us staring up at the top of the tent.

"His father was my first boyfriend," I say, explaining my situation to him. It feels good to tell him. I don't tell a lot of people much, but I want to tell Owen everything for some reason.

"He passed away when I was fifteen. Two weeks later, I found out I was pregnant with AJ. When my parents found out, they wanted me to put him up for adoption. They had four other children to care for besides me, and it was hard enough for them to put food on the table for all of us. There was no way they could afford an infant, but there was also no way I was going to give up my son. Luckily, Lydia came up with a compromise.

"She said if I agreed to give her legal custody after he was born, I could live with her and help raise him. She wanted reassurance that I wouldn't end up putting him up for adoption, and primary custody of him would give her that reassurance. She also said it would be easier for medical and insurance reasons. I didn't question her. I was young, I had no idea what any of it meant. I just knew it was my only guarantee that I could keep AJ, so I did it. I would have signed whatever she wanted if it meant I could be with him.

"Once AJ was born, she took over completely. She was never pleased with how I did anything. She made me feel ignorant. And after a while, I started to believe her. After all, I was young, and she had raised children before, so I assumed she knew more than me. By the time I graduated high school, Lydia was making all the decisions for him. And one of those decisions was that he was going to stay with her while I attended college."

Owen finds my hand and pulls it between us, holding on to it. I appreciate the encouraging gesture, because this is a hard confession.

"Instead of attending a four-year university, I decided to attend cosmetology school, since it was only a one-year program. I thought once I graduated and got my own place, she'd let him live with me. But three months before graduation, her husband passed away. She moved back to Texas to be closer to Trey, her other son. And she took *my* son with her."

Owen sighs. "That's why you moved to Texas? You couldn't stop her from leaving Oregon?"

I shake my head. "She has the legal right to take him anywhere she wants. She said Texas was a better place to raise a child and that if I wanted what was best for AJ, I would move here after graduation. My final class ended at five P.M.

on a Friday and I had moved into this apartment less than twenty-four hours later."

"What about your parents?" he says. "They couldn't do anything to stop it?"

I shake my head. "My parents have been supportive of my decisions, but they don't get involved. They don't really have a close relationship with AJ since I moved out of their house and into Lydia's when I was pregnant with him. Besides, they have enough to worry about. I would feel bad telling them how Lydia is treating me, because it would just make them feel guilty for allowing me to move out all those years ago."

"So you just pretend everything is okay?"

I glance up at him and nod, slightly worried as to what I might see in his eyes. Contempt? Disappointment? When our eyes meet, I don't see either of those things. I see sympathy. And maybe a little bit of anger.

"Is it okay for me to say that I hate Lydia?"

I smile. "I hate her, too," I say with a quick laugh. "I also love her, though. She loves AJ as much as I do, and I know he loves her. I'm thankful for that. But I never would have given up custody to her in the first place if I knew it would end up like this. I thought she wanted to help, but now I realize she's using AJ to replace the son she lost."

Owen scoots toward me until I'm looking straight up at him and he's staring down at me. "You'll get him back," he says. "There's no reason a court wouldn't want your son with you."

His compliment makes me smile, even though I know he's wrong. "I've researched all my options. A court wouldn't take a child away from someone they've legally been with since birth unless there's a legit reason. Lydia will never agree to let him live with me full-time. The only option I have, really, is to do whatever I can to appease her, all the while saving every extra penny I can to pay the lawyer I've hired to help me. But even he doesn't seem hopeful."

He rests his head in one hand and brings his other hand to my face. His fingers trail lightly across my cheekbone, and his touch makes my eyes want to fall shut. I somehow keep them open, despite the soothing feel of his skin against my cheek. "You know what?" he says with a smile. "I'm pretty sure you just made determination my favorite quality in a person."

I know I barely know him, but I definitely don't want him to move on Monday. I feel like he's the only good thing to happen to me since I arrived in Texas.

"I don't want you to move, Owen."

His eyes shift down, and he stops looking at me. His hand moves to my shoulder and he traces an invisible pattern with the tip of his finger, following it with his eyes. He looks apologetic, and it's more than just the fact that he's leaving. He's upset about something deeper, and I can see his confession wanting to fall off the tip of his tongue. He's holding something back.

"You didn't get a job," I say. "That's not where you're going Monday, is it?"

He still doesn't look at me. He doesn't even have to respond, because his silence confirms it. He answers anyway, though. "No."

"Where are you going?"

I watch as he winces slightly. Wherever he's going, he doesn't want to tell me. He's afraid of what I'll think. And honestly, I'm afraid of what I'm about to hear. I've had enough negativity for one day.

He finally lifts his eyes to meet mine again, and the regretful look on his face makes me wish I didn't bring it up. He opens his mouth to speak, but I shake my head.

"I don't want to know yet," I say quickly. "Tell me after."

"After what?"

"After this weekend. I don't want to think about confessions. I don't want to think about Lydia. Let's just spend the next twenty-four hours avoiding both of our pitiful realities."

He smiles appreciatively. "I like that idea, actually. A lot."

Our moment is disrupted by the fierce growl of my stomach. I clench it in my hands, embarrassed. He laughs.

"I'm hungry, too," he says. He exits the tent and helps me out as well by giving me his hand. "Want to eat here or my place?"

I shake my head. "I'm not sure I can wait fifteen blocks," I say, heading toward the kitchen. "You like frozen pizza?"

All we're doing is cooking pizza, but it's the most fun I've had with a guy since Adam. Getting pregnant at the age of fifteen doesn't leave a lot of time for social interaction, so saying I'm a little inexperienced could be an understatement. I used to grow nervous at the thought of getting close to another guy, but Owen has the opposite effect on me. I feel so much calmness when I'm around him.

My mother says there are people you meet and get to know, and then there are people you meet and already know. I feel like Owen is the latter. Our personalities seem to complement each other, like we've known one another our whole lives. I had no idea until today just how much I need someone like him in my life. Someone to fill the holes that Lydia has created in my self-esteem.

"If you weren't in such a hurry to graduate, what career would you have chosen other than cosmetology?"

"Anything," I blurt out. "Everything."

Owen laughs. He's leaning against the counter next to the stove, and I'm seated on the bar across from him. "I suck at cutting hair. I hate listening to everyone's problems while they sit in the salon chair. I swear, people take so many things for granted, and hearing all their whiny stories puts me in such a bad mood."

"We're kind of in the same business if you put it that way," Owen says. "I paint confessions and you have to listen to them."

I nod in agreement, but also feel like I could be coming off as ungrateful. "There are a few really good clients. People I look forward to. I think it's not so much the people that I don't like, but the fact that I had to choose something I didn't want to do."

He studies me for a moment. "Well, the good news is, you're young. My father used to tell me that no life decision is permanent other than a tattoo."

"I could argue with that logic," I say with a laugh. "What about you? Have you always wanted to be an artist?"

The timer goes off on the oven and Owen immediately opens it to check the pizza. He shoves it back inside. I know it's just a frozen pizza, but it's kind of a turn-on to see a man take over in the kitchen.

He leans against the counter again. "I didn't choose to be an artist. I think it kind of chose me."

I love that answer. I'm also jealous of it, because I wish I could have been born with a natural talent. Something that would have chosen me, so that I wouldn't have to cut hair all day.

"Have you ever thought about returning to school?" he asks. "Maybe majoring in something you actually have an interest in?"

I shrug. "One of these days, maybe. Right now, though, my goal is AJ."

He smiles appreciatively at my answer. I can't think of any questions I want to toss his way, because the silence is nice. I like the way he looks at me when it's quiet. His smile lingers, and his gaze falls all over me like a blanket.

I press my hands onto the countertop beneath me and look down at my dangling feet. I suddenly find it hard to continue watching him, because I'm afraid he can see how much I like it.

Without speaking, he begins to close the distance between us. I bite my bottom lip nervously, because he's coming at me with an intention, and I don't think his intention is to ask more questions. I watch as the palms of his hands meet my knees and then slowly slide upward. His hands graze my thighs all the way up until they come to rest on my hips.

When I look into his eyes, I get completely lost in them. He's staring at me with a level of need that I didn't know I was capable of producing in someone. He wraps his hand around my lower back and pulls me against him. I place my hands on his forearms and grip tightly, not sure what's about to happen next but completely prepared to allow it.

The faint smile on his face disappears the closer his lips come to mine. My eyelids flutter and then close completely, just as his mouth feathers mine.

"I've been wanting to do this since the moment I laid eyes on you," he whispers. His mouth connects with mine, and at first his kiss is like the one I gave him in the tent. Soft, sweet, and innocent. But then the innocence is stripped away the second he runs one of his hands through the back of my hair and slides his tongue against my lips.

I don't know how I can feel so light and so heavy all at once, but his kiss makes me feel weighted to a cloud. I slide my hands up his neck and do my best to kiss him the way he's kissing me, but I'm afraid my mouth doesn't even compare to his. There's no way I could make him feel like he's making me feel right now.

He pulls my legs until they're wrapped around his waist, and then he lifts me off the bar and directs us toward the living room without stopping our kiss. I try to ignore the smell of pizza being overcooked in the oven, because I don't want him to stop. But I'm also really, really hungry and don't want the pizza to burn.

"I think the pizza is burning," I whisper just as we hit the couch. He gently lowers me onto my back as he shakes his head.

"I'll make you another one." His mouth reconnects with mine, and I suddenly couldn't care less about the pizza.

He lowers himself onto the couch but not completely on top of me. He keeps his arms locked on either side of my head and doesn't do anything to show that he expects more than just this kiss.

So that's what I give him. I kiss him and he kisses me and we don't stop until a smoke alarm begins to sound. As soon as we realize the sound is coming from inside my apartment, we both separate and jump up. He rushes to the oven and opens it while I grab the cardboard pizza box and begin fanning the smoke alarm.

Owen pulls the pizza out of the oven and it's so burnt, it's completely inedible. "Maybe we should just go out to eat on the way back to my place."

The smoke alarm finally stops, and I toss the pizza box on the counter. "Or we can just eat some of the years' worth of food you bought at Target today."

He pulls the oven mitt off his hand and drops it onto the stove. He reaches for my hand and pulls me against him, lowering his mouth back to mine.

I'm pretty sure his kisses are the best form of dieting there is, because every time his lips touch mine, I forget all about the fact that I'm starving.

As soon as our tongues meet, there's a sudden, loud knock on the front door. Our mouths separate and we both turn and look at the door as soon as it swings open. When I see Trey standing in the doorway, I immediately back away from Owen. I hate that my first instinct is to separate myself from him, because the last thing I want Owen to think is that I'm involved with Trey in any way. The truth is, I would have backed away from him no matter who was at the door.

I just really wish it wasn't Trey.

"Shit," Owen mutters. I glance at him and his face has fallen, along with his shoulders. I can tell immediately that he must have the wrong idea about Trey's bursting through the front door.

I glance back at Trey, who, for some reason, is making his way toward the kitchen with a death stare directed at Owen. "What are you doing here?"

I look at Owen, and he isn't paying attention to Trey. He's looking directly at me. "Auburn," he says. "We need to talk."

Trey's laugh makes me wince. "What do you need to talk to her about, Owen? Have you not already told her?"

Owen's eyes close for several seconds, and then he opens them and fixes his stare on Trey. "When will it be enough for you, Trey? Fuck."

My heart is hammering away in my chest and I have a feeling I'm about to find out why they feel this way toward each other, but at the moment I'm not sure I want to know. It can't be good.

Trey takes two steps toward Owen, until he's inches from his face. "Get out of her apartment. Get out of her life. If you can do those two things, then I'll probably be satisfied."

"Auburn," Owen says firmly.

Trey takes several steps toward me, standing between Owen and me so that I can't see him anymore. I look into Trey's eyes now and see nothing but anger.

He points behind him. "This guy you brought back to your apartment? The guy you allowed near your son? He was arrested for possession, Auburn."

I shake my head with a disbelieving laugh. I don't know why Trey is saying these things. He steps aside and I can see Owen again.

My heart grows too heavy to hold, because the look on Owen's face says it all. I see the apology and the regret. This is what he was going to tell me earlier. This is the confession I told him could wait until Monday.

"Owen?" I say his name in almost a whisper.

"I wanted to tell you," he says. "It's not as bad as he's making it sound, Auburn. I swear."

Owen begins to take a step toward me, but Trey immediately turns and pushes him against the wall. His arm connects with Owen's neck. "You have five seconds to get the fuck out."

Owen's eyes are still locked with mine, despite the arm

that's pressed against his throat. He nods. "Let me get my things out of her room, and I'll go."

Trey eyes him carefully for several seconds and then he releases him. I watch as Owen walks into my room to retrieve his "things."

I know for a fact Owen didn't show up here with anything.

Trey is eyeing me now. "Your child's uncle is a fucking cop and you don't think to get a background check on the people you allow into your life?"

I have no response to that. He's right.

Trey shakes his head in disappointment, just as Owen exits my bedroom. Before Trey turns to face him, Owen briefly glances toward the tent. His eyes are telling me something he's not willing to say out loud. He brushes past Trey and walks out the front door without looking back.

Trey walks to the door and slams it shut. He stands with his hands on his hips, facing me, waiting for an explanation. If I didn't think he would go back to Lydia and tell her everything that just happened, I'd tell him to fuck off. Instead, I do what I always do. I say anything that will please them.

"I'm sorry. I didn't know."

He walks toward me and gently squeezes my forearms while he looks me in the eyes.

"I worry about you, Auburn. Please don't trust anyone until you run them by me first. I could have warned you about him."

He hugs me, and it takes everything I have to hug him back, but I do.

"You don't need his reputation coming between you and your son. It wouldn't be good for you."

I nod against his chest, but I want to push him away from me for the disguised threat. He's just like his mother. Always using my situation with AJ to manipulate me. It burns me and strips me of any confidence I momentarily gained from being in Owen's arms.

I pull away from him and attempt a smile. "I don't want anything to do with him," I say. The words are hard for me to say, because there might be actual truth in them. I can't even think about how angry I am at Owen right now when Trey is still standing in front of me. "Thank you for telling me," I say as I head to the door. I open it so that he'll take the hint. "I want to be alone for a while, though. It's been a long day."

Trey walks toward the door and backs out. "I'll see you Sunday night at dinner?"

I nod and force another fake smile to appease him. As soon as I close the door, I lock it and rush to my bedroom. I crawl inside the tent and find a piece of paper on my pillow. I pick it up and read it.

Please come by my studio tonight. We need to talk.

I read Owen's note so many times, I could likely rewrite it with perfectly matched handwriting. I lie down on the pillow and sigh heavily, because I have no idea what to do. There's nothing that could excuse the fact that he's going to jail, or the fact that he lied to me. But despite everything that just happened, every part of me is aching for him. I barely know the guy, yet somehow I can feel that familiar clench of a fist gripping at my heart. I have to see him one more time, even if it's just to say good-bye.

CHAPTER TWELVE

Owen

I should have told her. The second I was released from custody, I should have gone straight to her apartment and told her everything.

I've been pacing the studio floor for over an hour now. I only pace when I'm pissed, and right now I'm not sure I've ever been this angry. I'm going to burn a hole into this floor if I don't stop.

But I know she's read my message by now. It's been over two hours since I left it on her pillow and I'm starting to think she's already given up on me. I don't blame her. As much as I want to try to convince her that Trey's not good for her and

I'm not as bad as she now thinks I am, I have a feeling I won't even get that opportunity. There's no telling what she's been told about me by now.

Just as I begin to head toward the stairs, I hear a knock on the glass door. I don't rush to the door. I sprint.

When I open the door, her eyes meet mine briefly before she glances nervously over her shoulder. She grabs the door and quickly slips inside, shutting it behind her.

I hate that. I hate that she's scared to be here and scared who might have seen her walk in the door.

She doesn't trust me.

She turns and faces me, and I hate the disappointment flooding her eyes right now.

We need to talk and I don't want to do it right here, so I reach around her and lock the door. "Thank you for coming."

She doesn't respond. She waits for me to say something else.

"Will you come upstairs with me?"

She glances at the hallway over my shoulder and nods. She follows me across the studio and up to my apartment. It's crazy how different things are between us now. Two hours ago, everything was perfect. And now . . .

It's amazing how much distance one truth can create between two people.

I walk to the kitchen and offer her something to drink. Maybe if I pour her a drink, the conversation might last longer. There's so much I want and need to explain to her, if she will just give me that opportunity.

She doesn't want a drink.

She's standing in the middle of the room and it appears as if she's afraid to approach me. Her eyes roam around the room as if she's never been here before. I can see the look on her face. She sees me differently now that she knows.

I quietly watch her assess the room for a while. Eventually her eyes meet mine again, and there's a long pause before she works up the courage to ask me what she came here to find out.

"Are you an addict, Owen?"

She doesn't skirt around the subject at all. Her straightforwardness makes me cringe, because nothing is a simple yes-or-no answer. And she doesn't appear to want to wait around for the explanation with the way she's eyeing the stairwell.

"If I said no, would it even make a difference for us?"

She regards me silently for several seconds, and then she shakes her head. "No."

I had a feeling that would be her answer. And just like that, I no longer feel like explaining my side of the situation. What would be the point when my answer doesn't matter? Telling her the truth could just further complicate things.

"Are you going to jail?" she asks. "Is that why you said you're moving?"

I tilt the bottle and pour myself a glass of wine. I take a long, slow sip from it before answering with a nod. "Probably. It's my first offense, so I doubt I'm away for long."

She exhales and closes her eyes. When she opens them again, she's looking down at her feet. Her hands move to her hips and she continues to avoid eye contact with me. "I want custody of my son, Owen. They would use you against me."

"Who's they?"

"Lydia and Trey." She looks up at me now. "They'll never trust me if they know I'm involved with you in any way."

I expected something along the lines of good-bye when she

showed up here, but I didn't expect the hurt that would come along with her words. I feel stupid for not thinking about how this would affect her. I've been so worried about what she would think of me when she found out, it really didn't occur to me until just now that her relationship with her son could be jeopardized.

I pour myself another glass of wine. Probably not a good idea for her to witness me downing wine now that she knows about my arrest record.

I expect her to turn and walk out now, but she doesn't. Instead, she takes a few slow steps toward me. "Will they let you choose rehab, instead?"

I down the second glass of wine. "I don't need rehab." I place the glass in the sink.

I can see the disappointment take over. I'm familiar with that look. I've seen it enough by now to know what it means, and I don't like that her feelings have so quickly moved from wanting me to pitying me.

"I don't have an issue with drugs, Auburn." I lean forward until we're just a foot apart. "What I have an issue with is the fact that you seem to be involved with Trey. I may be the one with the criminal record, but he's the one you should be careful of."

She laughs under her breath. "He's a cop, Owen. You're going to jail for possession. Which one of you do I trust?"

"Your instincts," I say immediately.

She looks down at her hands, folded across the bar. She presses the pads of her thumbs against each other. "My instinct is to do what's best for my son."

"Exactly," I tell her. "Which is why I said to trust your instincts."

Sometimes I wonder if being dead would be easier than being his mother.

Owen Gentry

I'll love you forever.
Even when I can't.

She looks up at me, and I can see the hurt in her eyes. I shouldn't have brought this on her, I know that. I know exactly what she's feeling when she looks at me. Frustration, disappointment, anger. I see it every time I look in the mirror.

I walk around the bar and take her by the wrist. I pull her to me and wrap my arms around her. For a few seconds, she allows it. But then she pushes me away with an adamant shake of her head. "I can't."

It's just two words, but they only mean one thing.

The end.

She turns and heads straight down the stairs.

"Auburn, wait," I call after her.

She doesn't wait. I reach the top of the stairs and listen as her footsteps echo across the studio. This isn't how it's supposed to end. I refuse to let her leave like this, because if she leaves with this feeling, it'll be easy for her never to come back.

I immediately descend the steps and run after her. I reach her just as her hand meets the lock on the front door of the studio. I pull her hand away and spin her around, and then I press my mouth to hers.

CHAPTER THIRTEEN

Auburn

He kisses me with conviction and apology and anger, and it's somehow all wrapped up in tenderness. When our tongues meet, it's a momentary reprieve from the reality of our good-bye. We both exhale softly, because this is exactly how a kiss should feel. My knees want to buckle from the feel of his lips against mine.

I kiss him back, even though I know this kiss won't lead to anything. It won't correct anything. It won't right any of his wrongs, but I also know it could be the last time I ever feel this way, and I don't want to deny myself that.

He wraps his arm around me, sliding one hand up my neck

and into my hair. He cradles my head and it feels as if he's attempting to memorize every aspect of the way it feels when we kiss, because he knows after we stop, that's all he'll have. The memory of it.

The thought of this being good-bye begins to anger me, knowing he gave me hope and then allowed Trey to strip it away with the truth.

The kiss between us quickly grows painful, and not in a physical sense. The more we kiss, the more we realize what we're losing, and it hurts. It scares me to know that there's a chance I've come across one of the few people in this world who could make me feel this way, and I already have to give it up.

I'm so tired of having to give up the only things in life I want.

He pulls back and looks me in the eyes with a pained expression. He moves his hand from the back of my head and brings it to my cheek, brushing a thumb over my bottom lip. "This already hurts."

His mouth meets mine again, and he lands a kiss as soft as velvet against my lips. He slowly moves his head until his mouth is directly over my ear. "Is this it? Is this how it ends?"

I nod, even though it's the last thing I want to do. But this is the end. Even if he were to change his life completely, his past choices still affect my own life.

"Sometimes we don't get second chances, Owen. Sometimes things just end."

He winces. "We didn't even get a *first* chance."

I want to tell him it's not my fault; it's his fault. But I know he knows that. He's not asking me to give him another chance. He's just upset that it's already over.

He presses his palms against the glass door behind me, caging me in with his arms. "I'm sorry, Auburn," he says. "You have a lot to deal with in your life, and I absolutely didn't mean to make things more difficult for you." He presses his lips against my forehead and then pushes off the door. He backs up two steps and nods softly. "I understand. And I'm sorry."

I can't take the pained look in his eyes or the acceptance in his words. I reach behind me and unlock the door, and then I turn and leave.

I hear the door close behind me, and it becomes my least favorite sound in the whole world. I bring a fist up to my heart, because I feel exactly what he explained he feels when he misses someone. And I don't understand it, because I just met him a few weeks ago.

"There are people you meet that you get to know, and then there are people you meet that you already know."

I don't care how long I've known him. I don't care if he lied to me. I'm going to allow myself to be sad and feel sorry for myself, because despite whatever he's done in the past, no one has made me feel like he made me feel today. He made me feel proud of myself as a mother. Because of that, the fact that I have to say good-bye to him is worth a few tears, and I won't allow myself to feel guilty crying about it.

I make it halfway home, and just as I'm drying the last of the tears I've allowed myself to shed over this good-bye, a car pulls up beside me and comes to a slow crawl. I glance at it out of the corner of my eye and immediately see that it's a police car. I stop walking when Trey rolls the window down and leans across the seat. "Get in, Auburn."

I don't argue. I open the door and climb inside, and he begins to drive in the direction of my apartment. I don't like the vibe I'm getting from him right now. I can't tell if he's acting like a jealous boyfriend or an overprotective brother. Technically, he's neither of those things.

"Were you at his studio just now?"

I stare out the window and contemplate how I should answer. He'll know I'm lying if I say no, and I need Trey to trust me. Of all the people in the world, I need both Lydia and Trey to see that everything I do, I do for AJ.

"Yes. He owed me money."

I can hear his heavy breaths as he inhales and exhales. He eventually pulls over to the side of the street and puts the car in park. I don't want to look directly at him, but I can see him cover his mouth with his hand, squeezing the frustration from his jaw. "I *just* told you that he was dangerous, Auburn." He looks directly at me. "Are you stupid?"

I can only take so much. I swing the car door open, get out, and slam it shut. Before I can even take three steps, he's standing directly in front of me.

"He's not dangerous, Trey. He has an addiction. And there's nothing going on between us, I just went to collect my pay for working at his studio."

Trey studies my face, more than likely in an attempt to see if I'm lying to him. I exhale and roll my eyes. "If there was anything going on, I would have been at his studio for more than five minutes." I push past him and begin walking toward my apartment. "Jesus, Trey. You're acting like you have a reason to be jealous."

He's in front of me again, forcing me to stop. He stares down at me for several quiet seconds. "I am jealous, Auburn."

I immediately have to swallow the lump that forms in my throat. I also continue to stare up at him, waiting for him to take back what he said, but he doesn't. He's looking at me with nothing but sincerity.

He's Adam's brother. He's AJ's uncle.

I can't.

It's Trey.

I move around him and continue walking. We're only a block from my apartment, so it doesn't surprise me when I hear him fall into step behind me. I continue walking, trying to process the last two hours of my life, but it's a little difficult when my dead boyfriend's jealous brother is stalking after me.

When I reach my door, I unlock it and turn around to face him. Trey's eyes are like carving knives, digging into me, hollowing me out. I'm about to tell him good night when he lifts an arm and rests his hand against the door frame next to my head. "Do you ever think about it?"

I know exactly what he's referring to, but I play ignorant. "About what?"

His eyes fall to my lips. "Us."

Us.

Me and Trey.

I can honestly say no, I never think about it. But I don't want to hurt his feelings, so instead I don't respond at all.

"It makes sense, Auburn."

I shake my head, almost adamantly. I don't mean to appear so resistant, but it's exactly how I feel. "It makes *no* sense," I reply. "You were Adam's brother. You're AJ's uncle. It would confuse him."

Trey takes a step forward. His closeness feels different than when Owen steps toward me. Trey's closeness feels suffocating, like I need to punch a hole in the atmosphere just to breathe.

"I love him, Auburn. I'm the only father figure your little

boy has," he says. "He's living in my house with Mom, and if you and I were together . . ."

I immediately stand up straighter. "I hope you aren't about to use my son as an excuse for why I should date you." The anger in my voice surprises me, so I know it surprises Trey.

He runs a hand through his hair and looks at a loss for what to say. His gaze shifts down the hallway as he attempts his response. "Look," he says, meeting my stare again. "I'm not trying to use him to get closer to you. I know that's how it sounded. I'm just saying . . . it makes sense. We make sense."

I don't respond, because everything he's saying has some truth to it. Lydia trusts Trey more than anyone in the world. And if Trey and I were together . . .

"Think about it," he says, not wanting an answer from me right now. "We can start slow. See if we fit." He pulls his hand from the frame of the door and backs away, giving me room to breathe. "We'll talk about it Sunday night. I need to get back to work. Promise me you'll keep your door locked?"

I nod, and I hate that I nod, because I don't want him to think I was agreeing to all of the other things he just said.

But . . . he makes sense. He lives in the same house as AJ and Lydia, and the one thing I want is more time with my son. I'm at the point where I don't care what it takes to get more time with AJ; I just need it. I miss him so much.

I don't like the fact that I'm considering his offer. I don't feel for Trey even a fraction of what I felt for Adam. I can't even compare it to what I feel for Owen.

But he's right. Being with him would get me closer to AJ. And I feel more for AJ than anything or anyone in the world. I'll do whatever it takes to get my son back.

Whatever it takes.

Before I moved here, Lydia assured me that Dallas traffic wasn't all that bad. When I asked how long it would take to get from my potential new apartment to their house, she said, "Oh, it's no further than ten miles."

She failed to mention that ten miles in Dallas is a good forty-five-minute cab ride. Most nights I don't even get off work until seven. By the time I get in a cab to head to her house, it's AJ's bedtime. Because of this, she says it's an inconvenience for me to visit during weeknights. "It makes him restless," she says.

So Sunday-night dinners and any other day of the week I can talk her into allowing me to come over is all I get with my son. Of course, I stretch Sundays out as long as I can. Sometimes I show up at lunch and don't leave until after he goes to sleep. I know this irritates her, but I don't really give a shit. He's my son, and I shouldn't have to ask for permission to visit him.

Today has been an exceptionally long day with him, and I've loved every second of it. As soon as I woke up this morning, I showered and called a cab. I've been here since after breakfast, and AJ hasn't left my side. Right after we finished dinner, I brought him to the couch, and he fell asleep in my lap after half an episode of cartoons. I usually do the dishes and clean up after dinner, but I don't offer this time. Tonight I just want to hold my little boy while he sleeps.

I don't know if Trey is trying to prove a point about how domestic he can be, or if I'm seeing him in a slightly different light, but he actually took over and cleaned up the entire kitchen. From the sound of it, he just loaded and started the dishwasher.

I glance up when he appears in the doorway between the

kitchen and the living room. He leans against the frame of the door and smiles at the sight of us cuddled together on the couch.

He watches us quietly for a moment, until Lydia walks in and breaks up the peaceful moment. "I hope he hasn't been asleep for long," she says, eyeing AJ in my arms. "When you let him fall asleep this early, he wakes up in the middle of the night."

"He fell asleep a few minutes ago," I tell her. "He'll be fine."

She takes a seat in one of the chairs next to the couch and looks up at Trey, who is still standing in the doorway. "Do you work tonight?" she asks. Trey nods and straightens himself.

"Yeah. I need to get going, actually," he says. He looks at me. "You want a ride home?"

I glance down at AJ in my arms, not at all ready to leave yet, but not sure if I should do what I need to do with AJ still asleep in my lap. I've been working up the courage to talk to Lydia about our arrangement, and tonight seems as good a time as any. "I was actually hoping to talk to your mom about something before I go," I say to Trey.

I can feel Lydia glance at me, but I don't reciprocate her stare. You would think after living with her as long as I did, I wouldn't be so scared of her. However, it's hard not to fear someone when they hold all the power over the one thing in life you want.

"Whatever it is, it can wait, Auburn," Lydia says. "I'm exhausted and Trey needs to get to work."

I run my hand through AJ's hair. He has his father's hair. Soft and fine, like silk. "Lydia," I say quietly. I glance over at her, my stomach in knots and my heart in my throat. She always shuts me down every time I try to talk to her about this, but I have to get it over with. "I want to talk to you about custody. And I'd really appreciate it if we could talk about it tonight, because it's killing me not seeing him as much as I used to."

When I lived with them in Portland, I saw him every day. Custody wasn't such an issue then, because I came home from school every day to the same house as my son. Even though Lydia had final say over everything that involved AJ, I still felt like his mother.

However, since she took him and moved to Dallas several months ago, I've felt like the worst mother in the world. I never get to see him. Every time I talk to him on the phone, I'm in tears by the time I hang up. I can't help but feel like the distance she's putting between us is intentional.

"Auburn, you know you're welcome to see him any time you want."

I shake my head. "But that's just it," I tell her. "I'm not." My voice is weak, and I hate that I sound like a child right now. "You don't like it when I visit on school nights and you haven't even allowed him to spend the night with me."

Lydia rolls her eyes. "For good reason," she says. "How am I supposed to trust the people you allow at your place? The last one you had in your bedroom is a convicted felon."

My gaze falls to Trey, and he immediately breaks eye contact with me. He knows that telling her about Owen's past has just put a wedge between AJ and me. He can see the anger on my face, so he steps into the living room. "I'll put AJ to bed," he says.

I'm thankful for that, at least. AJ doesn't need to wake up and hear the conversation going on around him right now. I hand AJ off to Trey and turn and face Lydia this time.

"I wouldn't have allowed him to stay with AJ in the same apartment," I say in my defense. "He wouldn't even have been in my apartment if I knew you were bringing AJ over."

Her lips are pursed together, and her eyes are narrow slits of disapproval. I hate the way she looks at me.

"What are you asking me, Auburn? Do you want your son to have sleepovers at your apartment? Do you want to show up every night right before his bedtime and get him riled up to the point that he doesn't want to go to bed?" She stands up, exasperated. "I've raised that boy from birth, so you can't expect me to be okay with him being around complete strangers."

I stand up, too. She's not about to tower over me and make me feel inferior. "*We've* raised him from birth, Lydia. I've been there every step of the way. He's my son. I'm his mother. I shouldn't have to ask you for permission when I want to spend time with him."

Lydia stares at me, hopefully absorbing my words and accepting them. She has to see how unfair she's being.

"Auburn," she says, plastering a fake smile across her face, "I've raised children before, so I know how important routines and schedules can be for a child's development. If you want to visit him, that's perfectly fine. But we're going to have to work out a more consistent schedule so that he isn't negatively affected by it."

I rub my hands up and down my face, attempting to relieve some of the frustration I'm feeling. I exhale and calmly place my hands on my hips. "Negatively affected?" I say. "How can he be negatively affected by his own mother tucking him in every night?"

"He needs consistency, Auburn—"

"That's what I'm trying to *give* him, Lydia!" I say loudly. As soon as I raise my voice, I stop speaking. I've never raised my voice at her. Not once.

Trey walks back into the room and Lydia glances from him to me. "Let Trey give you a ride home," she says. "It's late."

She doesn't say good-bye, or even ask if the conversation is over. She walks out of the room like she just brought it to an end, whether I was finished or not.

"Ugh!" I groan, completely unsatisfied with how that conversation went. Not only did I not tell her I want my son to live with me, I couldn't even work out something in my favor. She always brings up "consistency" and "routines" like I'm trying to drag him out of bed at midnight to eat pancakes every night. All I want is to see my son more than she's allowing me. I don't understand how she can't see how much it's hurting me. She should be thankful I want to fill my role like I do. I'm sure there are people in her situation who would love for their grandchildren's parents to give a shit.

I'm torn away from my train of thought by Trey's chuckle. I face him, and there's a smile on his face.

I've never wanted to punch a smile so bad in my life, but if there were a more inappropriate time to laugh than right now, I'd hate to see it.

He can see I'm not amused by his laughter, but he doesn't hide it. He shakes his head and reaches into the entryway closet for his things. "You just yelled at my mother," he says. "Wow."

I glare at him while he attaches his holster to his police uniform. "I'm glad my situation amuses you," I say flatly. I walk past him and out the front door. When I reach his car, I climb inside and slam the door. As soon as I'm alone in the darkness, I break into tears.

I allow myself to cry as hard as I can until I see Trey making his way out of the house several minutes later. I immediately stop the tears and wipe my eyes. When he's in the car with the door shut, I stare out the window and hope it's obvious that I'm not in the mood for conversation.

I think he understands that he pissed me off, because he doesn't speak for the entire drive back to my house. And even though there isn't any traffic on the way home, twenty minutes is a long drive when it's this quiet.

When he pulls up to my apartment, he gets out of the car and follows me inside the building. I'm still pissed when I reach my door, but my attempt to escape inside my apartment without telling him good-bye is thwarted when he grabs my arm and forces me to turn around.

"I'm sorry," he says. "I wasn't laughing at your situation, Auburn." I shake my head and can feel the tension settling in my jaw. "I just . . . I don't know. No one ever yells at my mother and I thought it was funny." He takes a step closer to me and lifts a hand to the door frame. "In fact," he says, "I actually thought it was kind of sexy. I've never seen you angry before."

My eyes meet his in a flash. "Are you serious right now, Trey?" I swear to God, if there was any chance of my ever finding him attractive, he just completely ruined it with that comment.

He closes his eyes and takes a step back. He holds up his hands in surrender. "I didn't mean anything by it," he says. "It was a compliment. But you obviously aren't in the mood for compliments, so maybe we can try this again another time."

I welcome his departure with a quick wave as I turn around and close the door behind me. A few seconds pass before I hear Trey call my name through the door. "Auburn," he says quietly. "Open the door."

I roll my eyes but turn around and open the door. He's standing in the doorway with his arms folded across his chest. His expression has changed to one of regret. He rests his head against the frame of the door, and it reminds me of the night Owen stood in this exact same position. I liked it a lot more when Owen was standing here.

"I'll talk to my mother," Trey says. Those words make me pause and actually give him my full attention. "You're right, Auburn. You should be spending more time with AJ, and she's just making it hard on you."

"You'll talk to her? Really?"

He takes a step closer until he's standing in the doorway. "I didn't mean to upset you earlier," he says. "I was trying to make you feel better, but I guess I went about it the wrong way. Don't be mad, okay? I don't know if I can take you being mad at me."

I swallow his apology and shake my head. "I'm not mad at you, Trey. I just . . ." I inhale and exhale slowly. "Your mother just frustrates the living piss out of me sometimes."

He smiles agreeably. "I know what you mean," he says. He lifts himself away from the door frame and glances down the hallway. "I need to get to work. We'll talk later, okay?"

I nod and give him a genuine smile. The fact that he's willing to talk to Lydia for me is worth a smile or two. He backs up several steps before turning around and walking away. I close my apartment door after he disappears around the corner of the hallway. When I turn around, my heart jumps into my throat when I see Emory standing a few feet in front of me.

Holding a cat.

A very familiar-looking cat.

I point at Owen-Cat. "What . . ." I drop my arm, completely confused. "How?"

She looks down at the cat and shrugs. "Owen stopped by about an hour ago," she says. "He left this and a note."

I shake my head. "He left his cat?"

She turns around and walks toward the living room. "And a note. He said you'd know where to find it."

I walk to my room and immediately drop to my knees and climb inside the tent. There's a folded piece of paper on one of the pillows. I pick it up and lie down, and then I open it.

Auburn,

I know it's a lot to ask of you to keep Owen, but I didn't have anyone else. My father is allergic to cats, which may be why I got Owen in the first place. Harrison won't be back in town until Tuesday, but if you need to, you can drop her off there.

I know I've said it enough already, but I really am sorry. You deserve someone who can give you what you need, and right now that someone isn't me. If I had known you would show up at my door one day, I'd have done everything differently.

Everything.

Please don't allow anyone to make you feel less than what you are.

Take care.

PS: I know that one of these days, you'll have to let someone in to use your restroom. Just do me a favor and remove those cute little seashell soaps. The thought of someone else loving those soaps as much as I do is too much.

PPS: You only have to feed Owen once a day. She's pretty easy to keep alive. Thanks in advance for taking care of her, no matter how long or short you decide to do it for. I know she'll be in good hands, because I've seen you as a mother, and you're pretty damn good at it.

—Owen

I'm shocked at the tears that are falling down my cheeks. I close the letter and immediately walk out of my room. When I reach Emory in the living room, I scoop Owen-Cat up into my arms and I take her to my bedroom. I close the door behind me and I crawl onto the bed with her. She goes with the flow and lies down beside me, like this is exactly where she's supposed to be.

I'll gladly take care of her for however long Owen needs me to. Because having her connects me to him. And for whatever reason, I feel like I need that link to Owen, because it makes my chest hurt a little less when I think about him.

CHAPTER FOURTEEN

Owen

I look at my father, standing guiltily in the doorway to the holding room. I'm seated at a table very similar to the one I was seated at a few weeks ago when I was arrested. Only now I'm paying the price for that arrest.

I look down at my wrists and push the cuffs down half an inch to relieve some of the pressure. "What good is your law degree if you can't even get me out of this?"

I know that was a low blow, but I'm pissed. Frustrated. In a state of shock over the fact that I was just sentenced to ninety days in jail, despite this being my first offense. I know it had everything to do with the fact that Judge Corley presided over the case. Seems to be my luck, lately. My fate *would* be in the hand of one of my father's surface friends.

My father closes the door to the holding room, locking us both in. It's our last visit before I'm taken to my cell, and honestly, I'd rather he not even be here right now.

He takes three slow steps into the room and then comes to a stop as he hovers over me. "Why the hell did you refuse rehab?" he growls.

I close my eyes, disappointed in his focus. "I don't need rehab."

"All you had to do was a short stint in rehab, and this whole thing would have been removed from your record."

He's angry. He's yelling. His plan was for me to accept rehab, but I know for a fact that this was his way of making himself feel better about the fact that I've been arrested. If I were to spend my time in rehab rather than jail, it would be easier for him to swallow. Maybe I chose jail time just to spite him.

"I can talk with Judge Corley. I'll tell him you made the wrong decision and see if he'll reconsider it."

I shake my head. "Just go, Dad."

His expression is unwavering. He doesn't retreat from the room.

"Go!" I say, louder this time. "Leave! I don't want you to visit. I don't want you to call me. I don't want to speak to you while I'm in there, because I hope to God you're going to take your own advice."

He still doesn't move, so I take a step toward him, then around him. I beat on the door. "Let me out!" I say to the bailiff.

My father puts his hand on my shoulder, and I shrug it off. "Don't, Dad. Just . . . I can't right now."

The door opens, and I'm escorted down a hallway, away from my father. Once my cuffs are removed and the bars clank closed behind me, I take a seat on the cot. I rest my head in my hands and think back to the weekend I ended up here. The weekend I should have done everything differently.

If I had just found it in me to see that what I'm doing isn't protecting anyone. It's not helping anyone.

I'm enabling, and I've been doing it for years. *And now I'm paying the ultimate price, because it's costing me you, Auburn.*

THREE WEEKS EARLIER

I glance down at my phone and cringe when I see my father's number. If he's calling me this late, it can only mean one thing.

"I should go," I say as I silence the phone and slide it back into my pocket. I push the cup toward her and I see her expression fall with her nod, but she quickly turns around to hide it.

"Well, thanks for the job," she says. "And for walking me home."

I lean forward on the bar and drop my head into the palms of my hands. I rub them over my face, when really I want to punch myself. Things were going so well between us just now and the second I get a phone call from my father, I shut down and make it look like the exact opposite of what it is.

She thinks I'm leaving because whoever just called me was a girl. That's the furthest thing from the truth, and even though I hate that I just disappointed her, I love that she's jealous right now. People don't get jealous unless there are underlying feelings at play.

She pretends to busy herself by washing my coffee cup and she fails to notice I'm walking up behind her.

"It wasn't a girl," I say to her. The close proximity of my voice startles her and she spins around, looking up at me wide-eyed. She fails to respond, so I take a step closer and say it again to make sure she understands and that she believes me. "I don't want you to think I'm leaving because another girl just called me."

I can see the relief in her eyes and a small smile attempt to form on her mouth, but she faces the sink again in hopes that I don't notice. "It's not my business who calls you, Owen."

I grin, even though she can't see me. Of course it isn't her business, but she wants it to be her business as much as I do. I close the gap between us by placing both of my palms on the counter on either side of her. I rest my chin on her shoulder, and I want to bury myself against her neck and inhale her, but I grip the counter and remain where I am. It becomes even harder to control my impulses when I feel her lean into me.

There are so many things I want right now. I want to wrap my arms around her. I want to kiss her. I want to pick her up and carry her to my bed. I want her to spend the night with me. I want to confess to her all the things I've been keeping bottled up since she showed up on my doorstep.

I want them all so badly that I'm willing to do the last thing I want to do, which is slow down so that I don't scare her off.

"I want to see you again."

When she says "Okay," it takes everything I have not to pick her up and spin her around. I somehow remain calm and collected, even as she walks me to her door and we tell each other good-bye.

And when she finally closes the door for the last time, I want to knock on it again. I want to make her open it for a fourth time so that I can press my lips to hers and get a feel for what our future is hopefully about to consist of.

Before I can decide whether to leave and wait until tomorrow or go ahead and make her open the door so I can kiss her tonight, my phone makes the decision for me. I pull it out of my pocket after it begins ringing and answer my father's phone call.

"Are you okay?" I ask him.

"Owen . . . shit . . . this . . ."

I can tell by his voice that he's been drinking. He mutters something unintelligible and then . . . nothing.

"Dad?"

Silence. When I make it outside of the apartment building, I press my hand against my ear to try to hear him better.

"Dad!" I yell.

I hear rustling and then more muttering. "I know I shouldn't have done it . . . I'm sorry, Owen, I just couldn't . . ."

I close my eyes and try to remain calm, but he isn't making any sense.

"Tell me where you are. I'm on my way."

He mutters a street name that isn't far from his house. I tell him to stay put, and I run the entire way back to my apartment in order to get my car.

I have no idea what I'll find once I reach him. I just hope he hasn't done something stupid that could get him arrested. He's been lucky up to this point, but no one can have as much luck as he's had and continue to get away with it.

When I pull onto the street, I don't see anything. There are a few scattered houses, but it's mostly a barren area close to the subdivision he lives in. When I near the end of the road, I finally see his car. It looks like he's run the car off the road.

I pull over onto the side of the road and get out to check on him. I walk to the front of the car to assess any damage he might have done, but there isn't any. His taillights are on, and it looks like he just couldn't figure out how to get back on the road.

He's passed out in the front seat and the doors are locked.

"Dad!" I beat on the window until he finally wakes up. He fumbles with the buttons on the door and rolls the window halfway down in an attempt to unlock the car.

"Wrong button," I tell him. I reach through the window and unlock the door, pulling it open.

"Scoot over," I say to him. He leans his head against the headrest and looks at me with a face full of disappointment.

"I'm okay," he mumbles. "I just needed to take a nap."

I shove my shoulder into him to scoot him out of the driver's seat. He groans and climbs across the seat, slumping against the passenger door. Sadly, this is becoming routine. In the past year alone, this is the third time I've had to come to his rescue. It used to not be so bad when it was just the pain pills, but now that he's mixing them with alcohol, it's harder for him to hide it from everyone else.

I try to start the car, but it's still in drive. I put it in park and crank it with ease. I put the car in reverse and it pulls onto the road without a problem.

"How'd you get it to do that?" he says. "It wouldn't work when I tried."

"It was in drive, Dad. You can't start cars when they're in drive."

When I pass by my car still pulled over in the ditch, I hold my key fob up and lock it. I'll have to get Harrison to pick me up and follow me back out to the car after I drop my father off at home.

We've driven about a mile when the crying starts. He's huddled up against the passenger window and his whole body begins to shake from his tears. It used to bother me, but I've become immune to it. And I probably hate that I've become immune to his depression more than I even hate his depression.

"I'm so sorry, Owen," he chokes out. "I tried. I tried, I tried, I tried." He's crying so hard that his words are becoming harder to understand, but he keeps going. "Just two more months, that's all I need. I'll get help after that, I promise."

He continues to cry tears of shame, and this is the hardest part for me. I can take the mood swings, the withdrawls, the late-night phone calls. I've been dealing with them for years.

It's watching his tears that eats at me. It's seeing him still heartbroken over that night that makes me accept his excuses. It's hearing the depression in his voice that brings back the horror of that night, and as much as I want to hate him for being so weak, I also praise him for still being alive. I'm not sure I would have even had the will to live if I were him.

His crying comes to an instant halt the second the lights fill the inside of the car. I've been pulled over plenty of times to know that these things are usually routine when a car is out this late at night. But the condition my father is in right now makes me nervous.

"Dad, let me handle this," I say as I pull over to the side of the road. "He'll know you're drunk if you open your mouth to speak."

He nods and watches the cop nervously as he approaches the car. "Where's your insurance?" I ask my father, just as the cop reaches the window. My father fumbles with the glove box as I roll the window down.

The cop immediately looks familiar to me, but I don't place him right away. It isn't until he bends down and looks me straight in the eye that I remember him. Trey, I think is his name. I can't believe I even remember that.

Great. I would get pulled over by the one and only guy I've ever punched.

He doesn't appear to remember me, so that's a good thing. "License and insurance," he says stiffly.

I pull my license from my wallet and my father hands me his insurance card. When I hand both of them to Trey, he eyes my ID first. He smirks almost immediately. "Owen Gentry?" He taps my driver's license against my car and laughs. "Wow. Never thought I'd hear that name again."

I run my thumbs around the steering wheel and shake my head. He definitely remembers, all right. Not good.

Trey lifts his flashlight and shines it inside the car, running it over the backseat and then landing it on my father. My father shields his eyes with his elbow.

"That you, Callahan?"

My father nods but doesn't respond.

Trey laughs again. "Well this is just a real treat."

I assume Trey knows my father because he's a defense attorney, and I'm not so sure that's a good thing for us right now. It's not uncommon for the lawyers who defend criminals to be loathed by the officers who *arrest* those criminals.

Trey lowers the flashlight and takes a step back. "Step out of the car, sir." His words are directed at me, so I do what he says. I open the door and step out. Almost immediately, he grabs me by the arm and pulls until I willingly turn and lay my arms on the hood. He begins frisking me. "You got anything in your possession I should be aware of?"

What the hell? I shake my head. "No. I'm just driving my father home."

"Have you had anything to drink tonight?"

I think back on the drinks I had at the bar earlier, but that was a couple of hours ago. I'm not even sure if I should bring that up. The hesitation in my answer doesn't please him. He turns me around and shines the light directly into my eyes. "How much have you had to drink?"

I shake my head and try to look away from the blinding light. "Just a couple. It was earlier."

He steps back and tells my father to get out of the car. Luckily, my father gets the door open. At least he's sober enough to do that.

"Come around the car," Trey says to my father. He watches as my father stumbles from the passenger side, all the way to where I'm standing, holding the edge of the car for support during his journey. He's obviously drunk and I'm honestly not sure if it's illegal for a passenger to be intoxicated. As far as Trey knows, my father wasn't driving.

"Do I have permission to search the vehicle?"

I look at my father for guidance, but he's leaning against the car with his eyes closed. He looks ready to fall asleep. I debate whether or not to refuse the search, but figure that would just give Trey more reason to become suspicious. Besides, my father knows the repercussions of traveling with anything that could get him into trouble, so even though he was dumb enough to drive after drinking tonight, I seriously doubt he would actually have anything in his possession that could jeopardize his career. I casually shrug and then say, "Go ahead." I just want Trey to get revenge out of his system so he can be done with it and leave.

Trey orders us to stand near the rear of the vehicle while he leans across the front seat. My father is alert now, watching him closely. He's wringing his hands together and his eyes are wide with fear. The look on his face is enough for me to know that Trey is more than likely going to find something inside this car.

"Dad," I whisper, disappointed. His eyes meet mine and they're full of apologies.

I can't count the number of times my father has promised me he was going to get help. I think he waited a little too long.

My father closes his eyes when Trey begins making his way to the rear of the vehicle. He sets one, two, three bottles of pills on the car. He proceeds to open each one to inspect the contents.

"Looks like Oxy," Trey says, rolling a pill between his thumb and forefinger. He looks at me and then at my father. "Either of you have a prescription for these?"

I look at my father, hoping beyond all hope that he does, in fact, have a prescription. I know it's wishful thinking, though.

Trey smiles. *The bastard smiles like he just hit gold.* He leans his elbows on the car and begins putting the pills back into their bottles, one by one. "You know," he says, looking at neither of us, but speaking to us both, "Oxy is considered a penalty group one drug when obtained illegally." He looks up at me. "Now, I know you aren't a lawyer like your father here, so let me explain it to you in laymen's terms." He stands up straight and puts the caps back on the bottles. "In the state of Texas, being arrested for a penalty group one is an automatic state-jail felony."

I close my eyes and exhale. This is the last thing my father needs. If he loses his career on top of everything else he's lost, there's no way he would survive.

"I suggest, before either of you speak again, that you take into consideration what would happen if a defense attorney were to be charged with a felony. I'm almost certain that would result in the loss of his license to practice law."

Trey walks around the vehicle and steps between my father and me. He eyes my father up and down. "Think about that for a second. A lawyer, whose entire career consists of defending criminals, loses his career and *becomes* the criminal. Irony at its best." Trey then turns and faces me full on. "Did you work tonight, Gentry?"

I tilt my head, confused by his line of questioning.

"You own that studio, right? Wasn't tonight one of the nights you were open?"

I hate that he knows about my studio. I hate it even more that he's asking about it.

I nod. "Yeah. First Thursday of every month."

He takes a step closer. "I thought so," he says. He rolls the three bottles of pills between his hands. "I saw you leaving the studio with someone earlier tonight. A girl?"

Was he following me? Why would he be following me? And why would he be asking about Auburn?

My throat runs dry.

I can't believe I haven't put two and two together until this moment. *Of course* Auburn would have a connection to Trey. His family is probably the reason she's back in Texas.

"Yeah," I say, finding a way to downplay it. "She worked for me tonight, so I walked her home."

His eyes narrow at my response and he nods. "Yeah," he says dryly. "I don't particularly like her working for someone like you."

I know he's a cop, but right now all I see is an asshole. The muscles in my arms clench and his eyes immediately fall to the fists at my sides. "What do you mean someone like me?"

His eyes meet mine again with a laugh. "Well, you and I don't really have the best history, do we? You attacked me the first time we met. As soon as I pulled you over tonight, you admitted to driving under the influence. And now . . ." He looks down at the pills in his hands. "Now I find these in the vehicle you're driving."

My father steps forward. "Those are—"

"Stop!" I yell at my father, cutting him off. I know he's about to claim them, but he isn't sober enough to realize what that could do to his career.

Trey laughs again, and I'm honestly sick of hearing that noise. "Anyway," he says, "if she needs an escort home, she has me for that."

He slams the pills down on the hood. "So, which one of you belongs to these?"

My father looks at me. I can see the struggle in his eyes because he doesn't know what to say. I don't give him the chance.

"They're mine."

I close my eyes and I think about Auburn, because this moment and Trey's indirect threat to stay away from her is about to take away whatever chance we might have had.

Fuck me.

My cheek meets the cold metal of the hood.

"You have the right to remain silent . . ."

My hands are pulled behind me, and the cuffs are snapped into place.

Part Two

CHAPTER FIFTEEN

Auburn

It's been twenty-eight days since Owen was sentenced to ninety days in jail. A lot can happen in twenty-eight days.

I tuck the blanket tighter around his body and lean in to kiss AJ on the forehead. "I'll see you after school tomorrow, okay?"

AJ smiles at me, and like every time he does, my heart melts. He looks just like Adam. Other than having a red tint to his mostly brown hair, everything about him is Adam, right down to his mannerisms. "Are you coming over to eat with us?"

I nod and give him another hug. Saying good-bye to him, knowing he's not sleeping in a bed in my home, is the hardest part for me. I should be tucking him into bed in a home we share together.

However, whatever Trey said to Lydia worked, because I've been coming over more nights during the week and she hasn't said a single negative thing to me.

"Ready?" Trey says from behind me.

"Good night, AJ. I'll love you forever."

He smiles. "Good night, Mom. I'll love you forever."

I flip the light switch off as I exit the room and pull the door shut. Trey reaches for my hand and slides his fingers through mine as we walk toward the living room. I look down at our hands, linked together, and feel nothing but guilt. I've tried for the past few weeks to reciprocate the feelings he has for me, but so far it hasn't worked out like I'd hoped.

We make our way through the living room, and Lydia is seated on the sofa. Her eyes immediately fall to our hands. She smiles briefly, and I'm not sure what that smile means. Trey said she didn't really have a reaction when he told her he was taking me on our first official date last week, but I know she has to have an opinion about it. I'd almost think she would be happy, because having me linked to her through Trey in a positive way means there's less of a threat of me taking my son and moving back to Portland.

"Do you work tonight?" she asks Trey.

He nods as he releases my hand and reaches for the key that unlocks the entryway closet. "I'm on night shift for the next three weeks," he says. He inserts the key into the door and retrieves his gun from the case.

My attention moves from Trey to a picture of Adam hanging on the living room wall. He can't be more than fourteen in the picture. Every time I come here I do my best to avoid looking at it, but I'm shocked at how much AJ looks like his father. The older AJ gets, the more of Adam's features I see in him. But knowing that Adam never made it beyond the age of sixteen makes me wonder what he would have looked like as an adult. If he were alive now, would he look like Trey? Will AJ look like Trey?

"Auburn."

Trey's voice is so close, it makes me jump. When I look at him, he cuts his eyes briefly to the picture of Adam and then turns toward the front door. He looks disappointed that I was standing here staring at the picture, and it makes me feel somewhat guilty. It has to be hard for him, knowing I felt so much for his brother. I know it would be even harder for him if he knew how much I *still* felt for his brother.

"Good night, Lydia," I say as I make my way toward the front door.

She smiles, but there's something about her smile that's always been a bit off to me. Almost as if there's blame behind it. That could be my own conscience, but I've never gotten over the fact that I feel she resents me for the time I spent with Adam before he passed away. I don't think she liked how Adam felt about me, and I certainly know she didn't like the amount of time he wanted to spend with me.

And that worries me to an extent, because as much as she seems in support of Trey and me being in a relationship, I worry about what will happen if things don't work out between us. Which is exactly why I haven't made things official, because once I do, I need to be prepared for what could happen with AJ if Trey and I don't last as a couple.

Trey walks me to my front door, like he's done almost every night for the past week. I know he's still waiting for me to invite him in, but I'm just not there yet. I'm not sure when I will be, but I did finally allow him to kiss me last night, which wasn't exactly what I had in mind. He just sort of did it. I had unlocked my door and turned to face him and his lips were on mine before I could agree or object. And I wish I could say I enjoyed it, but I mostly felt uncomfortable, for a number of reasons.

I still feel uneasy about the fact that I used to be in love with his brother. I might still be in love with his brother, and that may never go away. I'm also uneasy about the fact that his brother is the only person I've ever had sex with. I'm also disturbed that AJ has known Trey as his uncle his whole life, and I don't want it to confuse him if it gets serious between us.

There's also the whole attraction thing. Trey is definitely a good-looking guy. He's confident and has a great career. But there's something about him that goes deeper than his muscular build or his perfectly groomed, dark hair. Something that is completely opposite from Adam. Something that actually turns me off.

There was a goodness about Adam. A calmness. When I was with him, I felt safe.

I got the same sense from Owen, which I think is why I was drawn to him. He had a lot of the same qualities that Adam had.

So far, I don't get that from Trey. I try not to think about the fact that I could be making a commitment to someone I'm afraid may not be a good person. But I've associated Trey with Lydia for as long as I've known him, so it may not be a question of Trey's character. I may have judged him unfairly, simply because I feel that his mother isn't a good person.

Because of that, I'm trying to open myself up to the idea of him. Which is why I allowed him to kiss me last night, because sometimes intimacy can give people a certain connection they wouldn't otherwise have.

I unlock my door and inhale a slow breath before turning around. I try to get in the mind-set that I want him to kiss me, that his kiss could feel good and exciting, but I know for a fact I won't feel even a fraction of what I felt when Owen kissed me.

That was a kiss.

I close my eyes and try to wipe the thoughts of Owen out of my head, but it's hard. When you connect with someone that fast and feel that much from their kiss, it's not so easy to just forget them when they do something to hurt you. And even though Owen turned out to have issues far beyond what I want to get immersed in, I still can't stop thinking about him. Maybe it's because the person I got to know and the person he turned out to be don't seem like they could be the same people. And as much as I try to forget about him, I can't help but worry. I worry about how he's doing. I worry about how long he'll be in jail. I worry about his studio. I worry about Owen-Cat, because I still have her and I know that as soon as Owen is released, I'll have to see him again in order to give him his cat back.

I worry about how I'm going to be able to hide that from Trey, because right now Trey thinks Owen-Cat belongs to Emory.

He also thinks the cat's name is Sparkles.

"Do you work tomorrow?" Trey asks.

I turn around and look up at him. He's a lot taller than me, and it sometimes intimidates me. I nod. "Nine to four."

He lifts his hand to my neck and leans in for a kiss. I close my eyes and do my best to enjoy his mouth when it comes to rest against mine. I imagine I'm kissing Owen for a second, and I hate that I do that.

This kiss is a short one. He's already late for work, so I'm spared the awkwardness of not inviting him inside.

Trey smiles down at me. "That's twice you've let me kiss you."

I smile.

"Call me when you get off work tomorrow," he says. "We'll make it three."

I nod again, and he turns to leave. I open my apartment door, but he calls my name before I close it behind me. He walks back to the door and looks at me with a serious expression. "Make sure your doors are locked tonight. I heard Gentry was released early, and I wouldn't put it past him to try and get revenge on me by coming here."

The air in my lungs depletes, and I have to hide my struggle for breath. I don't want him to see how his words have affected me, so I nod quickly. "Why would he want revenge on you?"

"Because, Auburn. I have what he can't have."

That makes me uneasy, because I don't like that Trey thinks he "has me." And that's another difference between Trey and Owen. I get the feeling Owen would never say he "has me."

"I'll keep it locked. Promise."

Trey nods and heads down the hall. I close the door behind me and lock it.

I stare at the lock.

I unlock it.

I don't know why.

Owen-Cat purrs at my feet, so I bend down and pick her up, then walk into my bedroom. The first thing I do, which is the first thing I did last night after kissing Trey, is brush my teeth. I know it's an absurd thought, but kissing Trey makes me feel like I'm cheating on Owen.

When I finish brushing my teeth, I walk back into my bedroom and see Owen-Cat make her way inside the tent. I didn't have the heart to take it down, mostly because I know as soon as AJ is allowed to stay the night here, he'll love it. I crawl inside the tent and lie on my back. I pull Owen-Cat onto my stomach and begin petting her.

My emotions are all over the place right now. I feel a rush of adrenaline, knowing Owen is no longer in jail and may very well be coming for his cat sometime this week. But I'm also filled with a nervous energy, because I don't know what will happen when I see him again. And I hate that the thought of possibly seeing him again fills me with more anticipation than Trey's kiss does.

Owen-Cat jumps off my chest when my phone receives a text message. I pull it out of my pocket and unlock the screen.

My heart tries to escape from my chest when I read the text from Owen.

Meat Dress.

I'm immediately off my feet and into the living room and swinging the front door open. As soon as our eyes meet, my heart feels like a fist is squeezing the life right out of it.

God, I missed him.

He takes a very hesitant step forward. He doesn't want to make me uncomfortable by being here, but I can see in his expression that he's feeling that same tight grip around his heart that I'm feeling.

I take a step back into my apartment, and I open the door further, silently inviting him inside. A small twitch of a smile plays on the corner of his lips, and he walks slowly toward my apartment door. Once he makes his way over the threshold, I step aside until he's all the way inside. He places his hand on the door and closes it, then turns around and locks it. When he faces me again, his expression is pained, like he doesn't know whether to turn and leave or take me in his arms.

I kind of want him to do both.

CHAPTER SIXTEEN

Owen

I wish she knew how much I thought about her. How every night, I questioned whether the tightness in my chest could actually be the result of missing her, or if it was simply the fact that I wasn't allowed to see her. Sometimes people want what they can't have and confuse that with feelings for another person.

Either way, the feeling is there. The pressure, the ache, the slow build in my stomach that's encouraging me to close the distance between us and take her mouth with mine. I would have done that by now if I hadn't seen Trey leaving her apartment on my way over. Luckily, he's an unobservant prick, so he didn't even notice me.

I definitely saw him, though. And it makes me wonder what he was doing here so late at night. Not that I have a right to know, but I certainly can't squash my curiosity.

He came to see me in jail last week. I was told I had a visitor, and I expected it to be my father. There was a very small part of me that was hoping it was Auburn. I never expected her to come see me while I was in jail, but I think the hope that it might happen kept me more positive than I would have been otherwise.

When I walked into the visitation room and saw Trey standing there, at first I didn't think he was there to see me. But once his glare fell on me, it became clear. I walked to my chair and took a seat, and he did the same.

He stared at me for several minutes without saying a word. I stared back. I don't know if he thought his mere presence alone was enough intimidation, but he never did speak. Just sat in his chair for ten solid minutes, staring at me.

I never wavered. I did want to laugh a few times, but was able to hold it together. He finally stood up, but I remained seated. He walked around the table, poised to head toward the exit behind me, but instead he paused and looked down on me.

"Stay away from my girl, Owen."

This is when he lost my eye contact. Not because he pissed me off or made me nervous, but because his words were an excruciating punch in the gut. The fact that he referred to Auburn as his girl is the last thing I wanted to hear, and that has nothing to do with my jealousy and everything to do with my instincts regarding Trey.

And while I have to admit I hate that I've screwed my life

up to the point that it would negatively affect us if we were together, I hate it even more that he gets to have her. Because she deserves better. *So* much better.

She deserves me.

If only she knew that.

She's staring up at me like she wants to throw her arms around me. Like she wants to kiss me. And believe me, if she did either of those things right now I would more than welcome it.

She's standing with her hands at her sides, like she doesn't know what to do with them. She lifts her right hand and brings it across her chest, squeezing the bicep of her left arm. Her gaze shifts to her feet.

"You're okay." Her voice comes out extremely unsure of itself. I'm not sure if she's asking me a question or making a simple observation. I nod anyway. She blows out a soft breath, and her relief is something I wasn't anticipating. I wasn't expecting her to be worried about me. I was hoping she was, but hoping for it and seeing it are two different things.

I'm not sure what's happening in this second, but we both simultaneously take a quick step forward. Neither of us stops until her arms are wrapped around my neck and my arms are wrapped around her back, and we're both gripping one another in a desperate hug.

I tilt my face toward her neck and inhale the scent of her. If her smell had a color, it would be pink. Sweet and innocent with a touch of roses.

After a long but still-too-short embrace, she takes a step back and grabs my hand. She pulls me toward her bedroom and I follow her. When she opens the door, my eyes fall to the blue tent still set up next to her bed. She hasn't taken it down and that makes me smile. She closes her bedroom door behind us and grabs the pillows off her bed, smiling gently as she tosses them into the tent and crawls inside.

She lies down in the tent, and I crawl in beside her and lie next to her. We face each other, and for several moments, all we do is stare. I eventually lift my hand and brush a lock of hair from her forehead, but I notice how she pulls away slightly. I drop my hand.

It's like she doesn't want to start the conversation because she knows the first thing that needs to be put out there is her relationship with Trey. I don't want to put her in an awkward position, but I also need to know the truth. I clear my throat and somehow release the words that don't want answers.

"Are you with him now?"

They're the first words I've spoken to her since we said good-bye a month ago. I hate that these have to be the words I chose. I should have said, "I missed you," or "You look beautiful." I should have said words she would appreciate, but instead, I said words that are hard for her to hear. I know they're hard for her to hear because her eyes cast downward and she can no longer look at me.

"It's complicated," she says.

If she only knew.

"Do you love him?"

She immediately shakes her head no. This fills me with relief, but I also hate that she's with someone for the wrong reasons.

"Why are you with him?"

She makes eye contact with me now and her expression has hardened. "The same reason I can't be with you." She pauses. "AJ."

This is probably the one thing I didn't want to hear, because it's the one thing I know I have no control over.

"He gets you closer to AJ, and I do the exact opposite."

She nods, but barely.

"Do you feel anything for him? At all?"

She closes her eyes as if she's ashamed. "Like I said . . . it's complicated."

I reach over and grab her hand. I pull it to my mouth and kiss the top of it. "Auburn, look at me."

She glances up at me again, and more than anything I want to lean forward and kiss her. That's the last thing she needs, though. It would only add more complication in her life.

"I'm sorry," she whispers.

I immediately shake my head. I don't need to hear how she's sorry we can't be together. The reasons we can't be together are all my fault. Not hers.

"I get it. I would never want to be a part of anything that could keep you away from your son. But you have to understand that Trey is not the answer. He's not a good person, and you don't want AJ to grow up with him as an example."

She rolls onto her back and stares upward. I don't like the distance she put between us just now, but I also know that my words aren't anything new to her. I know she knows what kind of person he is. "He loves AJ. He's good to him."

"For how long?" I ask her. "How long does he have to put on this act to win you over? Because it won't last, Auburn."

She brings her hands up to her face and her shoulders begin to shake. I immediately wrap my arm around her and pull her to my chest. I didn't want to show up here and cause her to cry.

"I'm sorry," I whisper. "I'm not telling you anything you

don't already know. I'm sure you've weighed your options, and this is the only one that works for you and I get that. I just hate it for you."

I brush my hand over her hair and kiss the top of her head. She allows me to hold her for several minutes, and I savor each and every one of those minutes because we both know the next thing she's going to say to me is good-bye.

I don't want her to have to say it, so I kiss her once more on top of her head. I kiss her cheek, and then I graze her jaw with my fingers, tilting her face to mine. I bend forward and gently press my lips to hers. I don't give her time to overthink it. I close my eyes, release her, and exit the tent.

She's made her choice, and even though it's not the choice either of us wants, it's the only choice that works for her right now. And I have to respect that.

I drop my cat off at my studio and decide there's no better time than midnight to go see my father. He honored my request and didn't visit or call while I was away. I'm surprised he didn't visit, but a small part of me is hopeful that he didn't because seeing his son being sent to jail for his mistakes might have been his rock bottom.

I've learned over the years not to allow myself to grow too hopeful, but I'd be lying if I said every part of me isn't praying he's been in rehab while I was away.

I expected he would be either asleep or gone, so I brought my house key with me. All the lights are off.

When I enter the house, I immediately see the faint glow of the TV. I turn toward the living room and see my father lying facedown on the couch. Knowing he's not in rehab sends a wave of disappointment through me, but I can't deny the small rush of hope that he's actually lying on the couch because he's not breathing.

And that is not something a son should feel for his father.

I sit down on the coffee table, two feet from him.

"Dad."

He doesn't immediately wake up. I reach over to my side and pick up his bottle of pills. The fact that I just spent a month in jail for him should have been more than enough to make him never want to touch another one of these. Seeing that it wasn't makes me want to walk out of this house and never look back.

My father is a good person. I know that. If he weren't a good person, it would be easier to walk away. I would have done it a long time ago. But I know he's not in control of himself. He hasn't been for years.

After the accident, he was in a lot of pain, physically and emotionally. It doesn't help that for the entire month he was in a coma, they had him doped up on meds.

When he finally woke up and began to recover, the pills were the only things to relieve his pain. When he began needing more than he was prescribed, the doctors refused his requests.

For weeks, I had to watch him suffer. He wasn't working, he wouldn't get out of bed, he was in a constant state of agony and depression. At the time, I didn't think my father was capable of allowing something as small as a pill to completely devour him, but I was naive. The only thing I saw when I looked at him was a man who was in pain and needed my help. I had been behind the wheel of the car that took the life of his son and his wife, and I would have done anything to make it better. To rectify what happened. I carried a lot of guilt for a long time over that accident, even though I know my father didn't blame me. That's one thing he did right: repeatedly tell me that it wasn't my fault.

Still though, it's hard not to feel guilt when you're a sixteen-year-old kid. I just wanted to make it better for him. It began with my being prescribed my own pain medication. It was fairly easy to fake back pain after a wreck of our magnitude, so that's exactly what I did. After several months of his continuously being in more and more pain, it got to the point where even my additional pills weren't enough for him.

That's also when my doctor pulled me off of the pills and refused to give me another prescription. I think he knew what was going on and didn't want to contribute to my father's addiction.

I had a friend or two at school who knew how to get the pills my father needed, so it started out with my bringing him the medicine from people I knew. That went on for two years until those friends either grew out of raiding their parents' stashes or moved off to college. Since then, I've been getting them from my only other source, which is Harrison.

Harrison isn't a dealer, but being around alcoholics for the majority of every day makes it fairly easy for him to know who to contact when someone needs something. He also knows the pills aren't for me, which is the only reason he's been willing to give them to me.

Now that he knows I went to jail over the very pills he's been supplying my father, he refuses to get any more for him. Harrison is done, which I was hoping would be the end of it for my father, since it meant the end of his supply.

But here he is with more pills. I'm not sure how he got these, but it makes me nervous that someone else out there other than myself and Harrison now knows about his addiction. He's being reckless now.

As much as I've tried to talk my father into rehab, he's afraid of what would happen to his career if he went and it were to become public knowledge. Right now, his addiction is just bad enough that it's destroying his personal life. However, it's almost to the point where it will destroy his professional life. It's just a matter of time, because alcohol is beginning to play a large role and the incidents I've been rescuing him from this past year are becoming more and more frequent. And I know that addictions don't just get better. They're either actively fought or actively fed. And right now, he's not doing a goddamn thing to fight his.

I open the lid and pour his pills into my palm and begin to count them.

"Owen?" my father mutters. He raises himself to a seated position. He's carefully eyeing the pills in my hand, more focused on what I'm going to do to them than he is on the fact that I've been released early.

I set the pills beside me on the coffee table. I clasp my hands together between my knees and smile at my father.

"I met a girl recently."

My father's expression says it all. He's completely confused.

"Her name is Auburn." I stand up and walk to the mantel on the fireplace. I look at the last family photo we ever took. It was more than a year before the accident, and I hate that this is the last memory I have of what they look like. I want a more recent memory of them in my mind, but memories fade a lot faster than photographs.

"That's good, Owen," my father mutters. "But it's after midnight. Couldn't you have told me tomorrow?"

I return to where he's seated, but I don't sit this time. Instead, I stare down at him. Down at this man who was once my father.

"Do you believe in fate, Dad?"

He blinks.

"Up until I saw her, I didn't. But she changed that the second she told me her name." I chew on the inside of my cheek for a second before continuing. I want to give him time to absorb everything I'm saying. "She has the same middle name as me."

He raises an eyebrow over his bloodshot eye. "Having the same middle name doesn't necessarily make it fate, Owen. But I'm happy you're happy."

My father rubs his head, still confused as to why I'm here. I'm sure it's not every night a son wakes his father up after midnight from a drug-induced sleep to rave about the girl he met.

"You want to know what the best part about her is?"

My father shrugs. I know he wants to tell me to fuck off, but even he knows it's in bad taste to tell someone to fuck off after they just spent a month in jail for you.

"She has a son."

This wakes him up a little more. He looks up at me. "Is it yours?"

I don't answer that. If he were listening, he would have heard me say I only recently met her. *Officially* met her, anyway.

I take a seat in front of him. I stare him directly in the eye. "No. He's not mine. But if he were, I guarantee you I'd never put him in the positions you've put me in the last few years."

My father's eyes fall to the floor. "Owen . . . ," he says. "I never asked you to—"

"You never asked me *not* to!" I yell. I'm standing again, staring down at him. I've never felt rage toward him like this. I don't like it.

I grab the bottle of pills and walk to the kitchen. I pour them down the sink and turn the water on. When all the pills are gone, I head toward his office. I hear him coming after me when he realizes what I'm doing. "Owen!" he yells.

I know he also receives a legal prescription, aside from what I'm able to get him, so I walk behind the desk and pull open the drawer. I find another half-empty bottle of pills. He knows not to try to stop me physically, so he steps aside, all the while begging me not to do this.

"Owen, you know I need those. You know what happens when I don't take them."

I don't listen to it this time. I begin pouring them down the drain, fighting him off while I do it.

"I need those!" He's yelling, over and over, trying to grab them as they disappear down the drain. He actually catches one between his fingers and shoves it in his mouth. It makes my stomach hurt. He seems so much less human when he's this desperate and weak.

When the last pill is gone, I turn and face him. He's so ashamed; he won't even look at me. He drops his elbows to the counter and cradles his head in his hands. I take a step closer to him and lean against the counter as I speak to him calmly.

"I watched her with her son. I've seen what she sacrifices for him," I say. "I've seen what lengths a parent should go to in order to ensure their child has the best possible life they can give them. And when I see her with him, I think of you and me, and how we're so fucked up, Dad. We've been fucked up since that night. And every moment since then, the only thing

I've wanted is to see you try to get better. But you haven't. It's just gotten worse, and I can't sit here and be a part of it. You're killing yourself, and I won't let the guilt of seeing you suffer excuse the things I do for you anymore."

I turn around and head for the front door, but not before walking by the mantel and taking the picture frame. I pass by him and walk out the front door.

"Owen, wait!"

I pause before descending the stairs and face him. He stands in the doorway, waiting for me to yell again. I don't. The second I see his lifeless eyes, the guilt seeps back into my soul.

"Wait," he says again.

I'm not even sure he knows what he's asking me. He just knows that he's never seen this side of me before. The resolved side.

"I *can't* wait, Dad. I've been waiting for years. I don't have anything else left in me to give."

I turn around, and I walk away from him.

CHAPTER SEVENTEEN

Auburn

"AJ, do you want chocolate chip or blueberry?"

We're grocery shopping. AJ, Trey, and I. The last time I was at this Target was with Owen, and that's been a while. Almost three months to be exact. Not that I'm counting. I'm totally counting. I do everything I can to make it stop. I've been trying to focus on this thing developing between Trey and me, but I'm constantly comparing him to Owen.

I barely knew the guy, but somehow he reached a part of me that no one has reached since I was with Adam. And despite the things Owen has done, I know he's a good person. As much as I try to get over the way my chest feels when I think about him, the feelings are still there and I'm at a loss as to how to make them go away.

"Mommy," AJ says, pulling on the hem of my shirt. "Can I?"

I snap out of my trance. "Can you what?"

"Get a toy."

I begin to shake my head, but Trey answers before I have the chance to. "Yeah, let's go look at the toys." He grabs AJ's hand and begins walking backward. "Meet us in toys when you're finished," he says, turning away.

I watch them. They're both laughing, and AJ's little hand is engulfed by Trey's and it makes me hate myself for not trying harder. Trey loves AJ and AJ obviously loves Trey and here I am being completely selfish, simply because I don't feel the same connection to Trey as I did with Owen. I spent two days with Owen. That's it. I probably would have found something I didn't like about him had I spent more time with him, so I could very well be caught up in the *idea* of Owen rather than actual feelings toward him.

Looking at it this way makes me feel somewhat better. I may not have had an instant connection to Trey but it's definitely growing. Especially with the way he treats AJ. Anyone who can make AJ happy makes me happy.

For the first time in a long time, I actually catch myself smiling over the thought of Trey rather than the thought of Owen. I grab most of the items on the list before heading toward the toy section. I take a shortcut through sporting goods and come to an immediate stop as soon as I round a corner.

If fate plays jokes, this is the absolute worst one.

Owen is staring back at me with as much disbelief registered on his face as I'm sure is on mine. In an instant, everything I've been trying to feel for Trey is reduced tenfold, and it's all directed toward Owen. I grip the cart with my hands and debate whether or not to turn in the opposite direction without speaking to him. He would understand, I'm sure.

He must be having the same internal struggle, because we both stopped walking as soon as we laid eyes on one another. Neither of us is speaking. Neither of us is retreating.

We're both just staring.

My entire body feels his stare, and I physically ache in every part of me. The main reason I've doubted what's happening between Trey and myself is standing right in front of me, reminding me of what true feelings for someone should be like.

Owen smiles, and I suddenly wish we were in the cleaning aisle, because someone is going to have to mop me up off this floor.

He glances to his left and then his right before his gaze lands back on me. "Aisle thirteen," he says with a grin. "Must be fate."

I smile, but my smile is robbed by the sound of AJ's voice. "Mommy, look!" he says as he tosses two toys into the cart. "Trey said I could have both."

Trey.

Trey, Trey, Trey, who is probably behind me right now, based on Owen's reaction. He stiffens and stands straight, gripping his cart with both hands. His eyes are on someone behind me.

An arm slips around my waist, gripping me possessively. Trey stands beside me and I can feel him eyeing Owen. He moves his hand to my lower back and then his lips meet my cheek. I close my eyes because I don't want to see the look on

Owen's face. "Come on, babe," Trey says, urging me to turn around. He's never called me babe before. I know he's only using the term in front of Owen to make our relationship seem more than what it is.

After another tug on my arm, I finally turn and walk with Trey.

We finish getting the few items that are left on my list. Trey doesn't speak to me the entire time we're shopping. He's keeping conversation going with AJ, but I can tell he's angry. My stomach is a ball of nerves because he's never given me the silent treatment like this before and I don't know what to expect.

The silent treatment continues through the checkout line, all the way to his car. He loads the groceries into the trunk while I buckle AJ into the backseat. When I have him strapped into his booster seat, I close the door and turn to find Trey leaning against the car, staring at me. He's so still, he doesn't even look like he's breathing.

"Did you speak to him?"

I shake my head. "No. I had just turned the corner right before you and AJ walked up."

Trey's arms are folded across his chest and his jaw is tense. He looks over my shoulder for several seconds before bringing his eyes back to mine.

"Did you fuck him?"

I stand up straighter, shocked at his question. Especially because we're standing right outside AJ's door. I glance inside the car at AJ but his focus is on his toys and not at all on the two of us. When I look back at Trey, I think I'm angrier than he is.

"You can't be mad at me for running into someone at a store, Trey. I don't control who shops here."

I try to move past him, but he grabs my arm and pushes me against the car with the weight of his chest against mine. He brings his hand up to the side of my head and lowers his mouth to my ear. My heart is beating erratically, because I have no idea what he's about to do.

"Auburn," he says, his voice a deep, threatening whisper. "He's been inside your apartment. He's been in your bedroom. He was in that stupid fucking tent with you. Now I need you to tell me if he's ever been inside *you*."

I'm shaking my head, doing whatever I can to calm him down, because AJ is just a foot away from us inside this car. He's gripping my wrist with his right hand, waiting for me to give him a verbal response. I'll say whatever I need to say to make sure he doesn't lose his temper right now.

"No," I whisper. "It wasn't like that. I barely knew him."

Trey pulls back a few inches and looks me in the eye. "Good," he says. "Because the way he was watching you made me think otherwise." He presses his lips against my forehead and relieves some of the pressure around my wrist. He smiles gently at me, but the smile has the opposite effect. It terrifies me that his temperament can switch as fast as it just did. He pulls me in for a hug and presses his face into my hair. He inhales and then exhales slowly.

"I'm sorry," he whispers. "Let's get out of here."

He opens the passenger door for me and shuts it after I climb inside. I exhale, relieved the moment is over but knowing full well that his reaction is a huge red flag.

As if my attention is being summoned, my eyes fall to a

car across the parking lot. Owen is standing next to it, staring in my direction. The look on his face makes it apparent that he witnessed everything that just happened. However, from across the parking lot it could have very well looked like a tender moment rather than what it actually was. Which could also explain the pained look on Owen's face.

He opens his car door just as Trey opens his. I keep my eyes focused on Owen long enough to see him lift a hand to his heart and clench it in a fist. The words he spoke to me about how much he missed his mother and brother replay in my head. *"Sometimes I miss them so much, it hurts me right here. It feels like someone is squeezing my heart with the strength of the entire goddamn world."*

Trey pulls out of the parking lot and right before Owen is out of my view, I inconspicuously lift my fist to my own chest. Our eyes remain locked until they can't anymore.

The incident at the grocery store yesterday wasn't mentioned again. Trey and AJ spent the entire evening at my house, and Trey acted as if nothing was amiss while he cooked AJ chocolate chip pancakes. In fact, if anything, Trey was in an extra-good mood. I don't know if it was a front to make up for the anger he expressed in the parking lot or if he really does enjoy spending the time he does with the two of us.

His sudden good mood could have also been because he knew he wouldn't see me for four days and he didn't want to leave on bad terms. He left for a conference in San Antonio this morning, and I could tell when he told me good-bye last night that he was uneasy about leaving me. He repeatedly asked me about my schedule and what plans I have for the weekend. Lydia is taking AJ to Pasadena for their weekend visit with her family. If I didn't have to work today, I would have gone with them.

But I didn't go, and now here I am with an entire weekend ahead of me and absolutely nothing to do; I think that makes Trey nervous. He obviously has trust issues when it comes to Owen.

Rightfully so. After all, here I am, two hours after Trey has left the city of Dallas, and I'm standing in front of Owen's studio. Every day that I walk by his studio, I inconspicuously slip a piece of paper in the slot. I've left over twenty confessions in the last few weeks. I know he's flooded with confessions, so there's no way he would know which ones were mine. But it makes me feel better to leave them. Most of the confessions are trivial things that have nothing to do with him. They usually have to do with AJ, and I never write them in such a way that Owen would be able to tell it was me. I'm sure he would never even guess that I leave them. But it feels like a form of therapy, anyway.

I look down at the confession I just wrote.

I think about you every time he kisses me.

I fold it in two and slip it through the slot, not thinking twice about it. Since that moment between us in the grocery store yesterday, I can still feel him. I want to hear his voice again. I want to see his smile again. I keep telling myself that leaving this confession is just to get closure so I can move ahead with Trey, but I know it's for purely selfish reasons.

I grab another piece of paper from my purse and quickly scribble words across it.

He's out of town this weekend.

I slide the paper through the slot without even folding it. As soon as it's out of my reach, my chest tightens, and I immediately regret what I just wrote. That wasn't a confession; it was an invitation. One that I need to rescind. Right now. I'm not that girl.

Why did I just do that?

I attempt to slip my fingers through the slot, knowing the paper has fallen to the floor by now. I grab another piece from my purse and write something to follow up the last confession.

Ignore that confession. That wasn't an invitation. I don't know why I wrote it.

I slide that piece of paper through the slot and immediately regret that one even more. Now I just look like an idiot. Again, I tear off another piece of paper and write on it, knowing I should somehow get this paper and pen out of my own reach.

You really should have a way for people to retract their confessions, Owen. Like maybe a twenty-second return policy.

I slide that one through the door as well, and shove the paper and pen into my purse.

What have I just done?

I slide the strap of my purse up my shoulder and continue toward the salon. I swear this has to be the most embarrassing thing I've ever done. Maybe he won't read them until Monday, and the weekend will be over.

It's been eight hours since my slipup this morning as I was walking past Owen's studio. I've had a lot of time to consider why I would even think it was okay to leave something like that for him to read. I know it was a weak moment, but it isn't fair of me to do that to him. If he really did develop feelings for me in the short time I knew him, the fact that I refuse to be with him is out of his control. And then I go and leave stupid notes like I've been leaving for the past few weeks, even though today was the first day I actually left confessions that pertained to the two of us.

I've made my decision though, and even if I don't feel for Trey the way he feels for me, I would never betray him. Once I make a commitment to someone, I'm the type of person who will honor that commitment.

We've had the discussion about not seeing other people, even though to me it still doesn't necessarily feel like *we're* even seeing each other. This means I need to somehow find a way to get over the thought of Owen. I need to stop worrying about him. I need to stop walking by his studio when I know there are different routes I could take. I need to put my focus and energy into my relationship with Trey, because if I want Trey to be a figure in AJ's life, I need to be committed to making that relationship work.

And Trey has been good to me. I know his bout of jealousy in the parking lot yesterday scared me, but I can't blame him. Seeing Owen and me together more than likely filled him with insecurity, so of course he's angry. And he's good to AJ. He could provide for us in a way that I can't do on my own. There isn't a reason in the world why I shouldn't want to make this work with Trey other than my own selfishness.

"I'm leaving," Donna says, peeking around the corner. "Do you mind locking up?"

Donna is the newest employee, and she's been here for about two weeks now. She's already got more clients than I do and does a way better job. Not that I'm bad at what I do, I'm just not that great. It's hard to be great at something you hate.

"No problem."

She tells me good-bye, and I finish washing the dye bowls in the sink. Several minutes after she leaves, the bell chimes, signaling someone has entered the salon. I step around the partition in order to let whoever it is know that we're finished for the day, but my words are caught in my throat when I see him.

He's standing by the front door, looking around the salon. When his gaze falls on me, the song playing through the overhead speaker comes to a timely end and a heavy silence fills the room.

If I could feel for Trey even a fraction of what Owen makes me feel just standing across the room from me, I could probably make that relationship work without issue.

But I don't feel this with anyone else. Just Owen.

He begins to walk toward me with quiet confidence. I'm not moving at all. I'm not even sure my heart is moving. I know my lungs aren't moving, because I haven't taken a breath since I stepped around this corner and saw him standing there.

He pauses when he's about five feet away from me. His stare hasn't deviated once, and I can no longer control the obvious rise and fall of my chest. His presence alone is causing me actual, physical turmoil.

"Hi," he says. His expression is cautious. He's not giving

away a single ounce of emotion. I don't know if he's angry about my confessions, but he's here, so he obviously knew they were from me. When I fail to return his greeting, he glances over his shoulder briefly. He runs a hand through his hair and then turns back to face me.

"You have time for a haircut?" he asks.

My eyes move to his hair, and it's significantly longer than after the last cut I gave him.

"You trust me to cut your hair again?" I'm shocked at the playfulness in my voice. No matter the circumstances, things just seem so easy with him.

"That depends. Are you sober?"

I smile, relieved that he's able to return the banter in the midst of our cold war. I nod and point to the back of the salon, where the sinks are. He walks toward me, and I walk around him, making my way to the front door to lock it. The last thing I need is someone walking in who shouldn't see him here.

When I return to the back, he's already seated in the same chair I washed his hair in last time. And just like last time, his eyes never deviate from my face. I test the water before running it over his hair. After wetting it, I dispense shampoo onto my palm and work my hands through his hair until it lathers. For a few seconds, his eyes fall shut, and I take this opportunity to stare at him.

He reopens them as soon as I begin rinsing his hair, so I quickly glance away.

I wish he would say something. If he's here, there's a reason he's here. And it's not to stare at me.

When I'm finished washing his hair, we silently walk toward the front. He takes a seat in my salon chair, and I dry his hair with a towel. I'm not sure if I breathe the entire time I'm cutting his hair, but I do what I can to focus on the hair and not him. The salon has never been this quiet.

It's also never been this loud.

I can't stop the thoughts from racing through my head. Thoughts of what it was like being kissed by him. Thoughts of how he made me feel when his arms were around me. Thoughts of how our conversations felt so natural and real that I never wanted them to end.

When I'm finished with the last cut of the scissors, I comb his hair out and then clean him up. I remove the protective smock and shake it out. I fold it and place it into the drawer.

He stands up and pulls out his wallet. He lays a fifty-dollar bill on the counter and slides his wallet back into his pocket.

"Thank you," he says with a smile. He turns to leave, and I immediately shake my head, not wanting him to go. We haven't even discussed the confessions. He didn't even tell me what made him stop by.

"Wait," I call out to him. Just as he reaches the door, he turns around, slowly. I try to figure out what to say to him, but nothing I really want to say will come out. Instead, I look down at the fifty-dollar bill and grab it, holding it up. "This is way too much money, Owen."

He stares quietly for what seems like an eternity before he opens the door and walks out without a word.

I fall into my salon chair, completely confused by my reaction. What did I want him to do? Did I want him to make a move? Did I want him to invite me back to his place?

I wouldn't have been okay with either of those things, and the fact that I'm upset that neither of them happened makes me feel like a horrible person.

I look down at the fifty-dollar bill in my hand. I notice

for the first time that there's writing on the back of it. I flip it over and read the message sprawled across the back in black Sharpie.

I need at least one night with you. Please.

I clench my fist and hold it up to my chest. The erratic beat of my heart and the rapid expansion of my lungs to make room for more air are the only two things I can focus on right now.

I toss the money on the counter and I bury my head in my arms.

Oh my God.

Oh my God.

I've never wanted to do the wrong thing so much in my entire life.

When I pause in front of his studio, I'm contemplating making a decision that I won't be proud of tomorrow. If I walk inside, I know what will happen between us. And while I know with Trey being out of town, the likelihood of his ever finding out about this is slim, it still doesn't make it okay.

The thought of his finding out about it also doesn't make me want to do it any less.

Before I can even make the choice for myself, the door opens and Owen's hand reaches out for mine. He pulls me inside the dark studio and closes the door behind me, clicking the lock into place. I wait for my eyes to adjust to the darkness and my conscience to adjust to the fact that I'm here. Inside his studio.

"You shouldn't stand outside like that," he says. "Someone might see you."

I'm not sure whom he's referring to, but there isn't a chance of Trey seeing me tonight, considering he's in San Antonio. "He's out of town."

Owen is standing less than two feet away, watching me with his head tilted to the side. I can see a faint smile cross his lips. "So I was told."

I look down at my feet, embarrassed. I close my eyes and try to talk myself out of this. I'm putting everything at risk by being here. I know if I could shut down the thoughts that have been going through my head, I would be able to see that this isn't smart. Whether we get caught or not, being with him won't make anything better. It'll just make it worse, because I'll more than likely want him even more after tonight.

"I shouldn't be here," I say quietly.

He's eyeing me with his same unwavering expression. "But you are."

"Only because you pulled me inside without asking."

He laughs quietly. "You were standing outside my door trying to decide what to do. I just helped make the decision for you."

"I haven't made any decision yet."

He nods. "Yes you have, Auburn. You've made a lot of decisions. You chose to be with Trey for the long haul. And now you're choosing to be with me for the night."

I bite my bottom lip and glance away from him. I don't like his comment, no matter how much truth is in it. Sometimes the truth hurts, and having him lay it out like that makes it seem more black and white than it really is.

"You're being unfair."

"No, I'm being selfish," he says.

"It's the same thing."

He takes a step toward me. "No, Auburn, it isn't. Unfair

would be giving you an ultimatum. Being selfish is doing something like this." His lips connect with mine with strength and purpose. His hands slide into my hair and wrap around the back of my head. He kisses me like he's giving me every kiss he wishes he could have given me in the past, and every kiss he'll wish he could give me in the future.

All of them, all at once.

His hands drop to my back and he pulls me against him. I'm not sure where my hands are at this point. I think I'm holding on to him for dear life, but every part of me other than my mouth has just gone completely numb. The only thing I'm fully aware of is his mouth on mine. His kiss is all I know in this moment.

All I want to think about.

But damn it if Trey doesn't force his way into my thoughts. I don't care how strong my feelings are for Owen, my loyalty is with Trey. Owen's actions forced me to make a choice, and now we both have to live with the consequences.

I break apart from him, finding strength to push against his chest. Our mouths separate, but my hands remain pressed against him. I can feel the deep rise and fall of his chest, and knowing he feels what I feel is almost enough for me to pull him back to my mouth.

"Trey," I say breathlessly. "I'm with Trey now."

Owen squeezes his eyes shut, like the sound of his name is painful to hear. He's breathing so heavily, he has to catch his breath before he responds. He opens his eyes and fixes his gaze on mine. "Your commitment is the only part of you that's with Trey." He lifts his hand and presses his palm over my shirt, against my heart. "Every other part of you is with me."

His words affect me more than his kiss. I try to inhale, but his hand pressed against my heart isn't allowing it. He takes a step closer until we're flush together. His palm is still pressed to my chest, but now his other arm is wrapped around my lower back.

"He doesn't make your heart feel like this, Auburn. He doesn't make it so crazy that it tries to beat through the walls of your chest."

I close my eyes and lean into him. I think my body makes the choice for me, because my mind has certainly lost all control. I press my face against his neck and listen quietly as our breaths fail to slow. The longer we stand here and the more he says, the heavier our need grows. I can feel it in the way he holds me. I can hear it in the desperate plea of his voice. I can feel it with every rise and fall of his chest.

"I get why you had to choose him," he says. "I don't like it, but I understand it. I also know that giving one night to me doesn't take away the fact that you might be giving him forever. But like I said . . . I'm selfish. And if one night with you is all I can get, then I'll take it." He lifts my head off his shoulder and tilts my face up to his. "I'll take whatever you're willing to give me. Because I know that if you walk out that door, then ten years from now . . . twenty years from now . . . we'll wish we had listened to our hearts when we think back on tonight."

"That's what scares me," I tell him. "I'm afraid if I listen to my heart once, I'll never figure out how to ignore it again."

Owen lowers his mouth to mine, and in a whisper he says, "If only I could be so lucky." His mouth connects with mine again, and this time I've very aware of every part of me. I'm pulling him to me with as much desperation as he's pulling at me. His mouth is everywhere as he kisses me with relief, knowing this kiss is me agreeing to whatever he's asking of me. It's my way of telling him he can have tonight.

"I need you upstairs," he says. "Now."

We begin to make our way across the floor of the studio, but neither of us can keep our mouths or hands off each other, so it takes us a while. Once we reach the stairs, he begins to back up them, making it even harder to continue kissing. When he sees we aren't getting anywhere, he finally grabs my hand and turns around, pulling me up the stairs until we're in his apartment.

When his mouth meets mine again, it's a completely different kind of kiss than the one we were just sharing. He cradles my head between both of his hands and he kisses me slowly. Soft and deep and full of highs and lows and depth.

He kisses me like I'm his canvas.

He grabs both of my hands and intertwines his fingers with mine. His forehead meets mine when his kiss comes to an end.

No one has ever made me feel this much. Not even Adam. And maybe the way I feel being kissed by him is a feeling that is so rare, it's something I'll never experience again after tonight.

That thought terrifies me, and also seals my fate until tomorrow morning, because whatever I feel with Owen shouldn't be taken for granted. Not even for the sake of loyalty to Trey.

And I honestly don't care what kind of person that makes me.

"I'm scared I'll never feel this again with anyone else," I whisper.

He squeezes my hands. "I'm scared you will."

I pull back and look at him, because I need him to know that my feelings for Trey will never match this. "I'll never have this with him, Owen. Not even close."

He makes a face that isn't full of relief like I expected. In fact, it's almost as if I said something he doesn't want to hear. "I wish you could," he says. "I don't want to think of you having to spend a lifetime with someone who doesn't deserve you."

He wraps his arms around me, and I bury my face in his neck again. "That's not what I meant," I say. "I'm not saying he deserves me any less than you do. I just feel a different kind of connection with you, and it scares me."

His hands grip the nape of my neck, and he moves his mouth to my ear. "You may not think he deserves you less than I do, but that's exactly what I'm saying, Auburn." His hands lower until he grips my thighs, and then he lifts me. He carries me across the room and lowers me down onto the bed. He slides on top of me, cradling my head between his forearms. He kisses me gently on the forehead, then again on the tip of my nose. His eyes meet mine, and he looks at me with more sincerity and honesty than I've ever seen in them before. "No one deserves you like I do."

His hands meet the button on my jeans, and he unbuttons them. His lips rest against my neck as he continues to convince me with his words that this is exactly where we need to be. "No one sees you like I do."

I close my eyes and listen to the sound of his voice. I wait as he removes my jeans, anticipating the touch of his hand against my skin. His palms slide up the sides of my legs and then his mouth is against mine again.

"No one understands you the way I do."

He presses himself against me at the same time his tongue

slips inside my mouth. I moan, and the room begins to spin, and the combination of his words and his touch and his body on mine are like gasoline on a fire. He begins to pull my shirt and bra over my head and I do nothing to help him or stop him. I'm useless against his touch.

"No one makes your heart beat like I do."

He kisses me, pausing only to remove his shirt. I somehow regain control of my senses when I realize my hands are pulling at his jeans, attempting to remove them so I can feel him skin to skin.

He presses his palm against my heart. "And no one else deserves to be inside you if they can't get there through here first."

His words trickle against my mouth like raindrops. He kisses me softly and then lifts himself off the bed. My eyes remain closed, but I hear his jeans meet the floor and I hear the tear of a wrapper. I feel his hands on my hips as he hooks his fingers beneath my panties and pulls them down. And it isn't until he's on top of me again that I finally find the strength to open my eyes.

"Say it," he whispers, looking down at me. "I want to hear you tell me I deserve you."

I slide my hands up his arms, along the curves of his shoulders, up the sides of his neck, and into his hair. I look him directly in the eyes. "You deserve me, Owen."

He drops his forehead to the side of my head and grabs my leg, lifting it, locking it around his waist. "And you deserve me, Auburn."

He pushes into me, and I'm not sure which is louder—his groan or my sudden outburst of "Oh my God."

He buries himself deep inside me and holds still. He looks

down at me breathlessly and smiles. "I can't tell if you said that because this feels incredibly good to you or if you're making fun of my initials again."

I smile between gasps. "Both."

Our smiles fade when he begins moving again. He keeps his mouth close to mine but far enough away that he can look down into my eyes. He moves in and out of me, slowly, as his lips begin to feather soft kisses across mine. I moan and need more than anything to close my eyes, but the way he's looking at me is something I want to remember every time I take a breath.

He pulls back again and pushes against me at the same time his lips meet my cheek. He begins to find a rhythm between each kiss, and he keeps his eyes focused on mine with every thrust.

"This is what I want you to remember, Auburn," he says softly. "I don't want you to remember what it feels like when I'm inside you. I want you to remember how it feels when I look at you."

His lips brush against mine so delicately, I almost don't feel them. "I want you to remember how your heart reacts every time I kiss you." His lips meet mine, and I attempt to ingrain every feeling I get from his kiss and his words into my memory. His hand slides through my hair and he lifts my head slightly off the bed, filling me with a deep kiss.

He pulls away so we can catch our breath. Looking into my eyes again, he says, "I want you to remember my hands, and how they can't stop touching you."

He works his mouth slowly up my jaw, until he reaches my ear. "And I need you to remember that anyone can make love. But I'm the only one who deserves to make love to you."

My arms lock around his neck with those words, and his mouth crashes against mine. He pushes into me, hard, and I want to scream. I want to cry. I want to beg him to never stop, but what I want even more is this kiss. I want to remember every part of it. I want to engrave the taste of him onto my tongue.

The next several minutes are a blur of moans, kisses, sweat, hands, and mouths. He's on top of me, and then I'm on top of him, and then he's on top of me again. When I feel the warmth of his mouth meet my breast, I completely lose myself. I let my head fall back and my eyes fall shut and my heart falls straight into the palms of his hands.

I'm so worked up, so dizzy, so grateful that I made the decision to stay, that I can't even tell when it's over. I'm still breathing so heavily, and my heart is pounding against my chest. I'm not sure that simply reaching a climax with Owen signifies the end of this experience. Because coming down from being with him feels just as incredible as it felt when it was occurring.

I'm lying against his chest and his arms are wrapped around me, and I never thought I'd be in this position again. A position where I know I'm right where I belong, but there's nothing I can do that can keep me there.

It reminds me of the day I had to say good-bye to Adam. I knew what we felt was more than what people gave us credit for, and being torn away from him before I was ready took me forever to get over.

And now, the same thing is happening with Owen. I'm not ready to say good-bye. I'm scared to say good-bye.

But I have to say good-bye, and it hurts like hell.

If I knew how to stop the tears, I would. I don't want him to hear me cry. I don't want him to know how upset I am that we can't have this every day of our lives. I don't want him to ask me what's wrong.

When he feels my tears falling against his chest, he doesn't do anything to stop them. Instead, he simply holds me with a much tighter grip and presses his cheek against the top of my head. His hand brushes softly through my hair.

"I know, baby," he whispers. "I know."

CHAPTER EIGHTEEN

Owen

I should have known she would be gone when I woke up. I felt her heartbreak last night when she was just thinking about having to say good-bye, so the fact that she left before having to do it doesn't surprise me.

What does surprise me is the confession lying on the pillow next to me. I pick it up to read it, but not before moving to her side of the bed. I can still smell her from here. I open the folded piece of paper and read her words.

I'll think about last night forever, Owen. Even when I shouldn't.

My hand falls against my chest, and I clench my fist.

I already miss her enough for it to hurt, and she's probably only been gone an hour. I read her confession several more times. It's easily my favorite confession now, but also the most painful.

I walk to my workroom, drag the canvas with her unfinished portrait to the middle of the floor, and set it up. I gather all the supplies I'll need, and I stand in front of her painting. I stare down at the confession, imagining exactly what she must have looked like when she wrote it, and I finally have the inspiration I need to finish the portrait.

I pick up my brush, and I paint her.

I'm not sure how much time has passed. One day. Two days. I think I stopped three times to eat, at least. It's dark outside, I know that much.

But I'm finally finished.

I rarely feel that any of my paintings ever make it to a finishing point. There's always something else I want to add to them, like a few more brushstrokes or another color. But there comes a point with every painting when I just have to stop and accept it for what it is.

I'm at that point with this painting. It's probably the most realistic painting I've ever laid out on canvas.

Her expression is exactly how I want to remember her. It's not a happy expression. In fact, she looks kind of sad. I want to think it's the same look she'll get on her face every time she thinks about me. A look that reveals how much she misses me. Even when she shouldn't.

I drag the painting to a spot against the wall. I find the confession she left on my pillow this morning, and I attach it to the wall next to her face. I pull the box of confessions she's left me over the last few weeks, and I attach those all around her painting.

I take a step back and I stare at the only piece I have left of her.

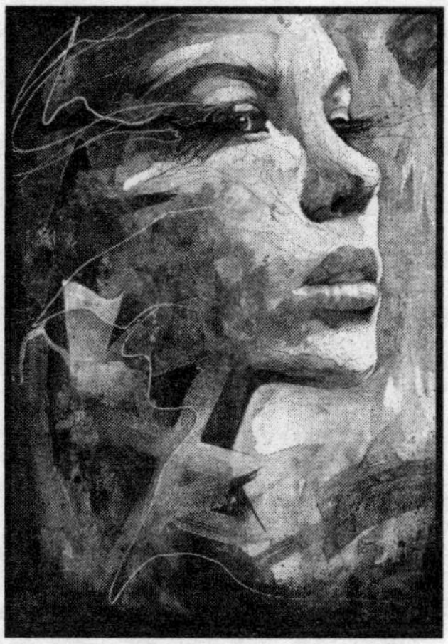

"What ever happened between you and Auburn?" Harrison asks.

I shrug.

"The usual?"

I shake my head. "Not even close."

He cocks an eyebrow. "Wow," he says. "That's a first. Pretty sure I want to hear the rest of this story." He grabs another beer and slides it across the bar toward me. He leans over and pops the tab. "Give me the condensed version, though. I close in a few hours."

I laugh. "That's easy. She's the reason for it all, Harrison."

He looks at me with a confused expression.

"You said condensed," I tell him. "That's the condensed version."

Harrison shakes his head. "Well in that case, I change my mind. I want the detailed version."

I smile and look down at my phone. It's already after ten. "Maybe next time. I've already been here for two hours." I lay money on the bar and take one last sip of the beer. He waves me off as I turn to head back to my studio. The painting I finished of her earlier should be close to dry now. I think this might be the first painting I ever hang in the bedroom area of my apartment.

I pull my key out of my pocket and slide it into the door, but the door isn't locked.

I know I locked it. I never leave here without locking it.

I push the door open, and the second I do, my whole world stops. I look to my left. To my right. I walk further into my studio and I spin around, staring at the damage that's been done to everything I own. Everything I've worked for.

Red paint lines the walls, the floors, covers every painting in the entire downstairs area. The first thing I do is rush to one of the paintings closest to me. I touch the paint smeared across the canvas and can tell it's already drying. It's probably been drying for about an hour now. Whoever did this was waiting for me to walk out of the studio tonight.

As soon as Trey comes to mind, that's when the real panic sets in. I immediately scale the stairs and head straight to my workroom. As soon as I swing open the door, I bend over and press my hands to my thighs. I exhale a huge sigh of relief.

They didn't touch it.

Whoever was here didn't touch the painting I made of her. After I allow myself a few minutes to recover, I stand and walk to her painting. Even though the painting hasn't been touched, something is different.

Something is off.

And that's when I notice the confession she left on my pillow.

It's missing.

CHAPTER NINETEEN

Auburn

"Are you expecting company?" I ask Emory. Someone is knocking on our door, so I look down at my phone. It's after ten.

She shakes her head. "It's not for me. Humans don't like me."

I laugh and make my way to the door. When I look through the peephole and see Trey, I sigh heavily.

"Whoever it is, you seem disappointed," Emory says flatly. "Must be your boyfriend." She stands and makes her way toward her bedroom, and I'm thankful she's at least learned the meaning of privacy.

I open the door to let him in. I'm a little confused as to why he's here in the first place. It's after ten at night, and he said he was out of town until tomorrow.

As soon as the door is open, he rushes inside. He kisses me briefly on the cheek and says, "I need to use your restroom."

His hurried appearance throws me off for a second as I watch him remove his things from his belt. Gun, handcuffs, car keys. He sets it all on the bar, and I can't help but notice the sweat dripping down his temple. He looks nervous. "Go ahead," I say, gesturing toward the restroom. "Make yourself at home."

He heads straight for the restroom and as soon as he opens the door, I experience a small moment of panic.

"Wait!" I say, rushing behind him. He steps away from the door, and I brush past him. I walk to the sink and pick up all the seashell soaps. I walk out of the restroom and he's eyeing my hands curiously.

"What am I supposed to wash my hands with now?" he asks.

I nod my head toward the cabinet. "There's liquid soap in there," I tell him. I look down at the soaps in my hands. "These aren't for guests."

He closes the door in my face, and I walk the soaps to my room, feeling a little ridiculous.

I have serious issues.

I set the soap down on my nightstand and pick up my phone. I have several missed text messages, and only one of them is from my mother. I scroll through them and they're all from Owen. I start at the bottom and work my way up.

Call me.

Are you okay?

It's important.

Meat dress.

Please call me.

If you don't respond to my text in five minutes, I'm coming over.

I immediately text him back.

Don't come over, Trey is here. I'm fine.

I hit send and then type him another message.

Are you okay?

He pings me back immediately.

Someone broke into my studio tonight. They destroyed everything.

My hand flies up to my mouth, and I gasp.

He took your confession, Auburn.

My heart is in my throat, and I quickly glance up to make sure Trey isn't standing at my door. I don't want him to see my reaction right now, or he'll want to know who I'm texting. I quickly send Owen another message.

Did you call the police?

His response comes through just as I hear the door to the bathroom open.

And tell them what, Auburn? To come clean up their mess?

I read the text twice.

Their mess?

I immediately hit delete on all the messages. I set the phone down and try to appear casual, but Owen's last message is playing over and over in my head. He thinks Trey did this?

I want to say that Owen is wrong. I want to say that Trey wouldn't be capable of doing something like what was done to Owen, but I don't know what or who to believe anymore.

Trey appears in the doorway and I study his eyes, trying to get a clue from them, but he gives me nothing but a wall.

I smile at him. "You're back early."

He doesn't smile back. My heart is trying to climb through the walls of my chest, and not in a good way.

He walks into my room and sits down on my bed. He kicks his shoes off and knocks them onto the floor. "What ever happened to that cat?" he asks. "What'd you say his name was? Sparkles?"

I swallow. Why is he asking about Owen's cat?

"Ran away," I say calmly. "Emory was devastated for a week."

He nods, working his jaw back and forth. He reaches a hand up and grabs my arm. I look down at it just as he pulls me to him. I fall against his chest, stiff as a board. He wraps his arm around me and kisses the top of my head. "I missed you, so I came back early."

He's being nice. *Too* nice. My guard stays up.

"Guess what?" he says.

"What?"

His hand moves to my hair and he runs his fingers through it. "I found a house today."

I pull away from his chest and look up at him, just as he tucks a lock of hair behind my ear. "I didn't realize you were looking for another house."

He smiles. "I thought I might get something a little bigger. Now that mom has moved back, I figured I could let her have that house, since it was hers to begin with. It's probably better if we had more privacy, anyway. The house I'm looking at has a fenced-in backyard. It's on Bishop, near the park. It's a really good neighborhood."

I don't say anything, because it sounds like he means he found *us* a house today. The thought of that terrifies me.

"Mom went with me to look at it. She really liked it. She said AJ would love it there."

I can't imagine Lydia saying AJ would love anything that isn't hers. "She really said that?"

Trey nods, and I find myself imagining what that would be like. Actually being able to live in the same house with AJ, in a good neighborhood with a backyard. And once again the thought makes its way into my head that it could be worth it. I'll never love Trey like I loved Adam, and I'll never feel the connection with him that I have with Owen, but Adam and Owen can't give me the one thing in my life that I need. Only Trey can do that.

"What are you saying, Trey?"

He smiles down at me, and I realize in this moment that maybe Owen was wrong. If Trey were responsible for destroying Owen's studio, he wouldn't be here saying the things he's saying right now. He would be livid, because he would know that confession was from me.

"I'm saying this isn't a game to me, Auburn. I love AJ and I need to know that you're in this with me. That we're in this together."

He shifts until he's on top of me, and then he leans forward and kisses me. We've been dating for over two months now and I've never let him do anything but kiss me. I'm still not ready to go further than this, but I know he is. And I know his patience has been wearing thin.

He groans and his tongue dives deeper into my mouth. I squeeze my eyes shut and hate that I'm forcing myself to pretend I'm okay with this. But internally, I'm just stalling, giving myself a moment to think about what move I need to make next, because Owen's texts are still in the back of my mind.

Not to mention the fact that Owen may very well be on his way here.

Trey's hands become needier as they grope and pull at me. His mouth moves roughly from mine, and he begins to kiss me all over as one of his hands works the buttons on my shirt.

I want to tell him to stop, but it's all happening so fast, I can't find a point at which to push him away. His hand is unbuttoning my jeans, and he's working his fingers inside my underwear when I can't take a second more of this. I dig my heels into my mattress and push him away as I attempt to scoot up on the bed.

He pulls away for a few seconds and looks at me, but words fail to come out of my mouth. When I say nothing, his mouth is immediately on mine again with even more force. He didn't get a verbal no, so I guess that means yes to him.

I press against his chest. "Trey, stop."

He immediately stops kissing me and presses his face into the pillow. He groans, frustrated, and I don't know what to say next. I just made him angry.

His hand is still in my jeans, and even though I'm not kissing him, he continues to slide his hand further until I have to physically push his hand away. He presses his palm into the bed beside me and lifts up until his face is just inches from mine. His eyes are full of anger, but it's not the anger that scares me.

It's the disgust.

"You can fuck my little brother when you're fifteen, but you can't fuck me as an adult?"

His words hurt. They hurt so much, I have to close my eyes and turn away from him.

"I didn't fuck Adam," I say. I slowly look in his direction

again, and I stare him straight in the eyes. "I made love to Adam."

He lowers his face until his mouth is directly over my ear. The heat from his breath makes my skin crawl. "What was it when Owen was fucking you in his bed? Was *that* love?"

I suck in a rush of air.

My entire body tenses, and I know if I try to run, he'll stop me. I also know that if I don't try to run, he'll more than likely hurt me.

I've never been more scared.

He remains on top of me, his mouth poised next to my ear. He doesn't speak again, but he doesn't have to. His hand is making his intentions clear as he works his way inside my jeans again.

For a split second, I wonder if I should let him do this. If I just shut up and allow him to take what he wants, maybe it'll be enough for him to forgive what happened with Owen. I can't let this come between me and my son.

But those thoughts only last for a split second, because there is no way in hell I'll allow AJ to grow up with a spineless mother.

"Get off me."

He doesn't. Instead, he lifts his head and looks down at me with a grin so cold, it sends a rush of chills over me. I don't know who he is right now. I've never seen this side of him before. "Trey, please."

His hand is rough, and I'm squeezing my legs together, but it doesn't stop him from forcing my thighs apart. I'm pushing him, but my weakness is laughable compared to his strength. His mouth is back on mine and when I try to turn away from him, he bites my lip, forcing his kiss on me.

I can taste the blood.

I begin to sob as soon as he begins unbuttoning his own jeans.

This isn't happening.

"She said stop."

It's not my voice, and it isn't Trey's, but the words force him to stop. I glance up to find Emory standing in the doorway, pointing a gun in our direction. Trey slowly turns to face the door. When he sees her, he carefully rolls onto his back with his palms face out.

"You do realize you're pointing a gun at a police officer," Trey says calmly.

Emory laughs. "You do realize I'm stopping an assault, don't you?"

He sits up, slowly, and she raises the gun even higher, keeping it trained on him.

"I don't know what you think is going on here, but if you don't hand me that gun, you'll be in a shitload of trouble."

Emory looks at me but keeps the gun aimed at Trey. "Who do you think will be in trouble, Auburn? The officer who was forcing himself on you or the roommate who shot his dick off?"

Luckily her question was rhetorical, because I'm crying too hard to answer. Trey runs his palm over his mouth and then squeezes his jaw, attempting to figure out how to get out of the mess he's just put himself in.

Emory focuses her attention back on him. "You're going to walk out of this apartment and all the way to the end of the hallway. I'll set your gun and your keys on the hallway floor once you're out of reach."

I can feel Trey look at me, but I don't look at him. I can't. He runs a gentle hand up my arm. "Auburn, you know I would never hurt you. Tell her she's confused." I can feel him reach up to my face, but Emory's voice stops him.

"*Get. The fuck. Out!*" she yells.

Once again, Trey raises his palms in the air. He stands, slowly, and buttons his jeans. He bends to grab his shoes.

"Leave them. Get out," Emory says firmly.

She slowly backs out of the doorway as he makes his way toward her. I watch the back of his head as he turns toward the front door and Emory follows him.

"All the way to the end of the hall," she says.

Several more seconds pass before she says, "Throw me his shoes, Auburn."

I reach across the bed and grab his shoes from the floor. I walk them to her and watch as she sets his shoes outside of our front door. She keeps a close eye on Trey at the end of the hallway as she lays the gun beside the shoes. As soon as it's out of her hands, she slams the door shut and dead bolts it, then fastens the chain lock. I'm now standing in the doorway of my bedroom, watching to make sure he's gone. She turns to face me, wide-eyed.

"I told you I liked the other guy more."

I somehow laugh between all my tears. Emory steps forward and hugs me, and as strange as she is, I'm more grateful to her than I've ever been to anyone in my life.

"Thank you so much for eavesdropping."

She laughs. "My pleasure." She pulls back and looks me in the eye. "Are you okay? Did he hurt you?"

I shake my head and pull my hand up to my lip to see if it's still bleeding. It is, but before I can turn to the kitchen, Emory is already tearing a paper towel off the holder. She turns on the faucet just as a knock lands against the door.

We both turn and look at the door.

"Auburn." It's Trey's voice. "Auburn, I'm sorry. I'm so sorry."

He's crying. That, or he's a really good actor.

"We need to talk about this. Please."

I know Owen is probably on his way over right now after all of his frantic texts, so I just want to get rid of Trey before they come face-to-face. That's the last thing I need tonight. I walk to the door, but I don't unlock it.

"We'll talk about this tomorrow," I say through the door. "I need space tonight, Trey."

A few seconds pass and he says, "Okay. Tomorrow."

CHAPTER TWENTY

Owen

I pull into a parking garage across the street from her apartment so Trey doesn't see my car.

When I'm out of my car and across the street, I keep running until I'm beating on her front door.

"Auburn!" I keep knocking. "Auburn, let me in!"

I can hear the locks begin to unlatch one by one, and with each lock that opens, I somehow grow more and more nervous. When she finally opens the door, and I see her standing in front of me, every part of me exhales, even my heart.

Remnants of tears line her cheeks, and the two seconds it

takes to enter her apartment and pull her to me feel like an hour too long. "Are you okay?"

Her arms wrap around me and I reach back to shut the door. I lock it and then pull her to me just as she nods.

"I'm fine."

Her voice is anything but fine. She sounds terrified. I push her away from me until she's at arm's length, and I take her in.

Her hair is a mess.

Her shirt is torn.

Her lip is bleeding.

Her head is moving back and forth and she's telling me no. She can see the fury in my eyes, just as I turn around and begin to unlock the door.

He can fuck with me all he wants. I draw the line when it comes to her.

Her hands are on my arms, pulling me away from the door. "Owen, stop." I swing open the door and step into the hall, but she pushes herself in front of me and puts her hands on my chest. "You're angry. Calm down first. Please."

I breathe in and out, attempting to calm myself down. But only because she said please. I hope she never finds out that hearing her say that one word could convince me to do anything she wants. Ever.

She urges me back inside her apartment. I walk to the counter and rest my arms on it, pressing my forehead against them.

I close my eyes, and I contemplate.

I think about what he might do next. I think about where he might go. I think about where she needs to be so that she's safe from him.

I don't have answers to any of those thoughts, other than

the last one. She needs to be with me. I'm not letting her out of my sight tonight.

I straighten up and turn around to face her. "Get your things. We're leaving."

I choose to take her to a hotel for the night because I don't trust her being at my studio with me. I'm still not sure what happened between the two of them and I don't know what he's capable of at this point.

She looks over her shoulder the entire way to our room, so I take her hand in mine and try to give her reassurance that she's safe for the night.

Once we're inside the hotel room and I shut the door, it feels as though the air is different in here. Like there's more of it, because she's finally able to breathe a sigh of relief. I hate that she's been so worried, and knowing that Trey is a huge part of her life makes me even more concerned for her.

She slips her shoes off and takes a seat on the bed. I sit down beside her and take her hand in mine again.

"Will you tell me what happened?"

She inhales slowly with another nod. "He showed up right before I saw your texts. At first, I didn't think he was capable of doing something like you were suggesting, but when he walked into my room, I saw it. There was something in the way he looked at me. The first thing he did was ask about Sparkles."

I don't want to interrupt her, but I have no idea what Sparkles means.

"Sparkles?"

She shoots me a quick, embarrassed smile. "I told him Owen-Cat was Emory's, and that her name was Sparkles."

I shake my head in confusion. "Why would he ask about my cat?" As soon as the question leaves my mouth, the answer becomes clear. "He was in my studio," I say. "He must have seen her and put two and two together."

She nods, but she stops talking. I wait for her to continue her story, but she doesn't.

"What happened next?"

She shrugs. "He just . . ."

She starts crying, quietly, so I give her a minute to continue at her own pace.

"He started talking about AJ and buying a house and . . . then he started kissing me. When I asked him to stop . . ." She pauses again and inhales a quick breath. "He said something about me and you being together in your bed, and that's when I knew he read my confession. I tried to get away but he held me down. That's when Emory walked in."

I should have gotten there faster, but thank God for Emory.

"That's all that happened, Owen. He stopped, and then he left."

I lift my hand to her lip and touch the area next to where she's bleeding. "And here? Did he do this?"

She glances down and nods. I hate seeing the shame in her expression. That should be the last thing she's feeling right now.

"Did you call the police? Do you want to call them now?" I begin to lift off the bed to get the phone for her, but her eyes widen and she begins shaking her head back and forth.

"No," she says. "Owen, I can't report this."

I pause for a moment, just to make sure I heard her right. I release her and sit up straighter, facing her directly. My head tilts in confusion.

"Trey attacks you in your own apartment, and you aren't going to report him?"

She looks away, more shame in her expression. "Do you know what would happen if I reported him? Lydia would blame me. She would never let me see AJ."

"Look at me, Auburn."

She turns her head and I take her face in my hands. "He attacked you. Lydia may be a bitch, but no one would ever blame you for reporting something like this."

She pulls away from my hands and shakes her head softly. "He knows I slept with you, Owen. Of course he's going to be angry after finding out I cheated on him."

I close my eyes. My heart is beating so hard; I think it needs out of this room. "You're *defending* him?"

The silence that follows crushes me. I stand up and walk away from the bed, toward the window.

I try to understand it. I try to make sense of it, but it makes no fucking sense at all.

"You didn't report him for breaking into your studio. It's the same thing."

I immediately spin around and face her. "That's only because I've ruined my credibility, Auburn. It would look like a pathetic act of revenge if I blamed Trey for that. He'd get away with it, and I would only make things worse for myself.

"You, on the other hand—he physically *attacked* you. There's absolutely no reason in the world why that shouldn't be reported. Not reporting it will make him feel like it's an invitation to do it again."

Rather than argue with me, she calmly stands and walks toward me. She wraps her arms around my waist and buries her face into my chest. I wrap my arms tightly around her in return. I'm suddenly a lot calmer than I was a few seconds ago.

"Owen," she says, her words slightly muffled by my shirt, "you aren't a father, so I can't expect you to understand my decisions. If I report him, things will only get worse. I have to do whatever I can to keep my relationship with my son intact. If that includes forgiving Trey and having to apologize to him for what happened between you and me . . . then that's what I have to do. I can't expect you to understand that, but I need you to support it. You don't know what it's like to give up your entire life for someone."

Not only do her words physically hurt me, they also terrify me. Even after this, she still doesn't see how dangerous that man is.

"If you love your son, Auburn . . . you will keep him as far away from Trey as possible. Forgiving him is the worst choice you could make."

She pulls away from my chest and looks up at me. "It's not a choice, Owen. If it were a choice, that would mean I have other options. I don't. It's just what I have to do."

I close my eyes and take her face in my hands. I press my forehead to hers, and I just stand there with her. I listen to her breathe, and I try to make sense of her words. She's telling herself that I don't understand because I've never been in her position. She thinks all the mistakes I've made in the past were made out of selfishness, rather than complete selflessness.

We're more alike than she thinks.

"Auburn," I say quietly, "I understand completely that you want to be with your son, but sometimes in order to save a relationship, you have to sacrifice it first."

She pulls herself from my grip. She takes several steps away from me before turning around. "What relationship have you ever had to sacrifice?"

I lift my head slowly, looking at her with everything that I have. "Us, Auburn. I've had to sacrifice *us*."

CHAPTER TWENTY-ONE

Auburn

I'm sitting on the bed with him, trying to absorb everything he's saying, but it's hard. "I just . . ." I shake my head. "Why didn't you just tell me all of this from the beginning? Why didn't you tell me that Trey knew they weren't your drugs?"

Owen sighs and squeezes my hands. "I wanted to, Auburn. But I barely knew you. Telling anyone the truth could have jeopardized my father's career. Not to mention the fact that Trey was threatening to cause trouble and the last thing I wanted was for you to have issues as a result of my relationship with my father."

If I thought I was through with Trey earlier tonight, I'm *definitely* through with him now. I can't believe he put Owen in this situation because he felt threatened by him. This whole time, I've been trying to see the good in Trey, but I'm starting to question if he even *has* any good in him.

"I feel like an idiot."

Owen shakes his head adamantly. "You can't be so hard on yourself. I should have told you sooner. I was going to, but after finding out you had a son, I realized just how much you had at stake. It made things complicated, because it was too late for me to go back and say the pills weren't mine, and there was no way Lydia and Trey would have allowed you to be with someone like me. We were stuck."

I fall against the bed and clasp my hands together over my stomach. I stare up at the ceiling, more confused about what to do than when we walked in here.

"I don't trust him. Not after this. I don't want him around AJ anymore, but if I tried to take them to court, Lydia would be furious. She would use my visits with AJ against me and I may never get to see him."

The reality of my situation begins to hit, and I bring my hands up and press my palms against my eyes. I don't want to cry. I want to remain calm and figure out a way around this.

Owen lowers himself beside me on the bed. He slips a hand to my cheek and urges me to look at him.

"Auburn, listen to me," he says, looking down on me with complete sincerity. "If I have to come clean about my father and take Trey to court, I'll do it. You deserve to be in AJ's life, and if we continue to allow Trey's threats to affect our decisions, he'll never stop. He'll never allow us to be together and he'll do whatever he can to keep you from AJ unless you're with him. It's all about the power with people like him, but we need to stop allowing him to have it."

He brushes away one of my tears with his thumb. "Whatever needs to be done, we'll do it together. I'm not going anywhere. And you aren't speaking to Trey again without me there, okay?"

His words are filling me with a mixture of relief and dread. It feels so good to know that he's on my side, but the thought of confronting Trey terrifies me. But it's the only choice we have at this point. We either have to work it out like adults, or I'll fight him in court.

And I won't stop until I win.

Owen pulls me against him and holds me quietly for so long, I fall asleep. The sound of the shower wakes me up, and I immediately look around the hotel room in an attempt to regain my bearings. When the haze clears and the events of the entire last day play out in my mind, I surprisingly feel a sense of calm fall over me. It's amazing how you don't realize just how alone and scared you were until you have someone by your side to support you. Owen has sacrificed so much for his father, and now he's doing the same for me. He's exactly the type of man AJ needs as a role model in his life.

I check my phone and find several missed calls from Trey. I don't want him suspicious or showing back up at my apartment tonight, so I shoot him a text.

I need some time alone, Trey. We can talk tomorrow, I promise.

I don't want him to think I'm as angry with him as I am. I just want to appease him for now until Owen and I can confront him together.

Okay.

I breathe a sigh of relief with his response and set my

phone down. I stand up and walk toward the bathroom, but I pause when I catch sight of Owen in the hallway mirror. The bathroom door is open slightly, as is the shower curtain. I see glimpses of him as he washes his hair, but it's enough for me to know I'd much rather be in there with him than out here alone.

I'm suddenly nervous and I don't know why I'm nervous. We've done this before.

I take off my shirt and lay it on the dresser, followed by my jeans. I take a look in the mirror and am embarrassed to see mascara streaked beneath my eyes. I wipe it away and then take a step back. There are faint bruises in various places on my body from the struggle with Trey and it almost makes me want to change my mind about what I'm about to do.

I don't, though. Trey has kept Owen and me apart enough, so I push the thought of him out of my head completely. I don't want to think about him again until we're sitting in front of him tomorrow.

I walk toward the bathroom and pause just outside the door. I slip off my bra and then my underwear. I debate whether or not to turn the light out. The one time I was with Owen, it was dark, so my insecurities were almost nonexistent. However, he's never seen me like this before. I've never seen *him.*

That last thought actually gives me the courage it takes to enter the bathroom.

"Auburn?" he says from the shower. He's questioning whether or not it's me walking in here right now, so I guess it proves we're both still a little on edge tonight.

"Just me," I say as I shut the door.

His head appears from behind the shower curtain, and the smile that's usually affixed to his face when he sees me vanishes when he sees *all* of me. My cheeks instantly flush and I reach next to me and flip off the light switch. I thought I could do it, but I can't. No guy, not even Adam, has ever seen me undressed with the lights on. I didn't realize just how much I lacked confidence.

I hear him laugh, but I can't see his face in the dark.

"Two things," he says, his voice firm. "Turn that back on. Get in here."

I shake my head, even though he can't see it. "I'll get in there, but I'm not turning the light back on."

I hear the shower curtain slide open and then wet feet splash against the tile floor. Before I know it, an arm is wrapped around my bare waist and the light is back on. His face is directly in front of mine and he's grinning. He leaves the light on and lifts me up, carrying me to the shower with him. He stands me inside the shower and I immediately cover what I can with my hands.

He takes a step back until we're a couple of feet apart and I can't help but notice how confident he is, standing completely naked in front of me. He has a right to be confident. Me . . . not so much.

He tilts his head back far enough to wash the soap from his hair, but not too far that he can't see all of me. His eyes roam over me while he rinses his hair with a satisfied smile.

"You know what I love?" he asks.

I keep my arms and hands in front of me, covering myself, and I shrug.

"I love it when you wash my hair," he says. "I don't know why. It just feels better when you do it."

I smile. "Do you want me to wash your hair?"

He shakes his head and turns around to rinse the soap off his face. "I already washed it," he says, matter-of-factly.

I can't help but stare at the back of him now. *Flawless.*

I tense up even more, knowing just how *not* flawless I am. And I don't feel this way because I have a case of low self-esteem, and I'm not pretending to be self-conscious just so he'll compliment me. It's just that I'm a girl who has had a baby, and bodies don't look the same after having babies. My stomach is covered in faint white lines and the scar from my cesarean is front and center, right above what should be one of the most attractive areas to a man.

I won't even talk about what pregnancy does to breasts. I close my eyes just thinking about it.

"It's kind of like when someone makes you a sandwich," Owen says.

My eyes flick open. He can see the confusion on my face, and he laughs.

"When you wash my hair." He says it like it's an explanation. "Sandwiches are the same way. I could use the same ingredients and make my sandwich the exact same way as someone else, but for some reason it just tastes so much better when I'm not the one who makes it. Just like when you wash my hair. It feels better when you do it. It also styles better."

Here I am, almost shaking I'm so nervous, and he's casually discussing sandwiches and shampoos.

He takes a step forward and places his hands on my elbows, turning me until I'm under the water. "I want to wash yours," he says, grabbing the travel-sized bottle of shampoo that's now half-empty.

He tilts my head back and runs his hands through my hair as the water saturates it. I'm not like him—I can't keep my eyes open while his hands are in my hair, so I let them fall shut. He lathers my hair, and I'm not sure what feels better, his fingers massaging my scalp or the part of him that's pressing against my stomach.

"Relax," he says as he begins to rinse my hair.

I don't relax. I don't know how.

As if he knows this, he moves closer. His closeness actually puts me more at ease. It's when he's several feet away and I'm under the scrutiny of his gaze that I'm the most nervous.

He begins to work the conditioner into my hair this time, and he's absolutely right. I've had my hair washed by other people before, a result of being in cosmetology school. And it does feel good, sort of like a massage. But this is more. His hands are so much more.

His lips press softly against mine and he kisses me. His hands move from my hair to my arms, and he pulls them away from my body, wrapping them around his waist until we're flush together. I finally open my eyes and look up into his as he begins to rinse the conditioner out of my hair.

"Feels good, doesn't it?" he says with a slightly wicked grin.

I smile. "I don't ever want to wash my own hair again."

He kisses my forehead. "Just wait until you taste my sandwiches."

I laugh, and the tenderness that enters his eyes at the sound of my laughter makes me realize that this is what I want. *Selflessness.* It should be the basis of every relationship. If a person truly cares about you, they'll get more pleasure from the way they make *you* feel, rather than the way you make *them* feel.

"I want you to know something," he says, kissing his way down my neck. "And I'm not saying this just to make you feel better." One of his hands slides up my waist until it meets my breast, and he holds it there. "I'm saying this because I want you to believe it." He pulls away from my neck to look at me directly. "You are so, so beautiful, Auburn. Everywhere. Every part of you. On the outside, on the inside, when you're beneath me, on top of me, painted on a canvas." His eyes are boring into mine and I close them, because there is way too much truth in his. "So beautiful," he whispers.

He begins to kiss his way down my throat until the warmth of his breath teases my breast. He takes me in his mouth, and I moan softly. I bring my hands to the back of his head and keep my eyes closed, hoping we end up in a bed before I collapse from dizziness.

His hands slide down my waist, down my thighs, until his mouth begins to follow their direction. When his tongue meets my navel, I gasp. Partly because of the sensation, and partly because I want him to stop heading in the direction he's headed. I don't want him near the parts of me I'm most self-conscious about.

He repositions himself until he's on his knees in front of me. He's no longer kissing me, and his hands are wrapped around the backs of my thighs. I can feel his breath against my stomach, and the fact that he's not doing anything makes me curious enough to open my eyes and look down at him.

He looks up at me. He smiles gently and brings a hand in front of him, trailing his fingers over the scar that marks my abdomen. "This," he says, looking at it. "This is the most beautiful thing I've ever seen on a woman."

The tears sting at my eyes and I refuse to cry at a time like this, but I think I just officially fell for this man.

His lips meet my stomach, and he presses a gentle kiss against my scar. He begins to work his way back up my body until he's standing straight, looking down at me again. "How many days have we actually seen each other since we met?" he asks.

I want to laugh at his randomness, because I think it's my favorite part of him. I shrug. "I don't know. Four? Five?"

He slowly shakes his head. "If you count today, it's seven," he says, sliding a hand through my hair. "So tell me, Auburn. How is it possible that I'm already falling in love with you?"

He catches my gasp with his mouth, and he picks me up, carrying me out of the shower and straight to the bed.

And this time, I don't get lost in his touch. I don't get lost in his kiss. I don't get lost in how it feels when he pushes himself inside me.

I don't feel lost in him at all, because it's the first time I've ever felt like someone truly found me.

"I'll park in the parking garage," he says. "Take my key and go through the back door."

He brings the car to a stop, and I open the door to get out. Before I do, he grabs my arm and pulls me toward him. His lips meet mine and his kiss feels like a promise.

"I'll be up in a second," he says.

I rush to the back door of his studio. I insert the key into the lock and shut it just as fast, then hurry up the stairs. Once I'm in his apartment, I can finally breathe a sigh of relief. I don't know why I would think Trey would be waiting out there. It's just disconcerting because he hasn't texted me since last night, when I told him I'd talk to him today. He's either giving me the space I need, or he knows I'm up to something.

Owen-Cat appears at my feet, and I pick her up and carry her into the kitchen with me. I set her on the bar as I reach for a bottle of wine. After the couple of days I've had, I definitely need a drink. I'm sure Owen, does too, so I pour him one, just as I hear him walk up behind me.

He wraps his arms around me from behind and pulls me against him. I lean my head back against his shoulder and rest my hands on his arms.

As soon as I touch him, my eyes flick open and my mouth attempts to form a scream, but I'm cut off by the words whispered into my ear.

"Can't even tell which man has his arms around you?"

Trey's voice stiffens my entire body. His grip around my waist tightens and that's when I feel the difference. The difference in their height. The difference in their hands. The difference in the way they hold me.

"Trey," I whisper, my voice shaky.

"Save it, Auburn," he hisses into my ear. He spins me around and shoves me against the refrigerator, pushing my arms against it. "Where is he?"

I swallow, relieved that he doesn't know where Owen is. Maybe Owen will hear him and be able to do something to protect himself.

I shake my head. "I don't know."

His eyes seethe with rage and he tightens his grip on my arms. "I'm not sure I can handle another lie from you. Where the fuck is he?"

I squeeze my eyes shut and refuse to answer. His mouth meets mine in an abrupt crash, and I attempt to push him off me. He breaks away and backhands me.

My legs instantly buckle, but he holds me up when I try to fall. His mouth returns to my ear.

"Call out his name."

I don't.

He wraps his hand around the back of my neck and squeezes. "Call out his name," he says again. I open my mouth to tell him to fuck off when I hear Owen's voice.

"Let go of her."

I open my eyes cautiously. The smile on Trey's face when he hears Owen's voice scares me more than what just happened between us. He pulls me to him, spinning me around, and presses his chest against my back. We're both facing Owen now.

Owen is standing just a few feet away, holding nothing but his cell phone and his car keys. His eyes are frantic as they fall from my head to my toes, assessing me for injuries. "Are you hurt?"

I shake my head, but Trey still has a tight grip around me. Owen is solid and still, watching Trey closely. "What do you want, Trey?"

A deep chuckle rises from Trey's throat and he turns his head to mine. He slowly runs his knuckles up my jaw. "You already tainted what I want, Owen."

I can see the rage wash over Owen and my eyes immediately grow wide with fear. I shake my head, trying to get him to calm down. The last thing he needs is something else to be arrested for. He's on probation, and attacking a cop is probably the one thing Trey is hoping he'll do. "Owen, don't. He wants you to hit him. Don't do it."

Trey presses his cheek to mine, and I watch as Owen's eyes follow the path of Trey's hand. He trails it down my throat, between my breasts, and over my stomach. By the time his hand settles between my legs, I can taste the bile in my throat. I squeeze my eyes shut, because the look in Owen's eyes proves there's no way he's going to stand here and allow Trey to do this.

I hear him lunge forward right before I'm tossed aside. I fall to the floor and by the time I turn around, Owen has already punched Trey. Trey is grabbing the counter for support with one hand and reaching for his gun with the other.

Owen is standing in front of me now, facing me, making sure I'm okay. My words don't come out, but I want to tell him to turn around, to run, to duck, but nothing will come out. Owen takes my face between his hands and says, "Auburn. Go downstairs and call the police."

Trey laughs, and Owen can see the onset of a new kind of fear in my eyes. He turns around and blocks me with his body, pushing me further away from Trey.

"Call the police?" Trey says, continuing with the laughter. "And who will they believe? The addict and the whore who got pregnant at fifteen? Or the cop?"

Neither Owen nor I speak as we both allow the words that just fell from Trey's mouth to sink in.

"Oh, and let's not forget the contraband you have hidden all over your studio. There's also that."

I can feel every muscle in Owen's body tense.

Trey set him up.

He broke into his studio not to steal stuff, but to leave stuff.

I fist my hands in the back of Owen's shirt, fearing the worst. "What do you want, Trey?" Owen asks. His voice sounds defeated. He's reached his breaking point with Trey, and that's not a good thing.

"I just want you out of the fucking picture," Trey says. "You've been a pain in my ass since the day we met, and you just continue to resurface." He takes several steps closer, and Owen pushes me further back, still shielding me with his body. "Auburn needs to be a mother to that boy, and he needs me to be his father. As long as you're brainwashing her, that'll never happen." Trey looks over Owen's shoulder, directly at me. "You'll thank me for this one day, Auburn."

Trey lifts the radio to his mouth. "En route to precinct six," Trey says. "Subject in custody for assault on an officer."

"What?" I yell. "Trey, you can't do this! He's on probation!"

Trey ignores me and begins spouting off an address into the radio. Owen turns to face me. "Auburn." His eyes are serious. Focused. "Tell them whatever he wants you to say. If he's telling the truth and he really did plant stuff in my studio, I'll go to jail for a long time. Let them arrest me for assault; it'll be a much lesser charge. I'll talk to my father in the morning, and we'll figure out where to go from there."

I refuse to agree with what he's saying. He hasn't done anything wrong. "If I just tell them the truth, you won't be in trouble, Owen."

He closes his eyes and exhales, practicing patience in a situation that warrants none. When he opens his eyes again, they're somehow even more focused. "He's angry. Trey knows what happened between us, and he wants his payback. And he's right. They'll never believe us over him. Not with my history."

My eyes begin to burn, and I try to remain as calm as he is right now, but it isn't working. Especially now that Trey is pulling him away from me. Owen puts his hands behind his back and Trey places the cuffs on them. Owen doesn't even resist, and I'm crying too hard to try to stop it.

I follow them down the stairs, across the studio, and out

the front door to Trey's police car. He shoves Owen in the backseat and then turns to face me. He opens the front passenger door. "Get in, Auburn. I'll give you a ride home."

I get in, but only because there is no way in hell I'm allowing Owen to spend another day in jail that he doesn't deserve.

CHAPTER TWENTY-TWO

Owen

I'm quiet. So is she.

I know that neither of us is speaking right now because we're trying to figure out a way to get out of this. There has to be a way for her to get her son and not have to go through Trey to do it. And there has to be a way for me to get out of the situation Trey has just put me in without it affecting Auburn and her relationship with AJ.

I watch from the backseat as she turns her attention to Trey.

"What do you think is going to happen now?" she asks him. "You think I'm just going to forget the fact that you attacked me? That you destroyed Owen's studio? That you're framing him?"

Don't, Auburn. Don't make him even angrier.

He turns to face her, and she doesn't back down, even through his silence.

"I'll never love you like I loved Adam."

As soon as the words come out of her mouth, he jerks the car over to the side of the road. He lunges forward across the seat and squeezes her jaw, bringing his face inches from hers.

"I'm *not* Adam. I'm *Trey.* And I suggest if you want to continue being the half-assed mother you are to my nephew, you'll say whatever the fuck I tell you to say."

A tear slides down her cheek. My fists are clenched, and I want to beat on the barrier in order to get him to release her, but I can't. My hands are cuffed behind my back and I can't do a goddamn thing from this backseat to stop him. I bring my feet up and start kicking his seat.

"Get your hands off her!"

Trey doesn't move. He continues to hold on to her jaw until she gives in and nods. He releases her and slides back to his side of the seat.

She glances at me from her position in the passenger seat, and I've never felt more helpless. I see the roll of her throat as she swallows.

She pulls her knees up to her chest, and her tears begin to fall even harder. Her head rests against the back of the seat while her back is pressed against the passenger door. I can see just how much pain she's in. How scared she is. I scoot closer to her and press my forehead against the glass, trying to get as close to her as I can. I look at her reassuringly, wanting her to know that whatever happens, we're in this together. She keeps her eyes locked with mine until we pull into the police station.

Trey kills the ignition. "This is what happened. You called me to pick you up at his apartment because the two of you got into a fight," Trey says. "And when I arrived, he attacked me. That's when I arrested him. Got it?" He reaches across the seat and takes her hand. "Owen needs to be behind bars where he belongs, and if I don't make sure that happens, I'll never forgive myself if you or AJ are hurt. He's the only reason I'm doing this, Auburn. You want your son to be safe, right?"

She nods, but there's something in her eyes. Something I know isn't consent, and that scares me. I don't want her to go in there and defend me.

"Do what he says, Auburn."

My door swings open, and I'm pulled out of the car. Right before I look away from her, she makes a fist and holds it against her chest.

CHAPTER TWENTY-THREE

Auburn

I didn't do what Trey asked me to do. In fact, I didn't do anything. I didn't say anything. I didn't answer a single question.

Every question that was fired at me, I pressed my lips together tighter and tighter.

Owen may not want me to tell them the truth, but if Trey thinks for a second that I'm going to lie for him, he's more delusional than I even imagined.

When they told me I was free to leave, Trey said he would drive me home. I told him no thank you, and I walked right past him. I'm now standing outside of the police station, waiting for the cab I just called to arrive. Trey walks up beside me and stands next to me. His mere presence causes me to rub my hands up my arms to wipe away the chills.

"I'll give you a couple of days to cool off," he says. "But then I'm coming over. We need to talk about this."

I don't respond to him. I don't know how he thinks I would ever be willing to forgive him after tonight.

"I know you're upset, but you have to see things from my perspective. Owen has a criminal record. I don't know what kind of hold he has over you, but you can't blame me for thinking about the safety of your son, Auburn. You can't be upset that I'm trying to do what's best by getting him out of your life, so that you can focus on AJ."

It takes everything in me not to respond. I continue to stare straight ahead until he sighs heavily and makes his way back inside the police station.

When the cab pulls up, I climb inside. The driver asks for the address just as I'm pulling my phone out of my pocket. I type "Callahan Gentry home address" into the search engine, and I wait for the results to return.

I don't know what I expected to find when I appeared at Callahan Gentry's front door last night, but the man who stood in front of me certainly wasn't it. He looked so much like Owen. His eyes were kind like Owen's, but they looked tired. That very well could have been because it was the middle of the night, but I felt like it was something more than that. It reminded me of when Owen said he watched the life seep out of his father's eyes, and I truly understood what he meant when I saw it firsthand.

"Can I help you?" his father said.

I shook my head. "No. But you can help your son."

At first, he appeared somewhat defensive after my comment. But then it was as if something clicked, and he said, "You're the girl he talked about. The one who has the same middle name?"

I nodded, and he invited me inside his home. When I sat on the couch across from him and began to tell him what had transpired, I grew more and more nervous, thinking my plan might not work out. But the second he agreed to help me, I instantly relaxed. I knew I couldn't fight this alone.

My hands are shaking right now, despite the fact that Owen's father is sitting right next to me. I don't think anything could calm me down in this moment, because if it doesn't work out in my and Owen's favor, I'll have just made things a whole lot worse. My heart is in my throat as we wait for her to arrive.

I've been awake for more than twenty-four hours now, but adrenaline is pumping through me, keeping me alert. I wasn't even sure if his phone call would convince her to show up today, but his secretary just buzzed through the speaker to let him know she's here.

In a matter of seconds, I'll be face-to-face with Lydia.

I expect she'll be angry. I expect she'll argue. What I don't expect to see when she finally walks through the door is the man standing behind her. When Trey's eyes meet mine, I can see the curiosity cloud his face. There isn't any curiosity on Lydia's face. Just a world of annoyance when she witnesses me sitting here.

She gives her head a shake as she pauses across the boardroom table from us. "This was the emergency?" she asks, waving her hand in my direction. She gives a huge roll of her eyes, and she turns and looks at Trey. "I'm sorry I dragged you into this," she says to him. "I didn't realize it had to do with Auburn."

Trey's expression is tight, and he glances from me to Owen's father. "What's this about?" he says.

Owen's father, who insisted I call him Cal the second he found out how I knew Owen, stands and motions for them to take two seats across from us. Trey chooses to remain standing, but Lydia sits directly in front of me. I can see her glance at the cut on my lip, but she doesn't ask about it. She darts her eyes to Cal as she folds her arms over the table. "I have to leave in half an hour to pick up my grandson from preschool. Why am I here?"

Cal shifts his eyes to mine briefly. I warned him about her, but I think he may have thought I was exaggerating. He straightens out the papers that are in front of him, and then he leans back against his chair.

"These are custody papers," he says, pointing at the papers laid out in front of him. "Auburn is requesting custody of her son."

Lydia laughs. She literally laughs and looks at me like I've lost my mind. She begins to stand up. "Well, that was fast," she says. "I think we're done here."

I hate that she so easily dismisses the notion. She turns to walk out the door, and I look at Trey, who is still eyeing me. He knows I'm up to something, and my confidence is scaring him.

"Trey," I say to him, just as Lydia reaches the door. "Tell your mother we aren't finished yet."

Trey's jaw grows tight, and his eyes narrow in my direction. He says nothing to Lydia, but he doesn't have to. Lydia turns and faces me, and then moves her focus to Trey. Trey won't look at her because he's too busy trying to threaten me with his glare, so she looks back at me. "What's going on, Auburn? Why are you doing this?"

I choose not to respond to her. Instead, I place my phone on the table. I open up the file, and I press play.

"You think I'm just going to forget the fact that you attacked me? That you destroyed Owen's studio? That you're framing him?"

I pause the recording and watch as all the color drains from Trey's face. I can almost hear his thoughts, they're written so clearly across his face. He's trying to think back on last night and what he might have said to Owen or me on the way to the police station. Because he knows whatever was spoken inside that vehicle, I now have it on my phone as evidence.

He doesn't move a muscle, other than tensing his arms and shoulders. "Should I play the rest of our conversation from last night, Trey?"

He closes his eyes and looks down at the floor. He lifts his leg and kicks the chair in front of him. "Fuck!" he yells.

Lydia flinches. She's looking back and forth between Trey and me, but he doesn't look at anything other than the floor. He's pacing back and forth.

He knows his entire career is in my hands now.

And the fact that Lydia is sitting down again proves that she realizes it, too. She's staring at my phone with a look of defeat, and as much as I want to say her expression pleases me, it doesn't. I never wanted it to come to this.

"I'll stay in Dallas," I tell her. "I won't move back to Portland. You can still see him. As long as you aren't living in the same house as Trey, I'll even give you weekend visitation. But he's my son, Lydia. He needs to be with me. And if I have to use your son against you in order to get my son back, then so help me God, I will."

Cal pushes the paperwork toward her. I lean forward across the table, and for the first time in my life, I'm not scared of the woman sitting across from me.

"If you sign the custody papers and Trey drops the charges against Owen, I won't forward the e-mail that contains this conversation to every single officer in Trey's precinct."

Before Lydia picks up the pen, she turns and looks at Trey. "If that happens and someone gets hold of whatever she has on that recording . . . will it affect your career? Is she telling the truth, Trey?"

Trey pauses his frantic pacing, and he looks directly at me. He nods a slow nod but can't even verbalize a response to her. Lydia's eyes close, and she exhales.

The choice is in her hands. Either she can allow me to be a mother to my son, or I'll make sure her son pays for what he's done to Owen. For what he almost did to me.

"You realize this is blackmail," Trey says.

I look up at him and nod calmly. "I learned from the best."

The room grows quiet, and I can almost hear him trying to come up with a way out of this. When Trey doesn't offer up an alternative, and Lydia realizes they have no choice, she picks up the pen. She signs each form and then pushes them across the table toward me.

I try to remain calm, but my hands are shaking as I hand the paperwork to Cal. Lydia stands up and walks to the door. Before she exits the room, she looks back at me. I can tell she's on the verge of tears, but her tears are nothing compared to the tears I've shed because of her. "I'll pick him up from preschool on my way home. You can stop by in a few hours. It'll give me time to get some of his things together."

I nod, unable to speak due to the sob I'm keeping lodged in

my throat. As soon as the door closes behind Lydia and Trey, I burst into tears.

Cal puts an arm around me and pulls me to him. "Thank you," I say. "Oh my God, thank you so much."

I feel him shake his head. "No, Auburn. I'm the one who should be thanking you."

He doesn't elaborate on why he's thanking me, but I can't help but hope that somehow, seeing the sacrifices his son has made for both of us will give him the strength to do what he needs to do.

CHAPTER TWENTY-FOUR

Owen

When I walk into the room and see my father's face rather than Auburn's, my heart sinks. I haven't seen or spoken to her in over twenty-four hours. I have no idea what's transpired or if she's even okay.

I take a seat in front of my father, not even concerned with whatever it is he wants to discuss with me. "Do you know where Auburn is? Is she okay?"

He nods. "She's fine," he says, and those words instantly put me at ease. "All the charges against you have been dropped. You're free to leave."

I don't move, because I'm not sure I understood him correctly. The door opens and someone enters the room. The officer motions for me to stand and when I do, he removes the cuffs from my wrists. "Do you have any belongings you need to retrieve before you leave?"

"My wallet," I say as I massage my wrists.

"When you're finished in here, let me know and I'll sign you out."

I look at my father again and he can see the shock still registered on my face. He actually smiles. "She's something else, isn't she?"

I smile in return, because *how did you do it, Auburn?*

The light is back in my father's eyes. The light I haven't seen since the night of our wreck. I don't know how, but I know she had something to do with this. She's like a light, unwittingly brightening up the darkest corners of a man's soul.

I have so many questions, but I save them until after I sign out and we're outside.

"How?" I blurt out before the door closes behind us. "Where is she? Why did he drop the charges?"

My father smiles again, and I didn't realize how much I missed that. I've missed his smile almost as much as I miss my mother's.

He hails a cab as it rounds the corner. When it stops, he opens the door and tells the cab driver her address. He takes a step back. "I think you should ask Auburn these questions."

I eye him cautiously, debating whether to get in the cab and head to Auburn or check him for fever. He pulls me in for a hug and doesn't let go. "I'm sorry, Owen. For so many things," he says. His hold around me tightens and I can feel the apology in his embrace. When he pulls back, he ruffles my hair like I'm a child.

Like I'm his son.

Like he's my dad.

"I won't be seeing you for a few months," he says. "I'm going away for a while."

I hear something in his voice that I've never heard before. *Strength.* If I were to paint him right now, I would paint him the exact same shade of green as Auburn's eyes.

He takes several steps back and watches me get inside the cab. I stare at him from the window and I smile. *Callahan Gentry and his son are going to be okay.*

Saying good-bye to him was almost as hard as this moment. Standing in front of her apartment door, preparing to say hello to her.

I lift my hand and knock on her door.

Footsteps.

I inhale a calming breath and wait for the door to open. It feels like these last two minutes have taken two whole lifetimes. I wipe my palms down my jeans. When the door finally opens, my eyes fall to the person standing in front of me.

He's the last person I expected to see here. Seeing him in the doorway to Auburn's apartment, smiling up at me, is definitely a moment I'm going to paint someday.

I don't know how you did it, Auburn.

"Hey!" AJ says, grinning widely. "I remember you."

I smile back at him. "Hey, AJ," I reply. "Is your mom home?"

AJ glances over his shoulder and opens the door wider. Before he invites me in, he crooks his finger and asks me to bend down. When I do, he grins and whispers, "My muscles are really big now. I didn't tell anybody about our tent." He cups his hands around his mouth. "And it's still here."

I laugh, just as he spins around at the sound of her footsteps approaching.

"Sweetie, don't ever open the front door without me," I hear her say to him. He pushes the door open wider, and her eyes lock with mine.

Her footsteps come to an immediate halt.

I didn't think seeing her would hurt this much. Every part of me hurts. My arms ache to hold her. My mouth aches to touch hers. My heart aches to love hers.

"AJ, go to the bedroom and feed your new fish."

Her voice is firm and unwavering. She still hasn't smiled.

"I already fed him," AJ says to her.

Her eyes leave mine and she looks down at him. "You can feed him two more pellets as a snack, okay?" She points in the direction of her bedroom. He must know that look, because he immediately retreats toward the bedroom.

As soon as AJ disappears, I take a quick step back because she's running at me. She jumps into my arms so hard and fast, I'm forced to take several more steps back and hit the wall behind me so that we don't fall. Her arms are locked around my neck and she's kissing, kissing, kissing me like I've never been kissed before. I can taste her tears and laughter, and it's an incredible combination.

I'm not sure how long we stand in the hallway kissing, because seconds aren't long enough when they're spent with her.

Her feet eventually meet the floor and her arms lock around my waist and her face presses against my chest. I wrap my hand around the back of her head and hold her like I plan on holding her every day after today.

She's crying, not because she's sad, but because she doesn't know how to express what she's feeling. She knows there aren't words good enough for this moment.

So neither of us speaks, because there aren't any words good enough for me, either. I press my cheek to the top of her head and stare inside her apartment. I look up at the painting on her living room wall. I smile, remembering the first night I walked into her apartment and saw it for the first time. I knew she had to have the painting in her possession somewhere, but actually seeing it displayed in her living room was an incredible feeling. It was surreal. And I wanted to turn to her that night and tell her all about it. I wanted to tell her my connection to it. I wanted to tell her my connection to her.

But I didn't, and I never will, because this confession isn't mine to share.

This confession belonged to Adam.

FIVE YEARS EARLIER

Owen

I'm sitting on the floor of the hallway, next to my father's hospital room. I watch as she exits the room next door. "You're just throwing them away?" she asks in disbelief. Her words are directed at the woman she just trailed into the hallway. I know the woman's name is Lydia, but I still don't know the name of the girl. Not for lack of trying, though.

Lydia turns around, and I see that she's holding a box in her arms. She looks down at the contents of it and then back at the girl. "He hasn't painted in weeks. He doesn't have any use for them anymore, and they're just taking up room." Lydia turns around and sets the box down on the nurses' desk. "Can you find somewhere to discard these?" she says to the nurse on duty.

Before the nurse even agrees, Lydia walks back into the room and returns a few seconds later with several blank canvases. She sets them on the desk next to the box of what I now assume are painting supplies.

The girl stares down at the box, even after Lydia returns to the hospital room. She looks sad. Almost as if saying good-bye to his things is as difficult as saying good-bye to him.

I watch her for several minutes as her emotions begin to trickle out of her in the form of tears. She wipes them away and looks up at the nurse. "Do you have to throw them away? Can't you just . . . can you at least give them to someone?"

The nurse hears the sadness in her words. She smiles warmly and nods. The girl nods back, and then turns and slowly makes her way back into the hospital room.

I don't know her, but I would probably have the same reaction if someone were to throw something away of my father's.

I've never attempted to paint before, but I do draw occasionally. I find myself standing up, walking toward the nurses' station. I look down at the box full of various types of paints and brushes. "Can I—?"

The sentence doesn't even finish leaving my mouth when the nurse shoves the box at me. "Please," she says. "Take it. I don't know what to do with it."

I grab the supplies and walk them into my father's room. I lay them down on the only available area of counter space. The rest of his hospital room is full of flowers and plants that have been delivered over the last couple of weeks. I should probably do something with them, but I still have hope that he'll wake up soon and see them all.

After finding room for the art supplies, I walk to the chair next to my father's bed and take a seat.

I watch him.

I watch him for hours, until I get so bored that I stand up and try to find something else to stare at. Sometimes I stare at the blank canvas on the desk. I don't even know where to start, so I spend the entire next day dividing my attention between my father, the canvas, and the occasional walks I take around the hospital.

I don't know how many more days of this I can take. It's as if I can't even properly grieve until I know he's able to grieve with me. I hate that as soon as he wakes up—if he wakes up—I'll more than likely have to go over every last detail of that night with him, when all I want to do is forget it.

"Never look at your phone, Owen," he said.

"Watch the road," my brother said from the backseat.

"Use your blinker. Hands at ten and two. Keep the radio off."

I was completely new at driving, and every single direction that came out of their mouths reminded me of that. All but the one direction I wished they had given me the most. "Watch out for drunk drivers."

We were hit from the passenger side, right when the light turned green and I made it out into the intersection. The wreck wasn't my fault, but had I been more experienced, I would have known to look left and right first, even though the light gave me permission to move forward.

My brother and mother died on impact. My father remains in critical condition.

I've been broken since the moment it happened.

I spend the majority of my days and nights here, and

the longer I sit, waiting for him to wake up, the lonelier it becomes. The visits from family and friends have stopped. I haven't been to school in weeks, but that's the least of my concerns. I just wait.

Wait for him to move. Wait for him to blink. Wait for him to speak.

Usually by the end of every day, I'm so exhausted from everything that's not happening, I have to take a breather. For the first week or two, the evenings were the hardest part for me. Mostly because it meant another day where he showed no signs of improvement was coming to an end. But lately, the evenings have grown into something I actually look forward to.

And I have her to thank for that.

It might be her laugh, but I also think it's the way she loves whomever it is she visits that makes me feel hopeful. She comes and visits him every evening from five to seven. Adam, I think is his name.

I notice that when she visits, his other family members leave the room. I assume Adam prefers it this way so he can get his alone time with her. I feel guilty sometimes, sitting out here in the hallway, propped up against the wall between his door and my father's door. But there's nowhere else I can go and feel the same way I do when I hear her voice.

His visits with her are the only time I ever hear him laugh. Or talk much, for that matter. I've heard enough conversations come from his room over the past few weeks to know what his fate is, so the fact that he's able to laugh when he's with her speaks volumes.

I think his imminent death is also what gives me a little bit of hope. I know that sounds morbid, but I assume Adam and I are around the same age, so I put myself in his shoes a lot when I start to feel sorry for myself. Would I rather be on my deathbed with a prognosis of only a few weeks to live, or would I rather be in the predicament I'm in?

Sometimes, on the really bad days, when I think about how I'll never see my brother again, I think I'd rather be in Adam's shoes.

But then there are moments when I hear how she speaks to him and the words she says to him, and I think, I'm lucky I'm not in his shoes. Because I still have a chance of being loved like that someday. And I feel bad for Adam, knowing the kind of love she has for him, and knowing that's what he's leaving behind. That has to be hard for him.

But that also means he was lucky enough to find her before his time was up. That has to make death a little more bearable, even if only by a fraction.

I return to the hallway and slide down to the floor, waiting for her laugh tonight, but it doesn't come. I scoot closer to his door and further away from my father's, wondering why tonight is different. Why tonight isn't one of the happier visits.

"But I guess I'm also referring to our parents, for not understanding this," I hear Adam say to her. "For not allowing me to have the one and only thing I want here with me."

As soon as I realize that this is their good-bye, my heart breaks for her and it breaks for Adam, even though I don't know either of them. I listen for a few more minutes until I hear him say, "Tell me something about yourself that no one else knows. Something I can keep for myself."

I feel like these confessions should stay between the two of them. I feel like if I were to ever hear one of them, Adam wouldn't be able to keep it for himself, because I would have it, too. Which is why I always stand up and walk away at these moments, even though I want to know her secrets more than I want to know anything else in the world.

I walk to the waiting area next to the elevators and take a seat. As soon as I sit down, the elevator doors open and Adam's brother walks in. I know it's his brother, and I know his name is Trey. I also know, simply based on the brief visits he makes with his brother, that I don't like him. I've seen him pass her in the hall a couple of times, and I don't like the way he turns around and watches her walk away.

He's looking down at his watch, walking in a hurry toward the room she and Adam are saying their good-byes to each other in. I don't want him to hear their confessions, and I don't want him to interrupt their good-bye, so I catch myself following after him, asking him to stop. He rounds the corner to the hallway before he realizes I'm actually speaking to him. He turns around and eyes me up and down, sizing me up.

"Give them a few more minutes," I say to him.

I can tell by the change in his eyes that I pissed him off when I said this. I didn't mean to, but it seems like he's the type of guy to get pissed off by almost anything.

"Who the hell are you?"

I immediately dislike him. I also don't like that he looks so angry, because he's obviously older than me and bigger than me and much, much meaner than me.

"Owen Gentry. I'm a friend of your brother's," I say, lying to him. "I just . . ." I point down the hallway toward the room she and Adam are in. "He needs a few more minutes with her."

Trey doesn't seem to give a shit how many minutes Adam needs with her. "Well, *Owen Gentry*, she's got a plane to catch," he says, agitated that I'm wasting his time. He continues down the hallway and walks into the room. I can hear her sobs now.

It's the first time I've ever heard her sob, and I can't bear to hear it. I turn and walk back to the waiting area, feeling her and Adam's pain in my own chest.

The next thing I hear are her pleas for more time and her "I love you"s as Trey is pulling her down the hallway by her arm.

I've never wanted to hurt someone so badly in my entire life.

"Stop," Trey says to her, agitated that she's still trying to get back to Adam's room. He wraps his arm around her waist this time and pulls her to him so she can't get away. "I'm sorry, but we have to go."

She allows him to hold her and I know it's only because she's so broken right now. But the way his hands move down her back forces me to grip the arms of the chair I'm in so that I don't physically pry him off of her. Her back is to me, which means he's facing me now that he has his arms wrapped around her. The smallest smirk plays across his mouth when he notices the anger on my face, and then he winks at me.

The bastard just winked at me.

When the doors finally open and he releases her, she glances back toward Adam's room. I can see her hesitation as Trey waits for her to step into the elevator first. She takes a step back, wanting to return to Adam. She's scared because she knows she'll never see him again if she steps into that elevator. She looks at Trey and says, "Please. Just let me say good-bye. One last time." She's whispering, because she knows if she tries to speak louder, her voice won't work.

Trey shakes his head and says, "You already said good-bye. We have to go."

He has no heart.

He holds the doors for her to step on, and she considers it. But then in the next second, she begins to take off in a sprint in the other direction. My heart smiles for her, because I want her to be able to say good-bye to him again. I know that's what Adam would want, too. I know how much it would mean to him just to see her run back into his room one last time and give him one last kiss and allow him to say, "I'll love you forever, even when I can't," just one last time.

I can see in Trey's eyes that he has every intention of stopping her. He turns to run after her, to pull her back, but I'm suddenly in front of him, blocking him. He shoves me, and I punch him, which I know isn't the right thing to do, but I do it anyway, knowing I'm about to get hit in return. But one punch is worth it, because it'll give her enough time to get back to Adam's room and tell him good-bye again.

As soon as his huge fist meets my jaw, I meet the floor.

Goddamn it, that hurt.

He steps over me to run after her. I grab his ankle and pull, watching as he falls to the ground. A nurse hears the commotion and comes running around the corner, just as he kicks me in the shoulder and tells me to fuck off. He's on his feet again and running down the hall, and I'm standing now.

I'm almost back to my father's room when I hear her say to Adam, "I'll love you forever. Even when I shouldn't."

It makes me smile, even though my mouth hurts and is covered in blood.

I walk into my father's room and go straight to the counter where the painting supplies are stacked up. I grab an empty canvas and rummage through the box, inspecting all the other supplies.

Who would have thought that my first fight over a girl would be for a girl who isn't even mine?

I can hear her still crying as she's pulled down the hallway again for what I know really is the last time. I sit down in the chair and stare at the box full of his art supplies. I begin to pull them out one by one.

It was eight hours later and almost daylight when I finally finished the painting. I set it aside to dry and fell asleep until dark. I know she won't be in his room tonight and that makes me sad for both of them, and even a little selfishly sad for myself.

I stand at his door for a little while, waiting to knock, wanting to ensure his brother isn't in the room. After several minutes of quiet, I knock softly on the door.

"Come in," he says, although his voice is so weak tonight, I have to strain to hear it. I open the door and take a few steps into the room. When he sees me and fails to recognize me, he attempts to sit up several inches. It looks hard for him.

God, he's so young.

I mean, I know he's about the same age as me, but death makes him look younger than he should. Death should only be acquainted with the old.

"Hey," I say as I slowly make my way into his room. "Sorry to bother you, but . . ." I glance back at the door and then to him again. "This is weird, so I'm just gonna say it. I . . . I made you something."

I'm holding the canvas in my hand, afraid to turn it around so that he can see it. His eyes fall to the back of it, and he inhales a breath and attempts to push himself further up on the bed. "What is it?"

I walk closer to him and point to the chair, asking for permission to sit. Adam nods his head. I don't show him the painting right away. I feel like I should explain it first or explain me or, at the very least, introduce myself.

"I'm Owen," I tell him after I take a seat in the chair. I motion to the wall behind his head. "My father has been in the room next door for a few weeks."

Adam regards me for a moment and then says, "What's wrong with him?"

"He's in a coma. Car accident."

His eyes become genuinely sympathetic, and it makes me like him almost immediately. It also lets me know that he's nothing like his brother.

"I was driving," I add.

I don't know why I clarify that to him. Maybe to show him that even though I'm not the one dying, my life isn't much to envy.

"Your mouth," he says, making a weak effort to point at the bruise that has formed since my scuffle in the hallway last night. "Were you the one who got into a fight with my brother?"

I'm taken aback for a moment, shocked that he knows about it. I nod.

He laughs a little. "The nurse told me about that. Said you tackled him in the hall when he was trying to stop Auburn from telling me good-bye again."

I smile. Auburn, I think to myself. I've been wondering for three weeks what her name is. Of course it would be Auburn. I've never heard of anyone else with that name; it suits her perfectly.

"Thank you for that," Adam says. His words come out in a pained whisper. I hate that I'm forcing him to talk so much when I know it hurts him.

I hold up the painting a little higher and look down at it.

"Last night, after she left," I say, "I guess you could say I was inspired to paint this for you. Or maybe it's for her. Both of you, I guess." I immediately look up at him. "I hope that's not weird."

He shrugs. "Depends on what it is."

I stand and walk the painting to him, turning it around so that he can see it.

He doesn't have any type of reaction to it at first. He just stares at it. I let him hold it, and I back away, a little embarrassed that I thought he would want something like this. "It's my first attempt at painting," I say, excusing the fact that he probably thinks it's horrendous.

His eyes immediately meet mine and the expression on his face is anything but indifference. He points to it. "This is your first attempt?" he says in disbelief. "Seriously?"

I nod. "Yeah. Probably my last, too."

He immediately shakes his head. "I hope not," he says. "This is incredible." He reaches to the remote and presses the button to lift the head of the bed a few more inches. He points to a table next to the chair. "Grab that pen."

I don't question him. I hand him the pen and watch as he flips the painting over and writes something on the back of the canvas. He reaches to the nightstand beside his bed and tears off a sheet of paper from a notepad. He writes something down on the notepad and hands me both the painting and the piece of paper.

"Do me a favor," he says as I take both of them out of his hands. "Will you mail this to her? From me?" He points to the slip of paper in my hands. "Her address is at the top and the return address is at the bottom."

I look down at the slip of paper in my hands, and I read her full name.

"Auburn Mason Reed," I say out loud.

What are the chances?

I smile and run my thumb over the letters in her middle name. "We have the same middle name."

I look back up at Adam, and he's lowering his bed again with a faint smile on his face. "That could be fate, you know."

I shake my head, dismissing his comment. "I'm pretty sure she's your fate. Not mine."

His voice is strained, and it takes a tremendous amount of effort for him to roll onto his side. He closes his eyes and says, "Hopefully she has more than one fate, Owen."

He doesn't open his eyes again. He falls asleep, or maybe just needs a break from speaking. I look down at her name again and think about the words he just spoke.

Hopefully she has more than one fate.

It makes me feel good to know that as much as he loves her, he also knows she'll move on after his death, and he accepts that. It even seems like he wants that for her. Unfortunately, if this really were fate, we would have been placed together under different circumstances and with way better timing.

I look up at him again, and his eyes are still closed. He pulls the covers over his arms, so I quietly back out of the room, painting in hand.

I'll mail this painting to her, because he asked me to. And then I'm going to throw away her address. I'll try to forget her name, even though I know I never will.

Who knows? If we're meant to be together and fate really does exist, maybe one of these days she'll wind up at my door. Maybe Adam will, in some way, be the one to make that happen.

Until that day comes, though, I'm pretty sure I have something to keep me occupied. I think with the inadvertent help of her and Adam, I may have just discovered my calling.

I look down at the painting in my hands, and I flip it over. I read the last words Adam will ever write to her.

I'll love you forever. Even when I can't.

When I turn the painting around to face me again, I run my fingers over it. I touch the space between the two hands, and I think about everything between the two of them that is pulling them apart.

And I hope, for her sake, that Adam is right. I hope she does have a second fate.

Because she deserves it.

Acknowledgments

First and foremost, a huge thank-you to Danny O'Connor for contributing the artwork for *Confess*. After searching high and low for art I felt could represent Owen, your work stood out above the rest. You have an incredible talent, and your fans (myself included) are lucky to be able to experience it.

As always, a huge thank-you to Johanna Castillo, Ariele Fredman, Judith Curr, Kaitlyn Zafonte, and the entire Atria Books team.

To my agent, Jane Dystel, and the entire Dystel and Goderich team.

To the Weblichs, for always making sure I'm stocked with pictures of Harry, cans of Diet Pepsi, and lots of positive energy. To the CoHorts, for giving me daily reminders as to why I do this in the first place. And to my biggest supporters, who are subjected to ten different versions of every chapter, but never complain: Kay Miles, Kathryn Perez, Chelle Northcutt, Madison Seidler, Karen Lawson, Marion Archer,

Jennifer Stiltner, Kristin Phillips-Delcambre, Salie-Benbow Powers, Maryse, and so many others.

To Murphy for being the best AsSISTERnt out there. To Stephanie, for being there from the beginning, as a boss and a best friend. To my mother, sister, husband, children, and everyone else who supports me endlessly and never complains.

To everyone who takes a chance and picks up one of my books, thank you for the opportunity to live my dream.

And of course, a huge thank-you to two of the people I am grateful this career brought into my life: Tarryn Fisher and Vilma Gonzalez. You guys have been my rocks this year.

About the Author

Colleen Hoover is the number one *New York Times* bestselling author of *Slammed*, *Point of Retreat*, *This Girl*, *Hopeless*, *Losing Hope*, *Finding Cinderella*, *Maybe Someday*, *Maybe Not*, and *Ugly Love*. She lives in Texas with her husband and their three boys. Please visit ColleenHoover.com.